Lexi Magill
and the
TELEPORTATION
TOURNAMENT

Lexi Magill

and the
TELEPORTATION
TOURNAMENT

Kim Long

RP|KIDS
PHILADELPHIA

Running Press Kids
Hachette Book Group
1290 Avenue of the Americas, New York, NY 10104
www.runningpress.com/rpkids
@RP_Kids

Printed in the United States of America

First Edition: October 2019

Published by Running Press Kids, an imprint of Perseus Books, LLC, a subsidiary of Hachette Book Group, Inc. The Running Press Kids name and logo is a trademark of the Hachette Book Group.

The Hachette Speakers Bureau provides a wide range of authors for speaking events. To find out more, go to www.hachettespeakersbureau.com or call (866) 376-6591.

The publisher is not responsible for websites (or their content) that are not owned by the publisher.

Print book cover and interior design by Christopher Eads and Frances J. Soo Ping Chow. Stock art on page 111 © Getty Images/Man_Half-Tube

Library of Congress Control Number: 2019933055

ISBNs: 978-0-7624-6698-6 (hardcover), 978-0-7624-6699-3 (ebook)

LSC-C

10 9 8 7 6 5 4 3 2 1

CHAPTER ONE

Lexi snatched the teleportation medallion off the counter and flipped it into the air. The half-dollar-sized gray medallion landed in her palm, and she clenched her fingers over it. A Tel-Med was the final thing she needed to enter the Teleportation Tournament, and now she had one. Granted, she had to blow her birthday dough and an entire year's allowance to rent it, but it's not like she had a choice. There was no way that she, Alexis Theresa Magill, teleport science whiz and Wisconsin's top junior scientist, was missing the chance to race around the world in *the* student science competition of the year.

"You're all set," the rental store employee said as he handed a smiling Lexi the receipt. "The store's closed Monday for the Memorial Day holiday, so it needs to be back on Tuesday to avoid a late fee."

Lexi nodded. "Got it. Thanks."

Tel-Med tucked safely in her pocket, Lexi strode to the exit. She checked her watch. 6:10 a.m. Right on schedule. In a few minutes, she'd be at the high school, where she'd grab a spot in the tournament check-in line and wait for her teammates. Sure, she was a tad

1

early, but it was worth it. Fifty teams of three kids each meant 150 entrants—the check-in line was going to get majorly long in a hurry.

Besides, early meant she'd get a chance to talk to Haley. Although they'd chatted on the phone and texted a few times, Lexi hadn't been able to spend any real time with her best friend since moving across town. There was so much Lexi wanted to catch up on—like finding out who Haley picked as her new lab partner after Lexi switched schools. Or if Haley *finally* figured out how to program Gary, the robotic grasshopper, to jump over a box of paper clips. Giggling to herself as she turned the corner, Lexi guessed a big "No" on that one. Lexi had created the original code, and Haley wasn't great at—

"Hey, Lexi!"

"Look! It's Lexi!"

Lexi glanced ahead. Down the block, kids from her former science academy waved from the parking lot. "Hey, everyone!" she yelled, picking up the pace.

Three boys wearing blue jeans and blue T-shirts with "Physics Phenoms" emblazoned across the front ran toward her. "You're here!" the middle boy said, eyes wide.

Lexi threw back her shoulders and grinned. "Hi, Tomoka! Of course! You didn't really think I'd miss this, did you?"

More kids rushed to greet her, and soon Lexi felt like her old self, chatting away about advancements in teleport science (underwater telepods for divers exploring the ocean floor!) and the newest tech gadgets (bionic gloves!). But as the conversations continued, a lump formed in her throat. She missed this. When her dad lost his job and moved her family to a smaller house across town, the pricey science academy was one of the first things to go under her parents' "major downsizing initiative."

Now Lexi was stuck at West Elm Middle School, where fitting in was like sound waves traveling in a vacuum: impossible. Not only wasn't there anyone who wanted to discuss the finer points of quantum physics, but the school didn't even have a science club. Plus, moving midyear made it impossible to find friends. So far, her semester had been filled with lonely lunch periods and loads of free time after school.

Lexi tightened her hands into fists, willing herself to stay focused. *Follow the plan.* She'd win the tournament and use the prize money to re-enroll in the academy. In the fall, she'd have her old life back.

A speck of a silver T-shirt and a bobbing blonde ponytail flashed in the distance. Instantly brightening, Lexi dashed toward the sparkly target.

"Haley!" Lexi shouted.

"Lexi!" Haley cried, wrapping her arms around Lexi's shoulders.

Lexi returned her friend's hug. "I've totally missed you."

"I know," Haley said. "Me too." Then, in a whisper, "I can't believe we're not racing together. It stinks that teammates have to be from the same school."

Lexi puffed out a breath. "Tell me about it. You would not *believe* what I had to go through to find teammates."

Haley peered past Lexi. "Oh no. Who did you end up with?"

"Just two kids from my history class." Lexi sighed. "They're nice and all, but they're not into science in the least. No science explorer camps, no junior science club . . . not even a science fair."

Haley winced. "Ouch. That doesn't sound good, though I suppose . . ."

"What?"

"Well, if they don't know anything about science, you won't have anyone to fight with over the answers."

Lexi laughed. Haley always had a way of twisting things around to find an advantage. "Yeah, well, maybe—"

"Sure," Haley said. "A bunch of us have been doing practice tournaments on the weekends, and OMG, Lexi. Andre argues about *everything*—even what telepod line is shorter! If I'm going to have to battle him on every puzzle, it'll eat up tons of time." She clutched Lexi's forearm. "I *so* wish you were still on my team. We'd be unstoppable!"

Haley continued her rant about Andre, but Lexi's mind drifted to the practice tournaments she had missed. She wished Haley had invited her. Even though they weren't teammates, it would have been fun to hang out like they used to. Lexi opened her mouth, but then closed it, remembering the stupid rental Tel-Med in her pocket. A year ago, she had her own, shiny gold Tel-Med and could go teleporting whenever she wanted. The new Magill family budget put an end to that.

A spinning Haley jolted Lexi out of her thoughts.

"Aren't our shirts awesome?" The shimmery letters shouting "Haley's Comets" blurred as Haley spun past Lexi.

"Oh wow. Yeah," Lexi answered half-heartedly. "Good idea with the glitter." She glanced away, trying to shake off the uneasy feeling that had taken root in her stomach from missing out. It wasn't Haley's fault she didn't have a Tel-Med anymore. In fact, that was probably why Haley hadn't bothered asking her—she knew Lexi wouldn't have been able to go.

Haley whirled to a stop and spread her arms out wide as she wobbled in place.

Laughing, Lexi gripped Haley's elbow to help her friend regain her balance. "Hey," she said. "So, tell me about Gary. Did you guys get him to jump?"

Haley steadied and tilted her head to the side, looking confused.

"You know, how we were trying to program him to hop over the box?" Lexi straightened her glasses. "And what's the new class project—"

"Attention, competitors!" an official announced over the speakers. "It's time to check in. Everyone, get in line with your teams!"

Haley jumped free of Lexi's grasp. "This is it! I have to find Emma and Andre. See ya!"

"Yeah, okay," Lexi mumbled, watching her friend dart through the crowd. "Hey!" she called. "We can catch up at the rest area! Save me a seat!" Haley didn't turn, and Lexi frowned. Oh well. She should find her teammates, too.

Lexi scanned the parking lot. Not surprisingly, nearly every team was color-coordinated, matching their shirts, pants, windbreakers, and sometimes even their gym shoes. More than half the teams had also sprung for identical backpacks. But as the teams assembled and check-in started, Lexi's team consisted of a single member: her. She scowled. *Two late teammates. Fantastic start.*

The line inched forward, and soon Lexi stood three back from the counter. As she turned to scour the area again, a tittering pulsed through the crowd. Lexi looked across the parking lot, where kids who had checked in were waiting. Teams gathered together, hands partially covering their mouths, whispering. Every few seconds, an arm shot out of a huddle with a finger pointed toward the circular drive reserved for buses. Wondering what the commotion could be, Lexi followed one of the fingers to its target.

She sighed with understanding. Her teammates were crossing the driveway, and if there were awards for oddest-looking racers, Ron and Mal would have won in a landslide.

For starters, Ron had to be carrying the largest backpack in the world. Bulging at every side, it seriously looked like his backpack had left a buffet where it had eaten all the other backpacks. Not only did it extend above his head to all the way down to his waist, but it was as wide as his body—his five-foot, five-inch, 160-pound body. And it didn't end there, as Ron was dressed as someone headed to tryouts: baggy green basketball shorts, loose-fitted green Green Bay Packers shirt, and gym shoes.

Mal, on the other hand, wore a pink T-shirt with, "Eat, Draw, Sleep, Repeat" scrawled across the front, a brown miniskirt, fuchsia leggings, and lime green ballet flats. Her long, glossy black hair was set in an elaborate braid, and a camera hung around her neck. A stylish purse backpack dangled over an arm, and to top it off, a gold scarf circled her wrist. She could have been going to a tea party or a fashion show, or, really, anywhere other than a teleportation tournament.

Lexi waved. "Hey, Ron. Hey, Mal."

"Lexi!" Ron boomed as he extended his arm over his head. "Never fear, the Filipino Flyer is here!"

"Sorry we're late," Mal said as she joined the line.

Thunk.

Ron dropped his pack onto the pavement. "Nah, it's perfect timing. Looks like we're next, huh?"

"Um, yeah," Lexi mumbled without looking. She pointed to the Milwaukee Brewers logo on her T-shirt. She'd used her favorite baseball team as inspiration for her team's wardrobe. "So, uh, I thought we were going with Brewers gear—or at least their colors of blue and gold? And pockets are kind of important—quick access to our Tel-Meds, IDs, and stuff."

Mal pinched her T-shirt. "Sorry. I really wanted to wear my drawing shirt." She raised her arm. "But I added a gold scarf, and I *do* have a pocket." Mal turned and directed Lexi to the back of her skirt, where the smallest heart-shaped pocket in the world resided.

"Oh," Lexi said.

7

"Yeah, and I looked for something Brewers, but no dice," Ron said. He stuck out his chest and smoothed the front of his shirt. "So, I went with Packers." He surveyed the crowd. "This is unbelievable. Almost everyone has team uniforms."

"I know," Lexi grumbled. "That's why I said—"

"Next!" shouted a tournament official at the counter.

Lexi nudged her teammates to the recently vacated station. "Names?" a voice from behind a box of file folders asked.

"Alexis Magill, Ronald Quinto, and Malena Moreno," Lexi answered.

The man raised his head, revealing a red handlebar mustache and big blue eyes. "Lexi! We've missed you!"

"Dr. Harrison! I miss you, too!" Lexi said. "Your physics classes are the best."

Dr. Harrison picked out their folders. "IDs and Tel-Meds, please." Lexi retrieved her Tel-Med, noticing the bright blue "RENTAL" stamp for the first time. Deftly flipping it to the other side, she handed it over with her school ID. Dr. Harrison opened the lid to a small black box and inserted the Tel-Med into a compartment. He closed the lid and pressed a button. *Click.* A second later, after checking the lights on the side of the machine, Dr. Harrison opened the lid and returned the Tel-Med.

"What's that for?" Lexi asked.

"We've installed a tracking and disabling chip," Dr. Harrison replied. "You'll hear more about it in a few minutes."

"Oh." Lexi studied the medallion. She didn't see any marks. *Whew.* There was no way she could afford a charge for damaging it.

Dr. Harrison repeated the process with Ron's and Mal's Tel-Meds. "Okay. Team name?"

"Team RAM," Lexi said, hoping Dr. Harrison wouldn't comment on how dorky it sounded. Most teams picked science-themed names, but Ron and Mal had nixed all of her suggestions.

"R-A-M?"

"Yeah, it's our initials," Mal offered. "Ronald, Alexis, Malena."

"Gotcha. Team RAM." Dr. Harrison handed them three navy blue–and–gold ribbon necklaces. "Go ahead and tie your badges through the ribbons."

"Brewers colors. Cool," Lexi said as she secured the badge with her name and photo to a necklace and hung it around her neck.

"And here's your first clue," Dr. Harrison said, passing a notebook-sized manila envelope to Lexi. "Don't open it until you're told to do so. It's an automatic disqualification."

"Okay," Lexi said, grabbing the envelope.

"All right, you three can wait in the main parking lot. We'll start the formal rules explanation in a little bit." He winked at Ron and Mal. "You guys really lucked out with Lexi. She knows her stuff. Good luck."

"Thanks," Lexi said, and she led Mal and Ron to a grassy area bordering the parking lot.

Mal aimed her camera at the check-in booth and snapped a few photos.

"What are you doing?" Lexi asked, unshouldering her pack.

"Grabbing a couple shots. I probably won't use them, but you never know."

Lexi squinted toward Mal, confused. "What do you—"

"Man, is this heavy," Ron interrupted. He hoisted his pack onto a picnic table and opened a few zippers. Hoodies, caps, and T-shirts spilled out.

"Holy cow!" Lexi said. "What's all that?"

Ron rocked back on his heels. "*Swag*, man. You know, merchandise. *Merch.* Haven't you heard? Europe's in love with the NFL. I've got jerseys, hoodies, hats—tons of Green Bay Packers stuff." He rubbed his hands together and pointed his thumbs to his chest. "This guy's gonna make a nice little profit this weekend."

Lexi stared at him, mouth agape.

"What?" Ron said. "I told you I'd do your science tournament thing *if* I got a chance to make some money. Football camp's this summer. My parents will pay for a week, but if I get more dough, I bet I can get them to let me go for two weeks. High school and college coaches love that stuff."

"I . . . uh, yeah," Lexi mumbled. "I remember you saying the money would come in handy, but I thought you meant *prize* money, like when we win. It's a race, remember? There's not going to be time to sell stuff."

Ron brushed her off. "No worries, Magill. My *swag's* gonna go quick. I'll need maybe five, ten minutes at each stop."

"But—"

Mal shrugged. "That works for me. That's when I'll take photos."

Lexi's breath caught in her throat. "Photos?" she croaked.

"For the state photo contest." Mal waved her arm to the side as if she were a model displaying a prize on a game show. "'Around the World' by Malena Moreno." She grinned. "Everyone's gonna have photos from around Wisconsin, *maybe* somewhere from a summer vacation, but all of Europe? No way. I'll definitely be the one to beat, not to mention I'll get automatic extra credit for my art class."

Lexi squeezed the back of her neck. "Oh yeah," she muttered as her conversation with Mal rushed back to her. "When you said you'd enter for extra credit, I thought you meant in science—you know, a report on physics . . ."

Mal laughed. "Nah, I meant art class. Why? Does it matter?"

"No. It's just . . . I know teleport science isn't your thing. And *believe* me, I'm grateful you guys said you'd come, and I'm all for, you know"—she pointed at Ron—"selling stuff"—she gestured to Mal—"and taking photos, but . . . we have to keep up with everyone else. They eliminate teams each day, and if we get cut, there'll be no swag *or* photos."

Ron cocked his left eyebrow. Then his right. Then his left. He switched back and forth at a steady pace. After the sixth or seventh time, Lexi couldn't help but laugh.

"Seriously," she said, lightly punching her fist into her palm. "I'm all for having fun, but we have to concentrate on the tournament. That's the whole point."

"Got it," Ron said. "Don't worry, Magill. It'll be fine. I'm looking forward to it. I love logic puzzles and stuff like that."

Mal adjusted her scarf. "Yeah, and I love traveling through Europe. I want to go to as many places as possible. We'll be super-fast."

Lexi let out a breath, feeling a little better. While she didn't expect Ron or Mal to know enough science to actually help during the tournament, there was a difference between not helping and slowing her down. "Okay. Thanks, guys."

Ron hopped onto the picnic bench and stepped atop the table. He looked over the crowd. "All right, so let's talk about this tournament. Who's our fiercest competition?"

"Good question," Mal said as she joined Ron on the tabletop.

Smiling, Lexi climbed up, too. She noticed Haley's Comets, the Physics Phenoms, Tesla's Techies, and several other teams of former classmates or summer science camp pros mingling in the lot. Jealousy rumbled through her. She'd give anything to be down there, laughing and talking about potential science problems they'd encounter in the tournament.

Next year. Next year, that'll be me.

"Earth to Lexi," Mal said, giving her a poke. "What do you think? Who do we have to watch out for?"

Everybody. Lexi motioned to the middle of the lot. "Well, everyone from the academy and STEM competitions will definitely be good."

"STEM?" Mal said. "That's Science, Tech—"

"—nology, Engineering, and Mathematics," Lexi interrupted. "There are competitions throughout the year." She identified the main teams before flipping her hand toward three sparkling silver shirts. "And that's Haley's team. She's my best friend and real smart, too."

"Hmmm," Ron said. "Who won last year?"

Lexi stared into the crowd. "The Mighty Sanbornes. David and Daniel are twins. They just turned fourteen, so this is the last year they can run. They're entering with their sister, Ashley. She's twelve, like us, so this will be her first tournament. I don't see them yet, though."

"Mighty Sanbornes," Ron murmured. He smoothed his hands together. "Good to know."

A horn blared, and Team RAM jolted. Lexi watched as Dr. Harrison proceeded to a makeshift stage at the front of the parking lot. With a squeal, she hurriedly leaped to the ground and grabbed her notebook. The tournament was about to start.

CHAPTER TWO

Dr. Harrison leaned into the microphone. "Welcome to Wisconsin's Sixth Annual Memorial Day Weekend Teleportation Tournament!" He laughed, stepping back. "Wow! It's nice seeing everyone up so early on a Saturday!"

Cheers erupted across the parking lot. Lexi smiled but didn't join. Standing tall, she stared straight ahead, clicked her pen, and rested a notebook on her arm, ready to write. Ron sidled up next to her . . . with a partially torn spiral notebook that was clearly a left-over from last semester. He flipped to a blank page about halfway in and dragged a chewed-off three-inch pencil out of his sock.

Mal leaned over. "I'll leave the note-taking to you two. I'm just gonna listen."

"Okay," Lexi said, side-eyeing her teammates. Apparently, she should have stressed the importance of note-taking more than once.

"All right," Dr. Harrison shouted. "Before we start, is there any-one who didn't provide their Tel-Med to the check-in booth?" The crowd hushed as kids looked at their neighbors. Dr. Harrison held his hands high over his head. "Please make sure. All Tel-Meds must have our tracking and disabling chip, and this is the only chance we have to install them. It's now or never." Again, kids glanced around the parking lot, nodding at their teammates to confirm their Tel-Meds were ready.

"Great. Let's move on. Since you were at our meeting last weekend, I'm going to make this short and sweet." Dr. Harrison lifted a badge—like the ones he had handed out at the check-in counter—off his chest. "First, this is your badge. It allows you to obtain teleport tickets free of charge and free access to museums and public transportation. So, whatever you do, don't lose your badge."

Lexi twirled the pen between her fingers. No need to write that down.

"Next," Dr. Harrison said, "are your Teleport Travel Request Forms. When your team wants to teleport to a new destination, complete the form and fill in the code of the teleport station where you want to travel. Hand in your form to a tournament official, and you'll get your tickets."

"What if we pick the code for a teleport station in Antarctica?" a kid shouted.

"Then you'll go to Antarctica," Dr. Harrison answered without missing a beat.

The teams hushed.

"Just kidding," Dr. Harrison said, and sighs of relief echoed through the crowd. "No one is going to give you a ticket for Antarctica or any other place that is wildly off course. That being said, we have tournament officials in stations that *are* off course because we expect some mistakes. If you end up traveling to one of those spots, you'll still have a chance to rejoin the race."

Dr. Harrison looked at the next note card. "Okay, now obviously everyone wants to go fast, but don't forget the mandatory checkpoints. Make sure you check in at the tournament booth every time you arrive in a new city. The booths will be located near the teleport stations and decorated with signs, so they should be easy to find."

Unable to keep still, Lexi started to doodle a baseball diamond. Dr. Harrison was just repeating the obvious. She scribbled a dugout next to the diamond, and then drew a row of seats behind it marking where her family's season ticket seats had been. Brewers tickets had been another casualty of the downsizing initiative—one particularly hard on Lexi and her father. Maybe there'd be enough prize money for them to go to some games this—

"Hey," Ron whispered, jabbing her with his pencil. "You're not writing any of this down."

Lexi flinched at the thought of missing something, but then Ron flashed his page. He had scrawled *Don't lose your badges, Don't go to Antarctica, and Don't forget checkpoints* on the first three lines.

She rolled her eyes. "You need to be reminded not to lose your badge?"

"And not to go to Antarctica?" Mal teased.

Scowling, Ron drew his notebook to his chest and stepped to the side.

"Fine," Lexi said, and with a sigh, she copied the three rules into her notebook.

Dr. Harrison continued, "Next are mandatory rest breaks. This is a three-day tournament, ending back in Wisconsin on Monday. You're going to be doing a lot of traveling over seventy-two hours. If a tournament official advises your team that you must stop for the day, then you'll be spending the night in that city's rest area. When the race reopens the next morning, teams will depart in the order they arrived."

Dr. Harrison ran his hand through his hair. "Also, remember that, due to regulations by the Wisconsin State Board of Education, there can be no teleporting between ten p.m. and seven a.m. As soon as you cross into a time zone where it's between ten p.m. and seven a.m., the chip we installed will disable your Tel-Med, so please keep aware of the time zones as you travel."

Lexi pursed her lips, wishing Dr. Harrison hadn't reminded her competitors about the different time zones. Time-zone screwups happened every year, and she had been hoping a few teams would fall behind from forgetting to factor in a time-zone change or skipping rest periods, leaving them exhausted from all the time-zone hopping. Now that was less likely.

"Okay," Dr. Harrison said. "The last thing is your team's Trek Tracker. There will be nine stops in the tournament, and your

Tracker has spots for nine stickers—one for each puzzle. As you complete a puzzle and collect a sticker, place it over the designated spot on your Trek Tracker. To win, your team must have all nine stickers in place. If a team crosses the finish line without all nine stickers, it will not be declared the winner. No skipping puzzles."

Lexi added *Nine puzzles* and *Collect nine stickers* to her notebook.

"And that's it," Dr. Harrison said. "I hear we have some special guests waiting to talk to you, but before that, let me see if there are any questions."

Several hands shot up. Dr. Harrison pointed to a boy near the front. "Can we work with other teams? You know, form alliances?"

Dr. Harrison shrugged. "Sure, if you want. But like I said, to be eligible to win, each team needs to collect its own stickers. And you should also know that we've designed it so only *one* team can win." Dr. Harrison bobbed his head back and forth. "In fact, I think it's fair to say it's physically *impossible* for there to be a tie. So yeah, if you want to hang out with your friends, go ahead. But know that when it comes to the finish line, it's the first team of three people: one, two, three."

If only I could hang out with my friends, Lexi thought for a split second before brushing it off. She had to stay focused. Eyes narrowed with determination, she wrote there couldn't be any ties.

"Can you tell us what the eliminations will be?" a girl shouted.

Lexi leaned in. Dr. Harrison hesitated, but then said, "We'll probably cut it down to thirty teams by tonight and then eliminate another half tomorrow night so that on Monday we'll start with fifteen teams. Then we'll narrow it down to a top five for the final puzzle."

"Wow, you weren't kidding when you said we had to keep up or be eliminated," Mal said.

Ron tapped the pencil to his page. "That's all right. I shouldn't need more than two days to sell everything."

Mal cocked her head to the side. "Good point. That should be enough for my photo exhibit, too."

Lexi gritted her teeth. The tournament hadn't even started and her teammates were talking about when it would be okay to be eliminated. She forced herself to take a deep breath. The tournament was going to come down to teleport science, and that was *her* expertise. She'd make sure they'd be racing on Monday.

Dr. Harrison stuffed his note cards into his sport coat. "Okay, if there's nothing else, then it's time for some good luck wishes." He snapped his fingers, and a screen rose behind him. "Who better to send those wishes than the scientists who invented teleport travel: Dr. James Bressler, Dr. Wallace Kent, and Dr. Viktoria Vogt!"

Lexi squeezed her notebook closed and sprung into the air. "NO WAY!" Heart racing, she ran a few feet toward the screen to get a better look. Sure enough, it was really them.

As the crowd simmered, the camera focused on Dr. Vogt. She set her glasses atop her head and brushed a few bangs off her forehead. Dressed in cargo pants and a black T-shirt, the seventy-year-old petite scientist vaulted toward the camera, leaving Dr. Kent and Dr. Bressler in the background. She winked and bent toward the lens.

"Guten morgen! It's so good to see such enthusiastic, young scientific minds!"

Lexi stood completely still as she tried to process the fact that Dr. Vogt was talking to her. Well, okay, a bunch of other kids, too, but she was one of them! She exhaled again.

Dr. Vogt continued in her German accent, "As you may know, Dr. Bressler, Dr. Kent, and I love working with young people. It's so exciting to hear fresh ideas from those with a real thirst for science. For that reason, we are happy to announce that one of you will have the opportunity to work as an intern in our lab this summer!"

Lexi's notebook slipped from her hands and fell to the ground as she placed her hands over her mouth. Her mind spun. An internship with the top teleport scientists in the world? She snatched her notebook off the ground but couldn't keep it still in her trembling fingers. She'd be the perfect intern. They had to pick her.

Dr. Vogt held up a finger. "But more about that later. For now, let's get to the tournament! Would anyone like a hint?"

As the other teams blared "Yes!" Lexi tried to steady her hands. *Focus.*

Dr. Vogt lowered her voice. "Listen closely. Every scientific invention starts with an idea, a spark. A scientist must, above all, have an imagination—an imagination that not only thinks of the impossible, but how to make the impossible *possible*." She shook her head. "But it's not easy. At the early stage of the spark, many will doubt you, even say you are foolish for believing such astounding things can become a reality."

Lexi nodded. Dr. Vogt knew what she was talking about. When she first published her teleportation theories, the scientific community scoffed. Everyone said teleportation was impossible—that there was no way enough energy could be generated to transport matter, much less a person, in mere seconds. In the end, Dr. Vogt proved everyone wrong. Her development of a teleportation medallion as an energy source advanced science tenfold. No one was laughing now.

Dr. Vogt balled her hand into a fist and glared into the camera. "You cannot let these doubters stop you. You must stand tall and protect your ideas." Steely-eyed, she inhaled deeply and pressed her hair behind her ears. "The world has always been full of those who dare to see things differently—those who followed their own course and their own dreams, despite what others said. For the first part of your trek, you'll be visiting some of these daring personalities." She leaned forward. "And here's a big hint—you might visit my home country along the way!"

With a wave good-bye, Dr. Vogt rejoined her colleagues, and the screen turned black. Lexi furiously wrote down all she could remember.

Dr. Harrison returned to the stage. "How did everyone like our special guests?"

Thunderous cheers filled the lot. "It's great, isn't it? Okay, so now that we know what's at stake, is everyone ready for your first puzzle?"

Lexi checked her watch. 7:20 a.m. Technically, the tournament wasn't supposed to start until 7:30 a.m. She wondered whether—

"Then what are you waiting for? Open your envelopes!"

Lexi turned to Mal and Ron, who both stared at her.

Riiiiiiiiiipppppp.

She whirled back around. A girl in a purple shirt stood a few feet away, torn envelope in her hand. Lexi rushed to her backpack and retrieved their envelope. An instant later, she tore the seal. The race was on.

CHAPTER
THREE

Lexi emptied the contents of the envelope onto the picnic table.

"Here it is," Ron said, sliding out a page titled "DESTINATION NO. 1."

Lexi reached for the clue, but stopped, remembering from her review of previous tournaments that the tournament directors sometimes buried hints in the starting package. She waved off Ron. "Go ahead and read it," she said, fanning through pages of rules and Travel Request Forms. "I'm gonna skim through the rest of this stuff real quick."

She spotted the Trek Tracker and picked it up.

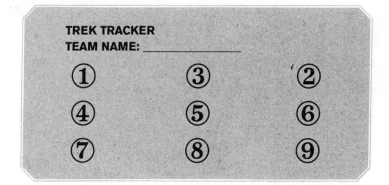

Making a mental note to remember that the order was incorrect in the first row, Lexi stuffed the Tracker inside her backpack.

She looked at Ron, who had remained silent. "Well? I thought you were going to read it?"

"I did," Ron replied as he extended his arm toward Mal. "To myself. Now, I need Mal's tablet to look something up."

Mal gripped her tablet between her hands. "No way. Let me see it, and I'll do the search."

Ron clicked his tongue. "Nah. How 'bout you just give me the tablet?"

The corner of Mal's mouth curled up. "Um, how 'bout for the obvious reason that it's *my* tablet? Use your phone."

"Screen's busted," Ron said. He lunged for the tablet, and Mal waved it behind her head and backed up. Ron swiped for it again, forcing Mal to sidestep his advances.

Lexi squeezed between her teammates and threw out her arms. "You guys! Stop!"

Mal retreated farther away as Ron faked a move to his left, then stepped toward her, his grabby hands outstretched in front of his body.

Lexi swiveled to block him, and as her teammates held their positions, she dug her fingernails into her palms in an effort to remain calm. Everything had gone so smoothly when she'd worked with Mal and Ron on their group project on ancient Egypt this past semester. Ron researched hieroglyphs and created his own puzzle,

Mal constructed and decorated a model of the Luxor Temple, and Lexi had explained Egyptian mathematics. Then they all contributed to their paper. The teacher gave them an A and complimented their teamwork. It was the main reason Lexi asked Ron and Mal if they wanted to race with her. This, though, was not a good start.

She swallowed. "Look, let's do what we did on our Egypt project. We can divide up responsibilities." She tilted her head toward Ron. "You can read the clues." She gestured to Mal. "And we all know Mal's a whiz on the computer. She can look stuff up."

Mal gave a curt nod, and a second later, Ron exhaled. "Fine," he said, holding the clue out in front of him. "Here's the important part: 'Some said I was silly, most called me mad, but if I inspired Cinderella Castle, how can I be that bad?'"

"Easy," Mal said. "I'll search for 'who inspired Cinderella Castle.'" Sliding onto the picnic table bench, Mal typed in the search. Moments later, she called her teammates close and whispered, "It's a castle in Bavaria called Neuschwanstein Castle." Mal shouted out tidbits as she scrolled through the text.

"It was built by King Ludwig the Second in 1869. He ruled from 1864 to 1886. They said he was irrational and eventually ousted him from the throne." Mal paused. "Wow."

"What?" Lexi and Ron asked at the same time.

"He became king when he was only eighteen, and then he built all these fancy castles. He kept spending money the country didn't have. That's the main reason they thought he was ridiculous—he's known as Mad King Ludwig. He died under suspicious circumstances a few days after he lost the throne."

Ron peered over Mal's shoulder and reached for the tablet. She yanked it away, giving him a dirty look. "What now?"

Ron flicked the clue with his finger. "It asks specifically about *Cinderella* Castle. You said he built several castles. I was going to check to make sure the New-stuff-one is the right one."

"*Neuschwanstein*," Mal corrected, still holding the tablet out of Ron's reach. "And yeah, I know what you said. This is it."

As Ron stiffened, Lexi rubbed her temples. The second awkward confrontation between her teammates in as many minutes was eating up valuable time. She had to find a way to keep everyone on track or they'd be lucky to solve a single clue before being eliminated.

"Give her some space, Ron," Lexi said as she adjusted her glasses.

Mal smiled as Ron spun to face Lexi.

Lexi spoke before Ron could say anything. "Mal's got this, though there is no harm in double-checking." She nodded to Mal. "Why don't you show us what you found?"

With a shrug, Mal tilted the screen in her teammates' direction. Lexi read a few lines. The website was clear that Disney's Cinderella Castle was inspired by King Ludwig's Neuschwanstein Castle.

Ron nodded. "Yeah, this is the one. Okay."

"Perfect," Lexi said as she headed to her backpack. "Now, all we have to do is find a teleport station near the castle."

"How do we—"

With a flourish, Lexi pulled out a stack of papers, silencing Mal. She unfolded the pages, which she had taped together to form a large poster, and spread them across the picnic table.

"What—" Ron started.

"—is that?" Mal finished.

Lexi chuckled. "I call it my Teleport Tableau." She circled to the opposite end of the picnic table and pointed to the first four pages. "This part is for the U.S. I organized it by state, and then under each state, I listed teleport stations in certain cities. I didn't include every city, of course, only the major ones or where something important to teleport science happened."

"And the other six pages?" Ron asked, eyebrow raised.

"Europe—organized by country, then cities within each country. Overall, I'd say there are about five hundred teleport stations on here."

Mal's jaw dropped. "Wow. That's a lot of work."

Lexi flattened the pages as much as possible. "Yeah, but public teleport travel has only been legal for a couple years, and it's hard to find all of the active telepods without a teleport locator computer program, which we don't have. This list should work just as well."

Ron and Mal remained frozen, staring at the tableau.

Lexi stifled a laugh, unsure if Ron and Mal were impressed or instead were thinking she came maybe a little *too* prepared. "It really was no big deal," she explained. "I love science and teleporting, remember? This was fun."

Mal waved her off. "Oh, don't worry. I get it. When it comes to design, I totally get into the details, too."

Lexi joined Ron as he leaned over the chart. "All right," she said. "Now we have to figure out where Bavaria is."

"Oh, I know that," Mal said. "Germany!"

Kneeling on the bench, Lexi looked at the Germany section, under which she had listed over twenty cities. She peeked at Mal, who fiddled with the tablet. "What's the closest city?"

Mal bounced her head from side to side. "Munich's the closest *major* city. But the castle's still a couple hours away by train."

Lexi found *Munich* on the tableau. She grabbed a Travel Request Form and started filling it out, but paused as she reached the blank for the station code. Two hours away? There had to be a closer station.

"Hey, Mal," Lexi said. "Can you look for—"

"On it," Mal said.

Tapping her pencil to the form, Lexi scanned the parking lot as she waited for Mal. Many teams remained, with the majority, like Team RAM, studying tablets. Of course they had tablet*s*, as in plural. Team RAM only had Mal's. Teams with three tablets would be able to work three times as fast.

With a small roar, the Mighty Sanbornes took off for the high school. So there they were—wearing incredibly ugly striped and polka-dot T-shirts. Seconds later, Haley's Comets, the Physics Phenoms, and several teams followed.

Lexi lingered on Haley, who had her arm draped over Comet Emma's shoulders. Lexi's heart panged. Since the first grade, she and Haley had always hung out after school, often experimenting in the robotics lab or inventing gadgets (like the extra-long hand gripper they used to steal Haley's brother's Doritos right out from under him from across the hall!), but sometimes just lounging around, watching movies.

Lexi tried keeping it up after she moved, but it was impossible getting rides to and from Haley's house after school. They video-chatted a few times for the first couple weeks, but then Haley kept missing their chat times and scheduling became harder and harder. For the most part, Haley had even stopped texting. To Lexi, the solution was as obvious as $e=mc^2$: to save their friendship, she had to get her butt back to the academy.

"All right, here we go," Mal said, jolting Lexi from her thoughts. "The closest cities to the castle are Schwangau, Waltenhofen, Füssen, Hohenschwangau, Enzen—" Mal stopped and eyed Lexi, who had just spun to face her. "Well?" Mal said. "This would go faster if you actually looked at your tableau thingy to see if any of these cities are on your list."

Lexi refocused on the tableau. "Sorry. Can you start over?"

"Schwangau. S-c-h-w-"

"Not on here. Next," Lexi said.

"Waltenhofen. W-a-l-t-"

Lexi slid a finger down the list of cities, then grimaced. "No."

"How 'bout Füssen? F-u (with two dots)-s-s-e-n."

Lexi raced through. Her eyes bulged. "Yes!"

"Great. There's actually a train station there—it's where the train from Munich stops. The teleport station's probably connected."

"Nice!" Lexi said, and she completed the form.

They bolted across the parking lot to the gymnasium, and Ron flung open the door. As her teammates ran to the temporary teleport station that had been erected at the far side of the gym, Lexi stood and stared, taking it all in.

A quantum computer, approximately two feet by three feet, stood by the bleachers. Lights beeped and flashed, and several keyboards poked out from its sides. A separate control panel was adjacent to the computer, where a telepod engineer punched keys into the display. Three portable telepods had been erected next to the wall. A kid in a blue shirt surged from the line, through a metal gate, and bounded up one of the platforms.

In a few minutes, she would be in his place, ready to travel across an ocean and to a new country in literally the blink of an eye.

"Earth to Lexi!"

Lexi jerked. Ron and Mal were waving frantically for her to join them in line. As another team raced through the doors from behind, Lexi took off for her teammates. She squeezed in line just before Edison's Excellencies passed her.

"Badges, passports, and Tel-Meds, please," the tournament official said. Team RAM handed everything over. "All right, everything seems to be in order. All I need is your Travel Request Form. Since this is a temporary teleport station, you won't need teleportation tickets. The telepod engineer will scan your destination code into the quantum computer directly."

Lexi provided the form and inspected the woman's face closely as she looked it over. The engineer's expression gave nothing away. If Team RAM wasn't supposed to be going to Germany, they'd find out once they got there. The engineer opened the gate, and Ron darted through.

"The one on the left, please," the woman called.

Ron advanced to the telepod, a clear square platform about a foot off the floor. He stepped up, carefully placing each foot in the marked area. After positioning his supersized backpack onto a smaller platform to the side, he bent over and unzipped the side of his gym shoe. Straightening, he held up his Tel-Med.

"Click it in place," the engineer said as a small metal shelf rose out of the platform. Ron placed the Tel-Med onto the shelf, and the shelf's rim flashed green.

"Straight as a board, arms at your sides," the engineer called while punching keys into the panel. "Hmph," she said. Then, "Try sliding your backpack a little closer to you." Ron obeyed, adjusting the pack so it was as close to his platform as possible, though still technically resting on the smaller side-platform.

The engineer pressed a few keys. Seconds later, a thin glass shield rose out of the platform and encircled Ron. A similar shield surrounded the platform containing Ron's backpack. Lights on the control panel glowed green.

"Ready," the engineer said.

Ron flashed a thumbs-up before dropping his arm to the side.

"Keep still. It's a three count . . . starting now. Three, two, one."

A bright light flashed, and the platform glowed purple. A violet streak stretched through the telepod, and Ron and his backpack vanished.

Lexi shuddered. It'd been over six months since she'd teleported anywhere, and she'd forgotten how amazing it was to see someone disappear.

"*Next*," the engineer said, tapping Lexi on the shoulder.

Lexi flinched. *Oops.* She got lost in her world again—Mal was already gone. She trotted to the telepod and snapped the Tel-Med in place. The shelf glowed green, and she straightened and focused on the engineer, waiting for the countdown.

"All set," Lexi called.

The engineer pushed a button, and the clear shield encased Lexi. "Okay. Stand straight and keep still. Ready. Three, two, one . . ."

Lexi slammed her eyes shut, and a fraction of a second later, her body tingled. An instant after that, the light feeling faded, and a bell dinged. She opened her eyes in Füssen.

CHAPTER FOUR

The blue-and-gold tournament booth was easy to spot—the orga-
nizers had obviously expected an onslaught of teams because at
least twenty tournament officials circled the check-in area. Within
five minutes of landing, Team RAM exited Füssen's station with
public transportation passes for Germany, a bus schedule to local
attractions, and a map.

Lexi needed only a second with the map. "Good news, the castle's on here—it's a short bus ride."

"Woo-hoo!" Ron said. "Am I an awesome puzzle solver or
what?"

Mal scrunched her nose. "Um, I'm the one who did the Internet
search. What'd you do other than read the clue?"

Not wanting to referee another spat between her teammates,
Lexi pushed her way through Mal and Ron and headed outside. She
crossed the train tracks to a row of red buses. "Come on," she called
over her shoulder. "Let's find our bus."

"Found it!" Ron said.

Lexi and Mal stopped suddenly and stared at Ron. He hadn't even glanced at the bus schedule. Smiling, Ron pointed to a bus at the end of the line. Several teams congregated outside the door, waiting for the driver to allow them to enter. "I'm thinking that one," he said. "Right?"

After a shared eye roll with Mal, Lexi strode past Ron to the last bus. The driver opened the door, and teams spilled inside. Lexi did a quick scan. No Sanbornes, Comets, or Phenoms. She peered down the road, wondering how far behind her team had already fallen. When she pivoted to the door, it closed in her face.

"Hey!" she shouted.

The door opened. "Full here," the driver said. "Next one will be along in about fifteen minutes."

Lexi threw out an arm and placed a foot on the stair. "What? No!" Panicking, she fumbled for words. "Please? There's only three of us. We can squeeze in anywhere. I promise."

The driver looked past Lexi toward Ron. "Looks more like four with that pack."

Lexi's stomach tightened. Ron's stupid swag was already causing problems. She opened her mouth to beg some more, but the driver stepped back and stared down the aisle. She squirmed, her mind racing for a more coherent argument, like maybe Ron's backpack could ride on the roof?

"All right," the driver said, returning to Lexi. "There's four seats scattered along the aisle. You'll have to sit separately."

"No problem," Lexi answered, motioning for Ron and Mal to follow.

As the bus left the station, Lexi peered out the window, searching for the Comets and other teams. She wondered how many buses ahead they were. Duh. She'd text Haley! Lexi dug out her phone, immediately noticing the battery was already down 50 percent. She'd begged her parents for a better one, but no luck. One quick text couldn't hurt, though. She pressed the message envelope and scrolled to Haley's name. Several unanswered texts from the last few days stared back at her.

With a sigh, Lexi returned the phone to her pocket. Who knew if Haley would even notice the text. Besides, Team RAM couldn't be that far behind. She'd see Haley at the castle.

Lexi leaned back and closed her eyes.

"Green Bay Packers shirts and hats! Take your pick! Once it's gone, it's gone," Ron belted.

Oh no. Lexi snapped open her eyes and spun in her seat. A man seated in the row behind her sneered in Ron's direction.

"Ron," Lexi whispered angrily. Ron didn't respond and continued his sales pitch to the back rows. Lexi called him again. Still no response, but Sneering Man shifted. Lexi turned back around, slinking into her seat. It was so important for teams to get off to a good start, and with who knew how many buses in front of them, Team RAM couldn't afford getting kicked off the bus.

Please. Lexi said silently as she crossed her fingers. *Please don't let anyone complain.*

Fifteen minutes later, when the bus finally stopped, Lexi shot up and exited. Mal followed, and, eventually, after everyone else disembarked, Ron walked out with his backpack.

"Woo-hoo!" Ron shouted. "*That* was an awesome ride! I made, like, a hundred and fifty dollars!"

"Good for you," Lexi mumbled. Eager to put the trip behind her and move on, she pointed to the ticket booth. "We're going to need tickets for the castle."

"I got it," Ron said. "Give me your badges. I'll be right back."

As Ron hustled to the ticket station, Lexi looked skyward. Castle Neuschwanstein was located in the center of the mountains on a ridge camouflaged by tall pines. Stone white bricks and towering turrets poked through the greenery. Blue-black roof shingles covered the tower peaks, atop which thin spires stretched into the sky. It certainly resembled pictures of every fairy-tale castle she'd ever seen.

"Let's cross the road," Mal said, nudging Lexi. She held up the camera. "I can get a better angle."

"Sure," Lexi said, biting her tongue. They had to wait for Ron and their tickets anyway—no harm letting Mal grab a few photos.

The girls crossed the road, and Mal snapped away. Lexi untied the sweatshirt from around her waist and hung it over her shoulders—the crisp mountain breeze made the air considerably cooler than it had been at the station. As she tied a knot in the sleeves around her neck, she glimpsed a horse-drawn carriage near a "Castle

Neuschwanstein" sign posted on a fence. She tapped Mal. "What's that? Do we have to get in line to take a carriage up the mountain?"

Mal lowered the camera from her eyes. "I don't know. I'll check it out."

Mal squeezed her thin, lanky body through the crowd, and Lexi lost sight of her until she broke out a couple minutes later. "Okay," Mal said. "There are two ways to reach the castle: hike up the side of the mountain or ride up in the carriage. If we take the carriage, we'd have to pay for it out of our own money."

Lexi winced. Since the tournament provided the essentials, she had figured she'd only need money for snacks and drinks and hadn't brought much. Spending it so soon wasn't the smartest move. She looked at the mountain trail again. It seemed long and winding, though some teams had already skipped the carriages and were hiking.

Mal nudged Lexi away from the carriages. "I say we walk. The line's real long, anyway. By the time we get a carriage, we can be at the castle."

"Good point," Lexi answered, relieved.

"Besides, if we walk, I can get a bunch of different angles. Come on, there's Ron!"

"Wait!" Lexi shouted after Mal. *Great.* One problem solved, but now she had to deal with Mal wanting to stop and take photos. She reached Mal and grabbed her arm. "Hey, we have to get to the top as quickly as possible. We're not gonna have—"

"Got 'em!" Ron interrupted, waving the castle tickets over his head. He returned their badges. "What do we do now? Wait in line?"

Mal pointed to the trail. "Nope. We're walking. Come on."

Team RAM started up the mountain, and it wasn't long before Lexi stopped worrying about how much Mal would slow them down. Turned out, *she* was the slow-mo. After the first turn, superstar jock Ron was far ahead. Not that Lexi was surprised. Ron was already being scouted by high schools, and the local newspaper had published plenty of articles about the Filipino Flyer's athletic prowess. But when Mal disappeared about a third of the way up, Lexi knew she was in trouble.

Trudging behind, she placed her hands on her thighs, dug down, and forced her legs to keep moving. To distract her mind from the constant ache, she quietly recited the Brewers' major league roster. It was a trick her dad had taught her for when she had to run laps in gym class—concentrating on something else made the time pass faster. By the time Lexi reached the top, her raw throat stung, her muscles burned, and she knew with 100 percent certainty that any Magill athletic gene had skipped her.

Wearing a satisfied smile, Lexi lumbered past a mob of tourists to an out-of-the-way railing and slid off her backpack. Her sweatshirt was next, and as she inhaled the fresh, pine scent, she used the sleeves to wipe off her sweaty forearms.

Spying her teammates near the back of the crowd, Lexi approached. "Well, we made it," she puffed as she removed her Brewers cap and tossed her head to dry her damp hair.

Mal fanned her shirt. "Yeah, that was a hike."

"*Willkommen! Willkommen!* Welcome to Castle Neuschwanstein!" a tour guide called, mingling through the crowd. "The next tour starts in five minutes, and it's the last English tour of the day, so please join us!"

"Sure," Ron said as he wiped his brow with his forearm. "Hey, wait," he called a second later, but the tour guide had already left to greet another group.

"What?" Lexi sputtered between gasps.

Ron squinted. "She said it was the last tour of the day? How is that possible?"

Lexi wriggled off her watch and reset the time, something she had planned to do upon arriving at each location. "Because it's four p.m. here. We skipped ahead seven hours when we teleported to Germany. I have a Time-Zone Cheat Sheet that correlates times back home with times in a bunch of different countries if you want to take a look later."

"All right, everyone. Gather 'round!" the guide announced.

The teams assembled, and the guide started the tour through the castle. Lexi studied her surroundings as best she could, looking for a statue of Ludwig, someone dressed as Ludwig, or anything that might resemble the king. But as the guide led them through the dull servants' dormitories into more regal parts of the castle, Lexi felt her attention sway to the extravagance around her. Extraordinary paintings stretched from floor to ceiling. Oak benches, ornate pottery, enormous chandeliers, copper and gold trim, embroidered linens, glass windows—opulent furnishings filled every nook and cranny. King Ludwig had clearly bought whatever he wanted, no matter the cost.

Eventually, the guide led everyone outside and began her final remarks. As soon as the tour ended, tourists clamored into carriages or started down the mountain. Everyone in the tournament, however, remained at the castle, mingling around and looking as clueless as Lexi felt. Apparently, her competitors hadn't found the king, either.

"Any ideas?" Lexi asked her teammates. "Did either of you see anything that looked like him?"

Ron shook his head. "Not unless he was a swan."

Lexi stifled a laugh. The tour guide had explained that King Ludwig was known as the Swan King, and his affinity for swans was evident in almost every room they had visited. Swan paintings, swan statues, swan cushions, swan tablecloths—the bird had been everywhere.

"I didn't see anything, either," Mal said. "But if you want to go back inside, I'm all for it. The architecture is exquisite, and while the décor is extravagant, it really displays Ludwig's fascination with the medieval world, from textiles to the color scheme, to—"

"Mal!" Lexi interrupted, hoping to jar her teammate's thoughts back to the race.

Ron laughed. "Getting a little carried away there, Moreno."

Mal exhaled. *"Fine.* Well, no, I didn't see him." She stepped toward an outcrop. "I wonder if he's outside."

Lexi looked over the balcony at the fields, forest, and mountains. The majestic view reminded her of one of her grandma's puzzles. "This view is incredible, but I don't see anything."

"Me neither," Mal said. She looked at Ron. "Does the clue say he's somewhere inside the castle?"

Ron shrugged off his backpack. "I think so." He pulled out the clue and flattened it against the pavement.

DESTINATION NO. 1

Some said I was Silly
Most Called Me Mad
But if I inspired Cinderella Castle
How Could I be that Bad?

To continue the trek, go to the castle I built that is considered my favorite home and find the room that contains my brother. Then, go with the flow.

"Oh no," Lexi said, glancing at Ron as her insides twisted.

"What?" Ron replied.

Lexi directed her teammates to the last three lines. Ron hadn't read them to her and Mal at the starting-point parking lot. He had only mentioned the part about Cinderella Castle. *He had entirely skipped the rest of the clue!*

A few seconds later, Mal gasped, and Lexi knew Mal understood.

Lexi watched Ron read through it again. Ron's eyes got huge as he traced his finger over the last three lines. Now they all knew.

Not only weren't they looking for Mad King Ludwig, but they were at the wrong castle.

CHAPTER FIVE

Mal removed the tablet from her backpack as Ron tugged his short black hair in all directions. A wave of nausea reverberated through Lexi. This was going to cost them. Big. Shuddering, she gritted her teeth and looked around to assess the damage, counting every team in sight.

Doppler Daredevils, Edison's Excellencies, an orange-shirted team, a pink-striped-shirted team, a team wearing gray hoodies . . . Lexi closed her eyes. In total, she'd seen about fifteen different teams at the base of the mountain, around the castle, or on the bus. That was less than half of the teams entered in the tournament. And she hadn't glimpsed any of the top teams—no Haley, no Sanbornes, no Phenoms.

Shoot.

Lexi opened her eyes and hung her head. Ron had screwed up, but she should have realized long before now that they were in the wrong place. She pounded a fist to her head. *Stupid.*

"How did I miss that?" Ron muttered. "I mean . . . what was I thinking? It's like, Puzzle Solving 101: Read the entire problem. I can't—"

"—believe it, either," Mal said, eyes narrowed. "But there's no way we're stopping now. One country does not qualify as a trip around the world. My photo exhibit will be laughed off the stage." She swiped the screen with enough force the tablet nearly flew out of her hand. "Here it is. Linderhof. King Ludwig lived most of his days at his hunting lodge at Linderhof. It's another castle, and it's the one he considered his favorite home."

Hands trembling, Lexi unpacked her Teleport Tableau so she could figure out which teleport station was closest to Linderhof. Her mind wandered to Haley, Tomoka, and her other former classmates who had clearly teleported to the correct castle. Ron's silly mistake was already putting her plan to rejoin them at the academy in serious jeopardy.

Ron continued to mumble. "'To continue the trek, go to the castle I built that is considered my favorite home.' It's as clear as day. The part about Cinderella Castle is there so we could figure out who *he* is. I'm sorr—"

"Enough," Lexi said with a scowl.

Ron stuffed the clue in his backpack. "I know. I'm sorry. Maybe I'll stay here and sell swag."

Lexi froze. That was exactly what she couldn't let happen. If Ron quit, it was the end of Team RAM. Teams had to have three members at all times, and the tournament didn't allow midrace replacements.

Swallowing her frustration, she tapped Ron's elbow. "Don't be silly," she forced out. "It's early. I'm sure we'll be okay." She nodded at Mal. "Where's this Linderhof place?"

"Right down the road."

"What?" Ron said, head spinning.

"Well, not *right* down the road," Mal clarified, rising to her feet. "About an hour away."

Ron's face fell. "An hour?"

Mal clicked her tongue. "What? It could be worse."

Lexi folded up the tableau. They'd take the bus back to the Füssen station and then find a bus to Linderhof.

"Wait!" Mal said.

Lexi startled. "What?"

"There's buses that travel between here and Linderhof. Apparently, it's very common for people to visit both castles on the same day."

"Oh wow," Lexi said.

Mal hustled to the trail, tablet still in hand. "Yep," she called, disappearing down the path. "Only thing is they stop running at five o'clock."

"Five?" Lexi said, twisting her watch. 4:45 p.m. "Fifteen minutes."

"Fifteen minutes?" Ron repeated. "We gotta book. Now!"

As Ron and Lexi chased after Mal, Lexi craned her neck every which way to see if any other teams had caught the mistake. The bus would be packed with tourists leaving for the day and wouldn't be expecting a bunch of teams. There wouldn't be room for everyone.

Lexi pivoted around a bend, and the town's narrow shop-lined streets came into view. A pair of red buses hummed off to the side. Not seeing any teams, Lexi slowed as she saw Mal step off the trail. Ron was already there. The Filipino Flyer had flown down the mountain in record time. Ron and Mal turned and faced her.

"Get in line! Get in line!" Lexi screamed, though with her huffing and puffing it sounded more like, "Get . . . li . . . n."

Ron and Mal didn't move. Lexi peeked at the buses. Smoke trailed from the exhaust pipes. She pumped her legs harder. Maybe they'd hear her now. She flung out her arm. "Get . . . line!" she shouted.

Mal nodded, tapped Ron's stomach, and the two sprinted toward the buses. Lexi slowed a smidge as she reached the base of the mountain—careening wildly into a mass of tourists would *not* be a good idea.

A tower clock chimed. Five o'clock.

Lexi hustled to the first bus. No driver. No passengers. No teams. She moved to the second, and as she approached, a man stuck his head out the door. "Last call for Linderhof!"

"Here!" Lexi gasped, swinging the pack from her back. She lifted the tournament badge off her chest and then flashed the public transportation pass.

The man grunted. "Go on."

Lexi pushed past him and climbed aboard. She searched the

rows. No teams—only tourists. She collapsed into the seat next to Mal as the bus took off.

"Good job finding the bus," she said as she grabbed a water bottle from her backpack. "We'll definitely save some time by not going back to the station."

Mal peered into her compact mirror and adjusted her impeccable braid by carefully tucking in loose strands of hair. "No problem, though from now on I suggest we *all* read the clues. That was ridiculous. It could have cost you your tournament and me my entire project."

Lexi took a swig of water. "Yeah, good point. Where's Ron?"

Mal gestured to a seat a few rows behind them. Ron sat hunched over Mal's tablet, his backpack taking up the entire seat next to him. "I gave him the tablet. He wanted to check out the next place," Mal said as she dabbed her chin with her scarf. "He wants to be ready as soon as we get there."

Lexi arched an eyebrow, wondering if getting ready meant selling swag or finding Ludwig's brother's room, but she decided not to ask. Between the mountain hike and keeping her teammates focused on the tournament, she was exhausted, and they'd only been racing a couple hours. Besides, she'd find out soon enough.

A little after six p.m. local time, the bus rolled to a stop. Lexi led her teammates off . . . and directly onto the mammoth Linderhof estate. They didn't need to hike a mountain to see this castle— Linderhof's white palace gleamed from the other side of an elaborate garden. A fountain stood in the center of manicured lawns, while flower gardens bordered stone paths that led to the palace's stairs.

"Holy moly," Mal said, stepping out of the way of exiting tourists. "This is beautiful."

Mal reached for her camera, but Lexi couldn't blame her teammate *too* much. The view was impressive, and the best part was the number of other teams on the grounds. Kids were everywhere—walking along stone paths, huddling outside the palace doors, and congregating around the fountain. *Yes!* Despite the bungled clue, Team RAM was totally in the thick of the hunt for the king's brother.

"Come on," Lexi said, charging forward as she spun her head side to side in search of Haley. "You can take photos on the way, but we need to get to the palace."

"No," Ron said softly.

Lexi scrunched her nose. "What?"

An odd smile crossed Ron's face. "The palace is a decoy—like an offensive lineman who checks in as an eligible receiver."

Mal lowered the camera and stared at Ron as Lexi wrinkled her brow.

"A what?" the girls asked.

Ron rolled his eyes. "Never mind. What I'm saying is that Otto isn't in the palace."

"Otto?"

"Otto. That's the king's brother's name, and from what I read, he's not going to be in the palace. He's somewhere else on the grounds." The girls didn't respond, and Ron stiffened and glared at them. "Look, I said I was sorry about earlier, but now it's crunch time. You either trust me or you don't."

Uh, don't? But with Ron's threat to quit still fresh in her mind, Lexi didn't want to say or do anything to nudge him over the edge. She studied the gardens. If Otto *was* inside the palace, certainly there wouldn't be so many teams still on the property walking around looking seriously confused. She scanned the area again. Unfortunately, Haley's team wasn't among them. Lexi sighed. Her friend was likely far ahead by now. She had to do something to catch up, and if Ron was convinced he had the right answer . . .

"Okay," Lexi said, silently hoping she wasn't making the stupidest mistake in tournament history. "Lead the way."

Ron picked a path and strode through the garden. As they passed several teams, Lexi made sure to keep an ear open. One team went on and on about King Ludwig's royal bed chamber, which was covered with gold, had painted walls, and housed humongous chandeliers. Another team raved about the dining room, which had a "magic" table that disappeared into the floor and sunk to the lower level kitchen, where workers would stack food before raising the table back into the dining room. There was even a hall of mirrors that created a mirage of an endless corridor.

But none of the teams had mentioned anything about finding Otto. Instead, her competitors were roaming the gardens, seemingly clueless about where to go next.

Unlike Ron.

Lexi eyed her teammate again and considered asking for an update, but she rejected the idea almost immediately. Ron walked with purpose. Tightening her grip on her backpack's straps, she plowed after him.

Bypassing additional fountains, trim gardens, and the palace entrance, Ron led Team RAM to a grass-covered hill behind the palace. As the three ascended the hill, Ron spun to the left and right, looking for followers. Lexi did the same, but no one was paying them any attention. They were quite a ways from the palace, and the other teams were no longer in earshot. The occasional click of Mal's camera provided the only background noise.

A narrow path leading to a cave came into view, along with a rope and several signs marking the cave's entrance. Ron stopped near one of the signs, crouched low, and retrieved his notebook from his backpack.

"Okay, this is what I found," he whispered, flipping to a page. "There were a couple websites that listed rooms inside the palace. I wrote them down, thinking we could use it to decide where to go first." Ron set the notebook on the ground, and Mal and Lexi stooped to read.

LINDERHOF CASTLE ROOMS:
LILAC CABINET
KING'S BEDCHAMBER
PINK CABINET

AUDIENCE CHAMBER
DINING ROOM
BLUE CABINET
YELLOW CABINET
VESTIBULE
WESTERN TAPESTRY CHAMBER
EASTERN TAPESTRY CHAMBER
HALL OF MIRRORS

"So?" Mal shrugged.

"Yeah, I thought you said we weren't supposed to go inside the palace?" Lexi added.

"We're not," Ron replied. "And this shows why. See—there's only one bedchamber, which is King Ludwig's. Look at the other rooms. If there were a shrine or statue or something of the king's brother, it'd say so, wouldn't it?"

Lexi skimmed the list again. Only one bedchamber was listed, and while one of the other rooms *could* contain a drawing or painting of Otto, if that was the case, the other teams would have found it and left.

"What are you saying?" Lexi asked, falling to her knees.

"This." Ron turned the page. "When I didn't see a second bedroom in the palace, I remembered what Mal had said when we were at the other castle—that maybe the king was outside somewhere. That led me to make a list of other stuff located on the grounds."

LINDERHOF GROUNDS:
MOROCCAN COTTAGE
MOORISH KIOSK
LINDEN TREE
NEPTUNE FOUNTAIN
WATER PARTERRE
EASTERN PARTERRE
WESTERN PARTERRE
VENUS GROTTO
HUNDING'S HUT

Lexi read the list silently.

"I still don't get it," Mal said. "None of these sound like a bedroom or refer to his brother, either."

Ron smirked. "*One* does. The clue says to find the room containing the king's brother, right?" Both girls nodded. "And we know Ludwig's brother was named Otto, right?" Lexi and Mal nodded again. Ron took out a pen and underlined one of the names:

VENUS GR<u>OTTO</u>

"Get it? The word 'Otto' is contained in the word 'Grotto.' The Venus Grotto is therefore a room that contains 'my brother.'" Ron stood and tossed his head back toward the cave behind him, more specifically the sign at the entrance that identified the cave as the Venus Grotto. "I think we're supposed to go in there."

A whoosh of adrenaline zapped Lexi, and she sprung up, passing Ron on the way into the cave. Her heart pounded at the thought that

Ron's puzzle solving pushed Team RAM past the teams still milling about the palace.

The cave opened to a narrow path adjacent to a small lake, where a shell-shaped boat floated in the middle of the water. A painted mural draped the cave's back wall. Rocks and stalagmites surrounded the entire grotto, which changed colors as overhead lights flashed over the water. Statues of swans decorated the landscape.

Eyes on the lake, Team RAM followed the curved path to its end on the other side of the grotto, where a small blue-and-gold tournament booth had been erected. A sign was tacked to the booth's base.

DESTINATION NO. 1

Screeching, Lexi jumped and high-fived Mal, who hopped in place, clapping her hands. Ron folded his arms across his chest, beaming. He held out a fist, and Lexi and Mal traded pounds as they whooped it up.

"No one else is here!" Lexi shouted, letting her emotions burst free. "With all those teams at the other castle *and* wandering outside the palace here, we have to be back in the top thirty."

"Hello there!"

A tournament monitor popped up from behind the booth, and Team RAM jumped. "Sorry," the man said with a chuckle. "I didn't mean to startle you." He handed over a manila envelope. "Here's your next clue, and so you know, there's a temporary teleport station near the bus stop, so there's no need to return to Füssen. Make sure to stop by the food tent on the way out—there's bratwurst and other German fare. Good luck."

"Heck yeah!" Ron shouted. "I'm starving."

Ignoring Ron, Lexi grabbed the envelope, slid a fingernail under the flap, and pulled out several pieces of paper. She read aloud the top page.

DESTINATION NO. 2

Congratulations! You have successfully solved clue #1.
Place the black swan sticker over the No. 1 circle
on your Trek Tracker.

To continue:

People thought King Ludwig's idea of a flying car was foolish, but this man had similar ideas three hundred years earlier, and he's considered a genius. Your next destination is a museum containing a replica of one of this genius's flying machines.

Hint: It's in the country that inspired King Ludwig's Venus Grotto.

Pages of sketches accompanied the clue, and Lexi showed them to her teammates. Most resembled oddly shaped airplanes, but a few depicted an airborne car. "Some of these are pretty cool," she said, tracing her finger over one of the more intricate drawings.

"It's gotta be Da Vinci," Mal said, already typing on her tablet. Seconds later, she added, "Yep. The Venus Grotto is modeled after the Blue Grotto in Capri, Italy. Italy and flying machines is definitely Da Vinci."

"Italy! Cool!" Ron said.

Lexi reread the clue to herself. Mal 100 percent sounded like she knew what she was talking about, but Da Vinci? Weren't clues supposed to relate to teleport science? Drawings of flying machines hardly qualified. She tapped her lips. To be fair, Dr. Vogt had said the first part of the race would feature daring personalities. No doubt Da Vinci and King Ludwig were that.

Lexi pictured Haley's reaction as she read the clue. Her best friend would be complaining big-time about having to track down an artist. Ha! Maybe the nonscience clues would trip up some of the academy teams and give her the opening she needed.

"Oh no," Mal said, giving the tablet another swipe. "We might have a problem."

"What?" Lexi and Ron asked.

Mal flicked the tablet. "There's more than one museum in Italy that has a Da Vinci flying machine. Hang on."

As Mal searched, Lexi reached inside the envelope and retrieved a round sticker picturing a black swan. She peeled off its back and placed it over the first circle on the team's Trek Tracker. *One down, eight to go.*

"Okay," Mal said. "I found three possibilities."

"Let's hear 'em," Ron replied.

"The first is the Leonardo Da Vinci Museum. It's in Florence. According to the website, it has life-sized versions of his inventions, including flying machines."

"That sounds good," Lexi said. "What're the others?"

"The National Museum of Science and Technology in Milan and the Da Vinci Museum in Rome. Both are also supposed to have models of his flying machines."

Lexi pulled out the Teleport Tableau and found the cities listed under Italy. "Well, the good news is I have codes for teleport stations in all three—so we'll be set with whichever we choose."

"Great," Ron said, rolling his eyes. "So now all we have to do is figure out which one it is." He tilted his head toward Mal. "What do you think? You've read about them. Does it seem one's more likely than the others?"

Mal shook her head. "I don't know. I mean, this is mostly a science tournament, so maybe the one in Milan since it's a science museum? Then again, the other two are specifically named after him." Mal met their eyes. "Way I see it, it can be any of them."

"How far apart are they?" Ron asked.

"About 145 miles between Rome and Florence, and then another 190 miles between Florence and Milan," Mal answered a few seconds later.

"Well, that cancels running to each one," Ron said. He blew out a breath. "Well?" He turned to Lexi. "Any ideas?"

Lexi squinted at the sketches again. There had to be a way to pick the right museum. The tournament directors wouldn't leave it to chance. But after another inspection, she hadn't noticed anything useful. "Any chance the museums have photos online?" she wondered out loud. "Maybe we can compare the flying machines in these sketches to the ones in the photos to see if there's a match?"

"Good idea!" Mal said, reaching for the sketches. She bumped the tableau, knocking it out of Lexi's hand. As Lexi retrieved it, her eye caught the abbreviation for Florence's teleport station.

"Wait!" Lexi cried. "The first clue—the one with Otto. Read it again. There was something we were supposed to do after finding Otto's room, wasn't there?"

Ron gasped. "Yeah, you know, there was. Hang on." He yanked the clue out of a side-zippered pouch and unfolded it. It says, "To continue the trek, go to the castle I built that is considered my favorite home and find the room that contains my brother. Then, go with the flow."

"Do you know what that means?" Ron asked.

Laughing, Lexi thrusted the tableau under her teammates' eyes. "Take a look at the code for the station in Florence."

ITA-FLO

"Get it? It's F-L-O, pronounced as *flow*. Like Team RAM is our initials. *Go with the FLO.*"

As Ron and Mal rocked back and grinned, Lexi folded the tableau and then filled out a Travel Request Form. "Florence, here we come!"

CHAPTER
SIX

"Ciao."

Lexi opened her eyes. A man with a bushy mustache filled her view. *"Benvenuti a Italia!"* He held out his hand, and Lexi took it and stepped off the platform. The man gestured to the corner, where blue and gold streamers hung over a small booth. A clock on the counter flashed 7:30 p.m.

Lexi's heartbeat quickened with the realization of how close they were to the end of Day One due to the time change. Team RAM had a lot of ground to make up—and fast.

"Where's Mal?" Lexi asked Ron as she approached.

"Bathroom." Ron tilted his head toward the booth. "I've got some bad news, too. Take a look."

Lexi stood on her tiptoes to see over the crowd of kids. Although several teams were present, no one was actually *at* the counter being checked in. Instead, everyone furiously typed on their tablets, talking to themselves. "What is it?" she asked out of the corner of her mouth.

"Listen," Ron whispered into her ear.

Lexi tilted her head to the side. Seconds later, she understood. Everyone was using their tablets to figure out how to translate English into Italian. She spotted a banner hanging from the ceiling: *Non parliamo Inglese/We Don't Speak English.*

"Get it?" Ron asked.

"Yeah. I wonder why. It can't be that hard to find people who speak English and Italian, right?"

"That's it! Great idea." Ron slapped Lexi on the back and then ran to the waiting area. He returned with a teenager and pointed him to the booth. As the kid walked toward the check-in counter, Ron explained, "He speaks English and Italian. I sent him to check us in."

Less than a minute later, the kid returned. "Sorry, but they said no. They want you to figure out how to communicate. They said it's part of problem-solving for your tournament."

"Oh," Ron and Lexi said.

"Thanks, anyway," Ron added, and he and the kid knocked fists.

Lexi loosened her pack's straps. "While we wait for Mal, we should write out what we want to say so it's all ready for her to type into a translation website."

Ron rocked off his backpack, nearly crushing a passing family in the process. "Good idea. I'll get my notebook."

"Hey!" Mal said, bounding toward them. "Sorry, but I *really* had to go." She paused. "Why aren't you guys in line?"

Lexi exhaled. "We have to speak Italian. We were waiting for you, since we'll need the tablet to find a translation website."

Mal narrowed her eyes. "No English?"

"Nope," Ron said, positioning himself behind Mal and grabbing the zipper to her purse.

Mal spun. "Hey!"

"Relax. I'm getting the tablet."

Mal swung the purse to her front. "Leave it," she said. She strode toward the booth. "Come on."

"No, seriously," Ron called.

"Yeah," Lexi added. "There's a sign and everything."

Lexi tried to follow, but she lost Mal's braid in the sea of stammering teams. She moved behind Ron and let him blaze a path.

They made it to the booth, where an irritated-looking Mal greeted them. "About time," she said, stretching out her hand. "Passports and badges." After her teammates didn't make a move, Mal shifted her weight and turned to the tournament worker, saying something that, judging from the conversation that followed, had to be fluent Italian.

Lexi gasped as she noticed the awed faces of the teams they'd passed. Mal had totally saved them. She tapped Ron, and both retrieved their passports and badges. The tournament worker completed the check-in, and Mal backed away.

"Let's go," Mal said. Minutes later, Team RAM was standing outside of the bustling station. Mal tipped her head toward a brick-paved street. "It's not far. We go right down *Vie de Servi*."

"Hold up," Ron said. "What was that back there? You speak Italian?"

"Yeah," Lexi added with a bounce to her step as she spied her frustrated competitors still hovering over the check-in counter. "I knew you spoke Spanish, but Italian? Do you realize how awesome that is? We skipped ahead of at least five teams!"

Mal delicately slid a loose hair into her braid. "I speak French, too. My dad gives art lectures all over Europe. Since my family spends tons of time here, my parents thought it'd help if I knew the languages." She resumed walking. "Come on. The museum's this way."

The brick road led to a large, open-air pedestrian plaza. As Mal led them through, Lexi rubbed her arms. While warmer than the mountains of Germany, Italy's weather was brisk. With night looming, it would only get colder. She fiddled for her sweatshirt, missing Ron's sudden stop and bumping into him.

"Look," Ron said, pointing.

Lexi raised her eyes. A gigantic domed building stretched for blocks. Mainly white with tinges of pink and green splashes throughout, the structure resembled an old church—except for the fact that, at least in Lexi's estimation, it was the size of at least ten churches. Spires jutted from the roof, reminding Lexi of the towers on King Ludwig's castle.

"Welcome to downtown Florence," Mal said. "We're in the city center. That's the Duomo, a cathedral built back in . . ." Mal scratched her chin. "Back in . . . well, I don't know when. Back a long time ago, like the 1400s or something." She snapped a photo. "This is a real popular area. I saw my first opera around the corner."

"It's huge," Ron said. "Hey, I'm gonna check—"

"Yeah, it's amazing," Lexi interrupted. "But let's keep moving." She stepped around Ron as he continued talking about the plaza and followed Mal down the street, all the while keeping one eye on the cathedral. "I can't believe how big it is."

The street tapered to a strip lined with three- and four-story buildings. Bicycles, motorcycles, and pedestrians hurried along the narrow corridor, which was framed by shops and restaurants. A block or so past the dome, Mal stopped in front of a beige building with an arched wooden door. A red "Leonardo da Vinci" banner hung above one of the windows, which displayed a "Museum Activities" sign.

"Ready?" Mal asked with her hand on the door. Before Lexi could answer, Mal peered past her. "Wait—where's Ron?"

Lexi spun. Ron wasn't there. "I . . . I have no idea. He was with us by the domo thing."

"Duomo. Yeah, I know."

The girls squinted down the street from where they had come. Pedestrians walked to and fro, but there was no sign of their teammate.

Lexi spoke through clenched teeth. "Where could he have gone?

There's no way he could have gotten lost. We were going straight the whole time."

Mal tapped Lexi's shoulder. "Well, he knows where we're going. Is it against the rules to get the clue and start without him?"

"No, but we won't be able to leave Florence. They won't give us tickets or check out partial teams." She turned again, hoping to catch a glimpse of Ron or his pack. "I can't believe he wandered off."

Mal opened the door and tugged Lexi inside. Passing the gift shop, they strode to the "Museum Entrance" sign in back. A directory showed that the museum was divided into five sections: Mechanisms, Earth, Water, Air, and Fire.

Lexi nodded to the Air section. "Da Vinci's flying machine is probably here."

"Or up there!" Mal pointed.

Lexi looked up. A wooden sculpture resembling a hang glider hung from the ceiling on the other side of the room. Tucked away in a corner underneath sat a blue-and-gold decorated tournament booth. The girls sprinted to it, and the official handed them a manila envelope.

Lexi tore it open.

Congratulations! You have successfully solved clue #2.
Place the eagle sticker on space No. 3 of your Trek Tracker.

To continue:

DESTINATION NO. 3

The museum where you are standing is dedicated to some of my inventions, but science was not my only passion. I had an artistic side as well. *Reflect* on what you know about me and one of the rooms in King Ludwig's Linderhof castle to find this painted portrait of a lady.

"What the heck is this?" Lexi wondered.

"What's what?"

Lexi passed the clue to Mal. "Any chance it's written in old-world Italian or something?"

As Mal read, Lexi placed the eagle sticker on the third circle of the team's Trek Tracker, leaving the second spot free. Eventually, this would make sense, but for now, she'd put them where she was told.

Mal handed the clue back to Lexi. "Sorry, but no."

"What? Are you sure?"

"Yeah." Mal tapped the paper. "Take a look. Half of the *letters* aren't even real letters. I have no idea what it says."

Rustling sounded from the entrance, and Lexi poked out her head, thinking Ron had finally decided to join them. Instead, the Solar Flares rushed inside. *Shoot.*

Lexi read the clue again. "Painted lady and Linderhof castle. I have no idea—"

"I have a bunch of art history stuff on my tablet," Mal said. "I'll scroll through and see what portraits Da Vinci painted. Maybe something will click."

Lexi eyed the flying machine overhead. "Good idea. While you do that, I'll take a closer look."

Constructed from wood, the flying machine had two bat-like wings that extended from opposite sides of a central plank where, according to the sketches accompanying the exhibit, the pilot would lie down. Cranks installed near the front and back of the board allowed the pilot to control the machine with his hands and feet. A tail, which was essentially a smaller version of one of the wings, protracted from the back. Lexi read the exhibit's description. A life-sized machine could have a wingspan of over thirty feet.

Lexi walked under the entire replica, searching for some kind of hidden message or hint. Not spotting anything, she decided to move on. The puzzle said to use their knowledge of Da Vinci—not only the flying machine. Maybe the clue was somewhere else.

In addition to the flying machine, the museum displayed replicas of Da Vinci's crane, rolling mill, bicycle, and tank. Lexi studied each one closely, but even though they sounded as fascinating as the flying machine, none of them offered any help in determining where they were supposed to go next. She moved to a model of Da Vinci's wooden car.

"Get anything, Lex?" a familiar voice called.

Lexi turned. Jacob, one of the Powerful Protons, drifted in from the opposite corridor. A big astronomy buff, Jacob organized the academy's annual April celebration in honor of Yuri Gagarin, the first human to launch into space.

"Hey, Jacob," Lexi said. "No, but we just got here. You?"

"Not yet, but Marley's workin' on it in the other room. How're you doing?"

"Okay, I guess. How was Yuri's Night?"

Jacob chuckled. "Not the same without you, Lex. No one would wear the Martian head."

Lexi laughed as she recalled the large papier-mâché alien costume she'd helped Jacob construct a couple years ago. Her stomach tightened as she remembered how she'd spent this year's Yuri's Night—watching space movies alone.

She peered past Jacob. "Are there any other teams in there with you? Have you seen Haley?"

"No, though I heard—" A muffled voice cried from the other room, and Jacob reversed direction. "That's Marley," he said. "Take it easy, Lex, and good luck. Oh, and rumor is the Comets, Sanbornes, and Phenoms tore through here a while ago."

Lexi blew out a breath. *Great.* Down a teammate and with no idea where to go, that was not what she wanted to hear. She rushed to Mal.

"Well?" Lexi asked, watching Mal scroll through a few pages on the tablet.

Mal beamed. "I think I got it!"

Lexi brightened. "Really? That's great. Where?"

Mal revealed the screen. "I went through the archive, and Da Vinci didn't paint a lot of female portraits, so I went back to the one *I* know. It's world-famous—the *Mona Lisa*. I think this has to be it."

"Where's it located?"

"The Louvre in France," Mal answered breathlessly. She stared into space. "Ahhh, Paris." She placed a hand over her chest and looked at Lexi expectantly. "The fashion capital of the world."

Lexi tried to think of an answer, but "hmmmmmm," was all that came out of her mouth. She needed a little more to go on than "Ahhh, Paris" to justify teleporting somewhere. "Well," Lexi finally said, doing her best to avoid Mal's excited eyes. "Maybe, but how's the *Mona Lisa* connected to Linderhof?"

Mal dropped her shoulders. "That I haven't figured out. But it could be, right?"

"True. The problem is our Linderhof expert is missing, along with his notes."

"Yeah. We need to find Ron."

Lexi scowled. "Let's go."

The girls exited the museum and hustled down the street,

peeping into shops and stores. Lexi kept an ear out, too, listening for shouts of Packers, football, *swag*, or anything that might lead them to Ron. But he was nowhere, and worse, as they retraced their steps from the Duomo back to the museum, they saw the Protons and several teams returning to the station.

Mal shook her head. "Do you think we should tell an official? Maybe something happ—"

Lexi clutched Mal's arm. "Wait. There!"

A ginormous brown backpack leaned against the window of a small café across the street from the museum. Lexi and Mal sprinted inside.

Feet up on a chair, Ron sat at a table with a bowl of soup in front of him.

Slurp.

"What are you doing?" Lexi screamed.

"You've got to be kidding me!" Mal added.

Ron flinched, knocking the table and spilling his soup. "Hey! Watch it!"

Lexi widened her eyes. "Watch it? Where were you? I can't believe you disappeared."

"Yeah," Mal said, lightly sliding the table into him. "*Not* cool."

"What?" Ron protested. He looked at Lexi. "I told you I was going to check out the vendors to see if I could entice them into buying my stuff."

Lexi thought back to the conversation in front of the Duomo.

Ron had said something, but she didn't recall the specifics, as she was anxious to get to the museum.

She exhaled. "I didn't hear you say anything about vendors."

"Yeah, it wás noisy and crowded," Mal said. "Next time make sure we hear you."

"Fine. I will. Next time." He rubbed his hands together and grinned. "So, want to hear how much I sold?"

"No," Mal said, slipping into a chair.

"Later," Lexi said. "We've already looked at the clue, and we're stuck. We need your notes on Linderhof." She took a seat, unpacked the clue, and tossed it onto the table. "Here. You did the hieroglyphics part on Egypt. What do you think of this language?"

He tapped the paper. "It's definitely some sort of code. I mean, it's obvious these funky-looking letters are symbols for other letters. It's like that movie my father loves, *The Da Vinci Code*. You got the clue at the Da Vinci museum, so I'm sure all we have to do is figure out how to interpret this."

Lexi searched the writing for hidden physics formulas, scientists, or elements from the periodic table, but nothing made sense. She returned it to Ron. "What about the part that says there's a connection between Da Vinci and one of the rooms in Linderhof. Do you know what it could be?"

"Hm. Maybe." Ron grabbed his notebook and flipped to the list of rooms. "Yeah, here it is. Reflect. The word 'reflect' is italicized in the clue, and—" He pointed to one of the rooms.

Hall of Mirrors

Lexi's pulse quickened as a spark of hope surged through her. "That makes sense." She turned to Mal. "Can you check—"

"Already on it," Mal replied, swiping the tablet. A few seconds later she bolted out of her chair and thrust the tablet over her head as if she was lifting a trophy. "Yes!"

"What?" Ron and Lexi asked.

Lowering the tablet, Mal returned to the table. "Mirror writing. Da Vinci was a genius, remember? He was afraid people would steal his ideas, so he wrote his notes *backward* so they would look like gibberish to anyone who saw them unless—"

"You used a mirror!" Lexi said, straightening.

Mal retrieved her compact and angled it over the clue. The unreadable symbols now appeared as letters.

Sheishousedinthecountrywherethefirstfemale recipientofthenobelpeaceprizewasborn. ohmadamewhereartthou

Lexi clapped excitedly. "I'll write it down," she said, grabbing her notebook.

Ron took off his cap and put it on backward as he set his feet on the edge of the table. "Mirror writing, huh? I'm gonna tell Coach we should do that with our playbook. You know, there was a rumor last year that Park North got ahold of one—"

"We're not done!" Mal interrupted, knocking Ron's feet off the table. "We have to read the *whole* clue." She tapped the now-decipherable passage. "To find the painting, we still have to figure out who the first female Nobel Peace Prize winner was and where she was born."

Lexi stifled a laugh, happy to see Mal wouldn't let them repeat Ron's Ludwig castle mistake. "Don't worry," Lexi said. "I know that one. It's Marie Curie, *Madame* Marie Curie. It was in physics. She discovered radium and polonium, which scientists use today to create the massive amount of energy needed to teleport." Lexi paused. "Oh, and she was born in Poland."

Glaring at Mal, Ron flipped his hand toward Lexi. "There, there's the other half of your clue. Jeez, Moreno. You're getting as bad as Magill. You two really need to do like my boy Aaron Rodgers says and r-e-l-a-x."

Lexi and Mal traded quick eye rolls. As Mal typed into her tablet, Lexi edged to her side, excited Mal was anxious to solve the clue. While Ron had run off to sell swag, Mal hadn't even mentioned taking photos. She was becoming a great race partner, and it was fun teasing Ron together. Lexi hadn't felt this comfortable around a classmate in a while.

Mal stopped swiping the screen and squealed. "This is it!" She tilted the screen so Lexi and Ron could see. "Da Vinci's portrait of *Lady with an Ermine* is housed at the Czartoryski Palace Museum in Kraków, Poland."

"Lady with an Ermine?" Ron leaned in for a closer look.

Lexi cocked an eyebrow at the image. "Yeah, what's an ermine?

Is that what she's supposed to be holding? It looks like a goat."

"Who knows, and who cares," Mal answered, pressing the tablet to her chest. She gazed into the distance. "Just think, in a few minutes, we'll be face-to-face with an original Da Vinci."

Lexi glanced at Ron, and both suppressed giggles.

"Anyway," Lexi said, pulling out her tableau and a Travel Request Form. She reviewed the cities listed under Poland and smiled. "Great! Kraków's on here! I'll write in the code, and we're good to go."

"Cool. Just a sec," Mal replied, running to the counter.

"What?" Lexi called as she completed the form.

"They gave me food vouchers when we checked in. Italian sausage soup and bruschetta. I'll get it to-go."

"Free food? Awesome!" Ron said, punching the air.

Lexi packed her things, catching a glimpse of the Stargazers as they raced past the café. Her excitement fizzled, and her stomach twisted. Tracking down Ron had eaten up valuable time.

"Hurry up, you guys!" she shouted, swinging her pack over her shoulder. She opened the café's door, poked out her head, and looked both ways down the street. Kids wearing dark blue, gray, and green T-shirts weaved their way down the road to the teleport station.

"Let's go!" Lexi called as she stepped into the street. She clenched her hand around her pack's strap and pursed her lips. If she had any shot at winning, she had to keep Team RAM moving, and right now they had some major catching up to do.

CHAPTER
SEVEN

Team RAM arrived in Kraków and hurried across the station toward the tournament booth. A clock on the counter flashed 9:01 p.m.

Ron poked Lexi. "Nine o'clock? For real? It doesn't feel like it."

Lexi nodded. "We jumped ahead seven hours when we teleported to Germany, remember? And we were in Italy a while."

A curtain behind the booth opened. "*Witamy w Polsce,*" greeted a tournament monitor as he stepped to the counter. He showed them his name tag. *Stanislaw.*

"Hi, Stanislaw. We need to go to the Czartoryski Palace Museum. Is it far?" Lexi asked as they supplied their passports and badges.

Stanislaw shook his head. "Not at all." He tapped a few keys on his computer. "Please be aware that this will be your team's last stop for the day."

Ron stretched his arms over his head and then waved his arm in front of him. "Nah. We're good. We can definitely keep going."

"Psst," Mal said from behind. "There's no teleporting after ten p.m. Remember?"

Ron spun to face her and Lexi. "But I'm not tired. It's stupid to stop now." He turned back around to Stanislaw. "Look, how about we do the rest periods on our regular time zone? We can keep racing, and whenever it's ten p.m. back home, we'll stop."

"Ron, he can't change the rules for us. Come on," Mal said.

Ron crossed his arms. "But—"

"Think about it," Lexi stated. "At ten p.m. back home, it'll be five a.m. here. Museums and other places aren't going to be open at five a.m. We have to follow the time zone where we are. And we *have* to use the time to rest. Otherwise, we'll be one of those teams who falls apart and doesn't finish the race because we're too tired."

Stanislaw gave Lexi a nod. "Your teammates are right. I can't change the rules, and you really should get rest when you can."

Ron tapped his chest. "Yeah, I know all about conserving energy and pacing myself. Have to leave something for those critical plays in the fourth quarter. All right."

"Good," Mal said, nudging Ron out of the way. "Do you have a map?"

Stanislaw slid a map across the counter. "Here you go."

Lexi noticed a block of info in the map's corner. She knew most places in Europe used a twenty-four-hour clock, but unless she was misinterpreting the times, it looked like the museum had already closed.

MUSEUM HOURS:

MON: CLOSED

TUES–SAT: 10–18

SUN: 10–16

She tapped a finger to the box. "This means it's open from ten a.m. to six p.m. on Saturdays, right?"

"Yes, but don't worry," Stanislaw replied. "They agreed to stay open longer specifically because of the tournament."

Lexi wiped her forehead. "Oh whew! For a second there—"

"It closes at ten," Stanislaw interrupted.

"Ten?" Lexi checked the clock. 9:06 p.m.

As if he could read her panicky mind, Stanislaw gently patted Lexi's hand. "Don't worry. It's not far." He pointed to an exit on the other side of the station. "Go out those doors and take a left." He tapped a finger to the map. "It's straight down this street. Stay on the sidewalk past the town square and restaurants, and you'll walk right into it. We have a few monitors along the way if you have any questions."

Lexi nudged Mal to go.

"Come back here when you're done," Stanislaw called. "The rest area's right through these curtains. We have cots and food waiting for you."

Lexi halted and did an about-face. She stared at the curtain. How many teams were already behind there and, more importantly, how many other teams had been allowed to continue to the next stop? She craned her neck to see around Stanislaw and peek through a teensy gap in the drapes, but the hole was too small for her to see anything. Knowing she was wasting time, she rejoined her teammates.

"Good luck!" Stanislaw shouted. "If you get confused, look for the McDonald's. It's a short stretch from there!"

"Oh man, I could go for some McDonald's," Ron said as they maneuvered through the crowded station.

"We are *not* stopping at McDonald's," Mal replied.

"Duh," Ron mumbled. "You heard him. The museum's closing soon. We're obviously in a rush."

Mal groaned. "That's not what I meant. It doesn't matter if we had all the time in the world. We're in a foreign country. You should eat something you can't eat back home. Not McDonald's."

Lexi thought a fudge sundae sounded pretty awesome, and almost said so, but she didn't want to say or do anything that would distract Ron from hurrying to the museum.

Ron waved off Mal. "Relax. I didn't say I was *stopping*. All I said was I could go for some McDonald's." He sped up, passed his teammates, and called over his shoulder. "Besides, as slow as you two walk, I can probably go there, eat, and *still* beat you to the museum."

Lexi and Mal quickened their pace to catch up to Ron, and Team RAM exited the station into Kraków's night air.

Like Florence, people congregated on the cobblestone streets, which contained rows of buildings, most five or six stories high, that seamlessly ran into one another. With the artificial light from the windows and streetlamps, the buildings' vibrant colors popped across the cityscape. Building fronts changed from tangerine to soft tan to pale green to red and on and on down the street until the block ended. It was as if Kraków's painters had been inspired by a rack of fresh spices.

Taking the lead, Mal blazed a path through a crowd listening to street musicians and vendors selling bagels. "This section of the city is called Old Town," she said, glancing at the map. "There's always music, and a lot of these cafés and pubs are really popular, especially on the weekends."

"That's for sure," Ron said as they passed the third club with customers spilling into the street. He repeatedly jostled his back-pack, and each time Lexi held her breath, hoping he wouldn't yank it off and start selling.

A short ways past a McDonald's, a large maize-colored build-ing with red brick panels came into view. The tournament official standing out front was a dead giveaway it was the museum, and Team RAM rushed inside.

A high-school-aged girl greeted them.

"*Cześć! Dobry wieczór. Witamy w naszym muzeum.*"

"Oh no," Lexi and Ron said. They looked at Mal.

Mal threw her hands in the air. "Don't look at me. I don't speak Polish!"

The girl giggled. "I speak English, too. My name is Martyna."

Team RAM sighed with relief as Martyna handed Lexi a map. "If you have any questions, let me know. Otherwise, we'll be closing at ten o'clock, so if you don't find what you need by then, you'll have to come back tomorrow."

"Got it," Lexi said. They walked to an information desk, where Lexi unfolded the map so they could figure out where to go.

The two-story museum consisted of over twenty rooms, each displaying a variety of crafts, armory, weapons, antiquities, and, of course, paintings, from several European countries. While sections of the museum exhibited historical relics, other rooms presented more modern work.

"It's got to be in one of the art gallery rooms," Mal said, reading the list.

Lexi noticed a room on the upper level labeled *Sala Leonarda da Vinci*. "Let's try here first."

Team RAM took off. Rooms dedicated to Polish military heroes and Polish poets decorated the ground floor. They passed through quickly, with only Ron pausing to view some of the older military uniforms. On the upper level, everyone slowed down, especially as they walked through rooms containing ornate ceramics from the Renaissance era. Lexi kept her arms at her sides, choosing to examine the various plates and vases from afar. No way could her family afford replacing a priceless piece of art on the new Magill family budget!

A room covered with painted portraits was next. "We're getting close," Mal said, taking a sharp left.

Sure enough, blue and gold from a tournament booth stuck out in the corner. They sped to it.

"Hi," Lexi said as they approached.

"*Cześć!*" replied the official.

Lexi reached for one of the envelopes stacked on the counter.

The official placed his hand on top of the stack. *"Nie."*

"No?" Lexi repeated. She swiveled toward Ron and Mal. "What do you—"

"Don't we have to find the painting first?" Mal asked.

Duh. Of course! Lexi glimpsed past Mal. A painting on the far side of the maroon room had been cordoned off with velvet rope. The three strode to it, and as they drew near, the subject came into focus. Surrounded with a gold frame, the painting was a portrait of a woman wearing a blue-and-golden robe cradling an animal in her arms.

"Still not sure what she's holding. Maybe a lamb?" Lexi asked.

"Hang on," Ron replied, stooping to read a sign below the painting. "It says she's holding a stoat."

"A what?" Lexi and Mal asked.

"A stoat." He pointed to the sign. "This is definitely the right painting."

Lady with an Ermine, Leonardo da Vinci (1452–1519)

As Ron and Mal read the plaque's description of the painting, Lexi focused on a blue-and-gold note below the portrait:

PUZZLE TIME!

Take one of the worksheets below and calculate your answer.

Then, select the corresponding ticket and bring it
to the tournament booth.

Lexi grabbed a worksheet.

MARIE CURIE

1. Take the year Madame Curie was born.
2. Multiply it by the number of Nobel Prizes she won in Physics.
3. Subtract the atomic number of Radium.
4. Add the melting point of Radium (Celsius), rounded to the nearest hundred.
5. Subtract the mass number of Polonium.
6. Add the number of neutrons in Polonium.
7. Add the number of neutrons in Radium.
8. Subtract the number of elements in the periodic table that exist naturally.
9. Subtract the year Madame Curie died.
10. Reverse the order of the numbers.

ANSWER: _____

"This is great you guys! The worksheet's a science problem. I totally got this!"

"An extra puzzle?" Mal complained. "Isn't it supposed to be a clue to our next destination?"

Lexi didn't break her smile. She'd answer fifty puzzles on science if she could. Previous tournaments she'd studied had as many as ten science worksheets spread throughout the race. She'd been counting on them, and it was about time the first made its appearance. This was how they would vault to the lead.

"No, they always throw worksheets in every once in a while. No biggie. It won't take long."

Lexi exited the room and steered toward an empty bench at the end of the hall. She plopped down, grabbed a pen, and set the worksheet to her side. Mal and Ron lingered in front of her, swaying into her light. As she started to ask them to move, an idea flashed to her. She checked her watch. 9:25 p.m.

"Hey, you know what? Since I'm doing this, why don't you guys go outside and do your thing?" Mal and Ron stared at her, mouths slightly agape. She continued, "Seriously. Ron, you can go sell stuff." Lexi turned to Mal. "And there must be a few interesting buildings nearby, right? Why don't you take some photos? Leave me the tablet in case I need it, and we can meet at the front of the museum in about twenty minutes? Say nine forty-five p.m.? Then we'll walk back together."

Lexi didn't have to ask twice. Without a word, Mal gave Lexi the tablet, and she and Ron tore down the hall. Lexi settled back on the bench. Now she could focus 100 percent.

She read the entire problem, underlining the specific calculations as she went along. Then, she read everything again, just in case the tournament directors included something sneaky. Not seeing anything out of the ordinary, she relaxed a bit and performed the requested computations until she arrived at her answer: 505.

10. Reverse the numbers.

Lexi paused. 505 was the same backward and forward. She rechecked her math and the formula she used to determine the number of neutrons in each element. *Mass number minus Atomic number equals number of neutrons.* Everything seemed right. 505. Maybe that was supposed to be the sneaky part.

She walked to Da Vinci's painting. Four stacks of tickets bordered the portrait:

A: 100–349   **B:** 350–549   **C:** 550–750   **D:** 800 and over

Her answer of 505 meant Group B. After a pat of the Brewers logo on her lucky T-shirt, Lexi snatched the B ticket and crossed the room to the booth.

"Hi," she said, tapping her paper.

"*Cześć!* What's it going to be?" the official greeted. He produced a tablet, which displayed four boxes on the screen, each one marked with an A, B, C, or D.

"B," Lexi answered, handing in the ticket and her worksheet.

The official initialed the bottom of her worksheet. "All right. You're set." He handed Lexi a set of earbuds. "I'll plug these in, you hit B, and you're ready to go."

Lexi accepted the earbuds, but stalled. *A video clue?* Maybe she should find Mal and Ron so they could listen with her. She pushed from the counter, then caught the time—9:35 p.m. If she left to retrieve her teammates, she'd lose her place in line.

Pulling out her notebook, Lexi returned to the counter. It wasn't like Mal and Ron were great notetakers. Heck, Mal hadn't even taken notes at the start of the race, and Ron had written the most obvious and silly things. Besides, if the clue had anything to do with science, neither teammate would be of any help. Convinced she was doing the right thing, Lexi inserted the earbuds and selected the box marked B.

Dr. Bressler flashed onto the screen. Clean-shaven with curly blond hair, he was the lone American on the teleport team. He designed the first telepod after Dr. Vogt developed the teleportation medallion.

"Hello, there!" Dr. Bressler said. "And congratulations! As Dr. Vogt told you earlier, the seed of any scientific invention is the spark of an idea and then holding true to your idea when others may doubt you. I'm here to welcome you to the *next* step in your journey—figuring out how to take your idea and make it a reality." Dr. Bressler pressed his fingertips together so that they formed a steeple. "It's not glamorous to be in the trenches, testing and tinkering day after day. But it's these long hours of trial and tribulation that prove crucial to ultimate success. As you continue, remember that many great discoveries were made only after hundreds of failed attempts. Don't get discouraged, and good luck!"

Lexi gaped at her notebook. Dr. Bressler talked fast. She had scribbled only a few phrases, and nothing pertinent to a destination. Perhaps the video was what he said it was—a good-luck message, much like Dr. Vogt's at the start of the tournament. She removed the earbuds, and the official handed her an unsealed blue envelope with "DESTINATION NO. 4" printed on the outside and a sticker of a stoat.

"Here you go," he said.

"Thanks," Lexi replied, backing away. She placed the sticker on the team's Trek Tracker. *Three down, six to go.* She took a breath. Based on previous tournaments, there would likely be three stickers a day. Team RAM should be on pace, though they were cutting it close and she still had no idea if they had made the top thirty.

Lexi exhaled again and reminded herself to think positive. It was perfectly possible Haley and the other teams were back with Stanislaw and waiting in the rest area. In a few minutes, Team RAM would be with them, and she and Haley would have the rest of the night to catch up.

Three teams stormed into the room.

With a new sense of urgency, Lexi jammed the Trek Tracker in her pack and scurried out. She had to collect Ron and Mal and get to the teleport station as soon as possible—just in case there was only one spot left.

The night breeze ripped through her hair, and Lexi pulled on her sweatshirt. Not seeing either teammate, she confirmed the time. 9:40 p.m. She clenched her fists and ordered her pounding heart to slow. The other teams still had to complete the calculations and watch the video. Even if they knew the elemental properties by heart like she did, it'd still take time.

Exhaling, she eased her grip on the envelope and peeked inside. As long as she had to wait, she might as well read the next clue.

Did you choose the correct answer?
MAYBE YES, MAYBE NO. If not, you'll be told at your next destination and given another chance to get it right along with another puzzle to solve. If your answer was correct, you'll proceed directly to the next stop.

To continue:

Travel to the country where Madame Curie became a citizen. If you need help determining exactly where to go, turn to the next page. Plot the fifty landmarks on the enclosed map via their longitude and latitude coordinates. Then, connect the dots as instructed on page three. Five of these lines will intersect at the location that serves as your next destination!

Lexi flipped to the next page and glimpsed the list.

LIST OF LANDMARKS

A. Taj Mahal
B. Roman Colosseum
C. Stonehenge
D. Grand Canyon
. . .

WHAT?!!

Eyes wide, Lexi stopped reading after the first few names. She knew Madame Curie became a French citizen, so their next destination was going to be somewhere in France—but figuring out exactly *where* in France they were supposed to go was going to take forever. Hands trembling, she unfolded the enclosed map. It was almost as large as her Teleport Tableau! Her breathing quickened, and she wiped her now sweaty forehead. According to the clue, she had to find the coordinates, plot the coordinates, and then connect them? She turned to the third page to skim that part of the puzzle.

1. Connect Point J to F to X
2. Connect Point K to G to ZZ
3. Connect Point L to AA to M

The page blurred before her, and Lexi closed her eyes. There had to be over fifty instructions on how to connect the fifty coordinates. This would take hours.

Hours. The thought of time nudged her to check her watch. 9:47 p.m. She surveyed her surroundings. Still no Mal or Ron. Scrambling, Lexi folded the map and stuffed it and the clue inside the envelope. Pack swinging in her hand, she stormed down the street to find her teammates.

Soon, Ron's voice bellowed from ahead. "Green Bay Packers! Shirts, caps, and jerseys. Right here. Right now! All the way from America! Get it while you can."

Panting, Lexi stomped to him. "Hey, you guys were supposed to meet me at the museum five minutes ago."

Ron didn't budge. "Sales, Magill."

Lexi shifted her weight and set a hand on her hip. "Well, no one's here now. Teams are right behind us. There's eliminations tonight, remember? And you should see the next clue we have to solve. We need to get back."

Ron sighed. "All right, all right. Chill." He stooped to repack his merchandise.

"Mal!" Lexi called, looking around. She didn't see her teammate. "Where is she?"

Ron heaved the pack onto his back. "What do you mean?"

"She wasn't at the museum. Isn't she with you?"

"Nope."

Great. "Fine. Let's go back. She's probably waiting for us."

Ron and Lexi hurried down the block toward the museum. Lexi furrowed her brow as they got closer, not seeing Mal anywhere in the vicinity.

"This is ridiculous," she said, glaring at Ron. "Do you have any idea where she went?"

"Nope. She didn't come out with me. She said she had to run to the bathroom first."

"Oh." Lexi eyed the entrance. She couldn't believe Mal was still inside, but she also couldn't imagine where else her teammate might have gone. She scratched her head. Forget tracking devices in the Tel-Meds. She needed them in her teammates! Groaning, she reached for the door handle.

The museum door banged open, and a purple team rushed out. A girl halted a few paces from Lexi. "Oh, hey—your teammate's not doing too good."

"What?"

"She's in the bathroom."

Lexi's heart thumped at the thought of having to quit if Mal couldn't race anymore. "She's sick?" Lexi asked.

The girl shook her head. "She can't find her Tel-Med."

"What?"

The girl ran toward her teammates, who hadn't slowed. She yelled over her shoulder, "She thinks she flushed it down the toilet!"

CHAPTER EIGHT

Lexi spun from the museum to Ron and then back to the museum, her hands shaking. "What? How?" she huffed, rubbing her forehead.

"Come on," Ron said, nudging Lexi to the door. "Let's check."

Lexi followed Ron to the restrooms, all the while convincing herself the purple-shirted girl was playing a cruel joke. Surely, Mal was snapping photos somewhere, and she and her Tel-Med were safe. Team RAM couldn't end like this. They reached the restroom door, and Ron stopped.

"What are you doing?" Lexi asked, stepping past him.

Ron's face contorted into a perplexed expression. "Duh, it's a women's bathroom. I can't go in there."

Lexi pushed open the door. "Are you kidding me? There's no one here except us, and the museum's gonna close in—" Lexi checked the time. "Four minutes! Come on!"

Ron didn't budge, and Lexi entered, leaving him in the hall.

Down on her hands and knees, Mal was crawling under the sinks. She had torn sheets of toilet paper and bunched them under each knee and hand so as not to touch the floor. Slowly, she inched along, peering to her left and right.

"Mal?" Lexi called as she dropped her backpack on a bench next to Mal's. "What on Earth are you doing?"

Mal reached the corner of the bathroom and stood. With scraps of toilet paper stuck to her knees, a rumpled shirt, and frazzled hair, fashion-show Mal had disappeared. A stressed-out girl with splotchy red cheeks and watery eyes stood in her place. She bundled up a wad of toilet paper that had been stuck to her knee and tossed it in the trash. "This is useless. I was hoping I was wrong, but it's got to be in the toilet. It's the only place left."

Lexi approached her teammate. "What happened?"

"My Tel-Med," Mal said, using the back of her hand to brush away a tear. "It was in my skirt pocket with my gum. As I was straightening my skirt, I saw the stick of gum sticking out of the pocket, so I pulled it out to put it in my purse. The Tel-Med came out with it. I heard it clink against the sink, or the floor, or something, but I can't find it." Mal spread out her arms. "I've gone over every inch of the floor, the sinks, the bench, everywhere. It's not here. It had to have flown into a toilet."

"You kept your Tel-Med in that tiny pocket?!" Lexi screeched before she could stop herself. "It's one thing not to wear cargoes, but—"

After another look at Mal's pitiful face, Lexi slammed her mouth shut. Yelling wasn't going to get them anywhere. She flexed her fingers. *Work the problem. That's what a scientist does. Keep your head and work the problem.*

She forced a small smile in Mal's direction. "Well, let's uh . . . let's see if we can find it, huh?"

Lexi walked to the bathroom stalls. She flung open each door and inspected the floor and behind the toilet. "I don't see it," she said, returning. "Did anyone use the toilets afterward?"

Mal wiped her nose with her wrist. "No. Another team was here, but they flushed before it happened."

"If no one went to the bathroom, I don't see how it could have been flushed away."

"I know, but where else could it be? Maybe it sunk into the toilet bowl and clanked down the pipe. We're not going to know unless we look." Mal wrung her hands. "I don't think I can do it. Can you?"

Lexi squirmed. Had she really been reduced to inspecting toilet bowls for Tel-Meds?

"Excuse me," a female voice said as Lexi stared into a stall and contemplated the most efficient way to perform the Tel-Med diving expedition.

Lexi turned. "Yeah?"

Martyna held open the restroom door. Ron slinked in beside her. Martyna gave a startled look at Ron before returning her eyes to Lexi. "I'm sorry, but it's ten o'clock. We're closing. You'll have to come back tomorrow." Martyna patted Ron's elbow. "And, sir, um, the men's room is across the way."

91

"I know," Ron said, crossing his arms. He tipped his head to Mal. "My friend lost her Tel-Med somewhere in here. I thought maybe I could help look."

"Oh my. I'm sorry, but—"

"It's got to be here," Lexi said. "Can you please give us five more minutes? *Please?*"

Martyna pursed her lips and started to shake her head, but stopped. "All right, five minutes. I'll be back."

Lexi adjusted her glasses and readied herself for her first dive. They had to get the Tel-Med now. Assuming they made the top thirty elimination tonight, returning tomorrow would put them too far behind. The top teams could already be at the next location. She stepped toward the toilet and crouched.

No.

Lexi shot up. Before she plunged her hand into toilet water, she had to make sure she exhausted all the other possibilities. Seriously—could Mal's Tel-Med really have flown over the top of a stall and fallen perfectly into a toilet?

The door banged open. "I'm sorry," Martyna called. "But security says you have to leave."

Heart in her throat, Lexi backed out of the stall. The guard approached. "Let's go."

Lexi yanked her arm away. "What? No!"

The guard shifted and, setting a hand on Lexi's back, nudged her toward the door. "This way, please."

Lexi gripped the edge of a stall, refusing to budge. "But we can't go yet. I have to find my friend's Tel-Med. It's somewhere in here."

The guard unclasped Lexi's fingers. He placed a hand on Lexi's shoulder and his other hand on Mal's elbow. "I'm sorry, but you'll have to come back tomorrow. Don't worry. We'll make a note for the lost and found. If our cleaning crew finds it, we'll leave it for you at the counter."

"But—" Mal started.

"Can't we—" Lexi said.

"Sir, please back up," the guard said to Ron as he led the girls to the door.

Ron darted his eyes around the restroom before settling on Lexi. Slumping, he backed out, clearing their path. As the guard prodded her forward, Lexi grabbed her backpack and whirled for one last look.

Nothing.

Stumbling into Ron and Mal, she exited, and soon Team RAM was on the wrong side of the locked museum door, their search for the Tel-Med coming to an abrupt end.

Laughter sounded in the distance, and Lexi glared in its direction. An orange T-shirt streaked ahead before disappearing into the night. It was the final straw. Hands clenched, Lexi faced Mal and erupted.

"How could you keep your Tel-Med in that tiny pocket? What were you thinking?" Lexi threw her hands in the air. "Do you realize what this means? Even if we somehow aren't eliminated tonight, we have to come back here tomorrow morning while everyone else gets to travel to the next stop." She set her hands on her hips. "And there's no guarantee we're even going to find the Tel-Med. I mean, *you* looked for it. *I* looked for it. With the cleaning crew in there tonight, it could get shoved down a drain or something. Or even farther down the toilet."

"Lexi, hang on," Ron started. "It's not like she did it on purpose."

"It doesn't matter!" Lexi shouted, panic consuming every ounce of her body. She whipped her cap off her head as visions of another year of public school, her lonely lunch table, and quiet nights inside her bedroom without Haley's e-mails, texts, and calls rushed over her. She stomped her foot. "Don't you realize what this means? We're out. It's over."

"Sorry, Lexi," Mal croaked. "But it really was an accident."

Tears burned Lexi's eyes. She could hardly catch her breath. She opened her mouth to continue, but caught Mal's look of distress. Lexi's stomach panged, and the knot of anger morphed into a ball of guilt. *Of course* it was an accident, and Mal obviously felt terrible about it.

"Hey, maybe we can borrow a Tel-Med from someone," Ron offered.

Lexi waved him off. "No," she scowled. "It won't have the tracking and disabling chip. Dr. Harrison was clear about that at the starting line, remember? He said that was the only time they could install them. If we can't find hers, it means no more racing."

"I'm so sorry," Mal repeated.

Lexi removed her glasses and wiped her eyes. "Yeah," she sputtered as she put her glasses back on. "I know."

"I should have helped you look in the toilets," Mal panted through her sobs. "Maybe then we would have found it before they kicked us out."

Lexi started to nod, but caught herself. Right before the security guard had interrupted them, she had been thinking Mal's Tel-Med *couldn't* have flown into a toilet. Straightening her Brewers cap, she blinked toward Mal.

"Wait. You said you checked the floors, before I got there, right?"

Mal nodded.

Lexi tapped a finger to her chin. "Right." Her confidence grew as her fuzzy mind cleared. *Work the problem.* "And you said you were in front of the mirror when you slid out your gum?"

"Yeah." Mal took a few steps, and then angled her body toward Lexi. "I saw the gum sticking out here." She pointed to her skirt's smallest pocket in the world. "I took it out"—Mal repeated the motion, holding an imaginary stick of gum—"and then I heard the clink."

Exactly. Lexi's heart raced. She was definitely on the right track. "Just *one* clink—not two or three, right?"

"Right."

"Did you hear a rolling sound, like a penny across a surface?"

"No."

"Did you hear a splash of water?"

Mal tilted her head. "Actually, no, I didn't. It was a single clink."

Lexi gazed skyward as she reimagined the layout of the restroom. "And you're positive you took the gum out like you demonstrated— in one quick motion, right?"

"Yes."

An idea zoomed to Lexi, and she twirled Mal around so she could look at her purse. "Your bag-purse thing was on the bench by the door, right?"

"Right."

"Can you take it off for a sec?"

Mal handed Lexi her backpack purse. Lexi wiggled it. Nothing. She set it on the pavement. One of the pack's side pockets was half unzipped. With a silent prayer, Lexi closed her eyes and stuck her fingers inside. Seconds later, she pulled out Mal's Tel-Med.

"What!?" Ron screamed, reaching for Lexi's arm.

"Holy cow!" Mal yelled, vaulting toward Lexi.

Lexi grasped her forehead with one hand and used her other hand to latch on to her teammates, hoping they'd keep her upright. Her knees nearly buckled as the tension oozed out of her body.

Mal snatched the Tel-Med out of Lexi's hand. "That was amazing! How did you think of it?"

Lexi rocked back and smiled. "Physics! Based on where you said you were standing and the force you described in removing the gum, it's unlikely the Tel-Med could have flown into a stall or a toilet. It's also safe to say that the Tel-Med came to a rest at some point because otherwise you'd have seen it rolling around. Since you heard only the one clink, the object that brought the Tel-Med to a state of rest would have had to have muffled that sound." Lexi shrugged a shoulder. "The only object in there capable of muffling a metal medallion was your backpack. The Tel-Med clanked against the counter or bench or wall—which was the clink you heard—and then hit the backpack, coming to rest inside the pocket."

Mal and Ron gaped at Lexi. "Wow," Ron said. "That's smart, Magill. Nice save!"

Lexi tapped the Brewers logo on her shirt. "Like Dan Plesac!"

"Who?" Ron and Mal asked.

Lexi giggled. "The Brewers' all-time record holder for most saves—he's one of my dad's favorite players."

Mal reached for Lexi and pulled her in for a hug. "Thank you," she whispered. "I don't know how I would have told my parents."

Lexi's face fell. She'd been so stuck on the fact they'd have to quit that she never considered Mal could have gotten in big-time trouble. Her stomach reeled at what Mal must have been going through as Lexi had continued to scream at her.

She squeezed Mal. "I . . . I'm so sorry I lost it back there." Tears pricked her eyes. "I panicked, and—"

"It's okay," Mal said. "I get it. I was mad, too."

The girls smiled at each other and both sighed heavily. As they laughed at their timing, Ron cleared his throat.

"Hate to break up this love fest, but shouldn't we get to the rest area and check-in?"

After another sigh, Lexi and Mal turned to their teammate.

"The museum's closed, and we were the last ones to leave," Lexi said. "We can't change anything now." She stared down the street as her stomach fluttered. "But yeah, let's go see if we made the cut."

Stanislaw checked in Team RAM and directed them through the curtain. As she walked through, Lexi spotted Haley, along with the Phenoms, Mighty Sanbornes, and other top teams. Her shoulders eased a bit. That meant the tournament directors made *everyone* stop at the Poland rest area. The only question now was whether Team RAM had made it into the top thirty.

"Well?" Ron asked. "What do you think?"

"I don't know," Lexi replied, quickly counting teams.

"Twenty-five!" Mal called from behind. Ron and Lexi spun. Mal stood with Stanislaw as he showed her a clipboard. She left his side and joined her teammates. "I figured I might as well ask, right?"

Ron and Mal high-fived each other and reached out to Lexi. Lexi returned the congratulations, but she couldn't ignore that they'd *barely* made it, and tomorrow morning there'd be twenty-four teams teleporting to France before them.

France. Lexi slumped as she remembered the amount of work ahead of her plotting all those points. She checked the time. 10:24 p.m. She yawned in spite of herself. Even though it was only 3:24

p.m. back home, the day's drama combined with eight hours of racing had wiped her out.

"Let's pick cots and then get something to eat," Mal said, heading to the sleeping area.

Lexi dropped to a cot.

"Lexi?"

Lexi raised her eyes. "Huh?"

"Don't you want to eat?" Mal gestured toward the buffet and laughed. "Ron's already in line, backpack and all."

Lexi patted her rumbling stomach, wishing she could relax and eat, but those coordinates weren't going to plot themselves. "In a minute. I want to take another look at the next clue."

Mal scooched beside her. "Oh! I didn't even know you got it. Let's see!"

"Sorry. I forgot to tell you with all the commotion." She handed the blue envelope to Mal. "We're going to France, but—"

"France? France!" Mal yanked the envelope out of Lexi's hands and leaped off the cot. "Where? Oh my gosh—imagine the photos! People go gaga over France!"

Yeah, tell me about it.

Mal clutched the envelope against her chest. "I can see it now," she said dreamily. She held out the envelope as if it were a trophy. "And the award for most outstanding exhibit goes to . . ." She paused and lowered her hand. "Wait. Where in France? I hope it's not a place like the Eiffel Tower—anyone can find photos of *that* on the Internet."

Before Lexi could answer, Ron loped toward them carrying a plate of food.

"Really?" Mal teased, eyeing the mound. "Think you took enough?" Smirking, Ron stuffed a kielbasa into his mouth and dropped onto the cot across from Lexi. Mal lightly kicked Ron's foot. "Guess what? We're going to France!"

"Ohthttttawwwwsmmm," Ron said with his mouth still full. Lexi and Mal shared a sympathetic eye roll as Ron licked his fingers. "Where? Some place with a bunch of American sports fans, I hope."

"Fine with me, as long as it's not *too* touristy," Mal replied. "It needs to be special." She fanned herself with the clue's envelope. "The French Riviera might be cool. It has tons of designer shops!"

Lexi pushed herself up off the cot. If she stayed for this conversation any longer, she was going to lose it again. She'd be up half the night plotting, missing her chance to hang out with Haley, and all Ron and Mal could talk about was swag and photos. She glanced toward the dining area.

Several teams had slid their tables together. The Mighty Sanbornes, Haley's Comets, Physics Phenoms, Tesla's Techies, and a team wearing red shirts were smiling and joking between bites of food. Lexi stared longingly at the group. She took a step, and then glanced back at Mal, who was still waving the clue around and rambling about France.

"I'm going to say hi to Haley," Lexi said, hoping her friend had saved her a seat like she had asked. "I'll be back in a minute."

"We'll get started," Mal said, plopping onto the cot.

Lexi paused. "What?"

"Go on and get something to eat," Mal said, sliding the papers out of the envelope. She poked Ron and laughed. "Come on, Ron. I'll read the clue this time, and you can use my tablet."

Ron let out a loud belch. "I don't know. I think I'm ready for seconds."

"Eww," Mal waved her hand in front of her nose. "For real?"

Lexi stifled a laugh. "Mal, you sure you want to? The puzzle's long. We have to plot all these points and then—"

"Well, there's no reason you should be stuck with it," Mal said. "Besides, you're the whole reason I'm here and we even get to go to France. Go on. We'll start."

Lexi's chest tingled as she watched her teammates together on the cot. Part of her wanted to slide right beside them and get cracking on that problem, but the other part longed to visit with her old friends. It was like she was an electron that had two atoms competing for her.

Laughter erupted from behind, and Lexi whirled. No one sitting at any of Haley's tables was working on the clue, that was for sure. She wondered when they had arrived at the rest area.

"Okay," Lexi said to Mal and Ron. "You guys can start looking up the coordinates. I'll be back."

Lexi strode to the makeshift banquet table. The closer she got, the more it brought her back to her old life at the academy.

The teams were debating which teleport scientist they liked the best.

"Dr. Bressler—no question!" Comet Andre said.

"Nah, for me it's Dr. Kent. He's been all over the world," a Sanborne added.

"They've *all* been all over the world," Haley chimed. "They've teleported everywhere. They have telepods in their labs! Imagine— every day we went to work we'd have the chance to travel somewhere new!"

Anxious to join in, Lexi advanced to the edge of the table. "Dr. Vogt is my fave," she said. "If it wasn't for her invention of the Tel-Med, none of the other stuff would matter."

Everyone at the tables turned, and a chorus of "Hey, Lexi!" followed. Lexi's heart warmed. She looked for an empty seat near Haley, but Haley hadn't saved her one. No matter. It was kind of cool to stand at the head of the table and have everyone's attention. She glanced at Haley. "Dr. Vogt's your favorite, too, isn't she, Hale?"

"Of course! I actually met her in February at a conference in London. She *loved* my question—said it showed real insight. I'm thinking she has to remember me."

Before Lexi could respond, a roar sounded from the sleeping area, and everyone turned to look. Ron stood with a football tucked under one arm and his other arm extended as if blocking a defender. Stanislaw was next to him, seemingly enthralled with the demonstration. Mal snapped photos, egging Ron on for more poses.

"Your teammates are hilarious," Proton Jacob said.

"Yeah, they seem fun," Tesla's Techie Jeannette added.

Lexi held her tongue. Hilarious and fun were not going to win the tournament.

"You guys must have fallen way behind," Haley said. "I didn't see you anywhere."

"Yeah," Lexi said with a sigh. "We had a few issues, but we survived the cut. We'll be racing tomorrow."

Haley winced. "But barely."

Lexi clenched her teeth. She didn't come over to talk about her team or how badly they'd done. She wanted to talk about teleport science or physics or math or anything that she hadn't had a chance to discuss in the last five months.

She nodded at Tomoka. "I bet you'd get a kick out of working with Dr. Kent, given his current research on rockets. How is yours coming along?"

The table tittered, and Lexi flinched. "What?"

"It's busted," Tomoka said. "We sort of had a . . . *meltdown*."

The tittering morphed into full-blown laughs. Lexi stood still, not getting the joke, and, even worse, feeling incredibly awkward at being the only one *not* getting it. Somehow, even though she was with her old friends, she felt like the same outcast she was at her new school.

"It's a long story, Lex," Tomoka said. "I'll have to—"

"How's everyone doing?" Dr. Harrison asked, striding to the table.

Haley vaulted out of her seat. "Dr. Harrison, have you talked to Dr. Vogt recently? Does she remember me?" Haley clenched her hands together in front of her chest. "Don't forget to mention I got an A-plus on my paper on her and was featured in the junior scientist journal."

Dr. Harrison waved off Haley. "I remember, I remember." He tipped his head toward Lexi. "I also remember Ms. Magill over here is a pretty big Dr. Vogt fan herself."

Lexi grinned.

"That's not all," Haley started, but the rest was drowned out as everyone else started blurting out their achievements, too.

Dr. Harrison put an end to it quickly. "Okay! Stop it, please! Don't worry. The scientists will know all about you when it comes to the internship." He passed the table and strode to the curtain. "Now get some rest."

As soon as Dr. Harrison exited, chatter erupted at the table. Lexi stepped away to grab a chair so she could slide in and join, but as she returned, most of the kids had scattered and only Haley, the Phenoms, and a couple others remained.

At last. A little one-on-one time with Haley was exactly what she needed. They could do some major catching up, and with a little luck everything would be—

"Comets, Phenoms, and Techies—the movie's set up. We're

ready!" Haley's teammate Emma called from the sleeping area.

"We're on our way," Haley said, rising.

"Be right there," Tomoka added as he and his teammates stacked their garbage.

Lexi tightened her grip on the back of the chair.

"I'm sure it'll be one of the Guardians movies," Haley said. She glanced at Lexi. "She loves them as much as you do."

Haley left, and Lexi's heart sank.

Tomoka frowned. "Sorry, Lex. I'll tell you about the rocket some other time."

Lexi released the chair. Trying to disguise her disappointment at not being invited, she shrugged. "Oh, that's okay. I have to get back and plot those coordinates, anyway."

Tomoka halted his trash pickup and exchanged glances with his teammates. Turning toward Lexi, he slid his team's blue envelope out from under his tray.

In an instant, Haley reappeared and clapped her hand on top of it. "Yeah, you should get going," Haley said, meeting Lexi's eyes. "That takes a while."

Tomoka picked up the envelope with his tray and left, Haley following a step behind.

"Good night," Lexi called, a tad confused by their reactions.

She watched Haley grab a seat next to Emma and wondered if Emma was Haley's new lab partner. Jealousy rumbled through her again, but Lexi quickly snuffed it out. Someone had to be Haley's partner now that Lexi wasn't around. It didn't mean it would stay that way once she returned. Once they fell into their old routine, she and Haley would be inseparable again.

Nodding to herself, Lexi made her way to the buffet and scooped a *gwampshi* and pierogi onto her plate. Haley was right—she didn't have time for a movie, anyway. She needed to plot those points so Team RAM could teleport first thing in the morning with the other teams. It was time to get to work.

CHAPTER NINE

Neither of her teammates was around when Lexi returned to her cot. She set her plate on a small folding table and scanned the area for the envelope. Not seeing it, she lifted up her flimsy pillow. Nope. She crouched and checked under each of the cot's four corners. Nothing. Irritated, she crossed the narrow aisle to the cot where Ron and Mal had been sitting. Ron had probably used it as a plate for one of his umpteen trips for food.

"Lookin' for this?"

Lexi turned. Ron waved the blue envelope in front of her face.

She rolled her eyes. "No. Actually, I'm looking for the map. I thought you guys were going to start plotting?"

"We were," Ron said, bending over to whisper. "But then we found something interesting." He paused and made his eyebrows dance. "*Quite* interesting. So we stopped and waited for you."

Lexi's insides fluttered with joy. Her teammates' decision to wait and include her in what they found was the complete opposite from how Haley had so easily blown her off moments earlier. Excited, she lowered her voice and replied to Ron, "Really? What?"

Ron showed her the clue, and Lexi reread it.

> *Did you choose the correct answer? MAYBE YES, MAYBE NO.*
> *If not, you'll be told at your next destination and given*
> *another chance to get it right. If your answer was correct,*
> *you'll proceed directly to the next stop.*
>
> **To continue:**
>
> Travel to the country where Madame Curie became a citizen. If you
> need help determining exactly where to go, turn to the next page.
> Plot the fifty landmarks on the enclosed map via their longitude and
> latitude coordinates. Then, connect the dots as instructed on page
> three. Five of these lines will intersect at the location that serves as
> your next destination!

"Yeah?" Lexi said. "So?"

"So," Ron said. "Notice anything interesting about this piece of paper?"

Lexi arched an eyebrow. "Such as . . ."

He referred her to the top of the page. "It's missing an important word, don't you think?"

Lexi tried cocking the other eyebrow to make her eyebrows dance like Ron's, but she failed. "What are you talking about?"

Ron signaled to the cot, and they sat. "Okay, so we saw all these points you have to plot and everything, right?"

"Yeah," Lexi said, glancing at her watch. Ron wasn't saying anything she didn't know.

"But look. The word, 'Destination' isn't at the top of the page like with the other clues."

"Huh?"

"Trust me. I've been on enough football teams to know that every circle, x, and arrow is there for a reason. I'm telling you, that there's a word missing *means something*."

Lexi stared at the envelope. "You think they gave us all these coordinates to trick us into traveling somewhere we're not supposed to?"

Ron shook his head. "Not necessarily, though that's what Mal thought, too." He flipped over the blue envelope, where *Destination No. 4* was scrawled and tapped it with his finger. "Look. The word 'Destination' is on the *envelope* this time instead of the clue. I think that means the envelope by itself might be enough to tell us where we're supposed to go."

Lexi considered the clue and then the envelope. Part of her wanted to dismiss Ron's idea outright and get to plotting the coordinates, but something held her back. This was exactly the type of sneaky thing the tournament directors would do to throw off teams. Maybe Ron was onto something.

"Was anything written on the other envelopes?" she asked.

"Nope. They were blank."

"Okay," Lexi said. "So maybe it *is* the actual envelope and we only plot points if we can't figure it out. Did you guys find anything about where it could be?"

Ron sighed. "Unfortunately no. We both looked for small writing, but didn't see anything other than 'Destination Number Four.' Mal even snapped a photo and downloaded it to the computer. She zoomed in and checked with her fancy photography program, but she didn't find anything, either. We were wondering if there were any other papers inside."

"No, just the clue and the map."

"Hmph." Ron held the blue envelope up to the light. "I still don't see anything."

Lexi extended her hand. "Let me look." She flipped the envelope a hundred different ways, but didn't see anything, either.

Ron examined the inside of the envelope again, then turned it upside down and shook. Nothing fell out. "I don't know."

Lexi grabbed the envelope. "Let's implement a scientific approach. We'll go step-by-step. How's this envelope different from the other ones?"

Ron pinched a corner of the envelope. "For starters, it's blue."

"Right." Lexi flipped it over. "And it has 'Destination Number Four' on the back."

After neither spoke in the following seconds, both grinned. "I think we already established those things," Ron said. "You're the one that got the envelope at the museum. Was there anything unusual about it?"

Lexi fiddled with the envelope, pressing it between her hands. The top bent back and grazed against her chest, exposing the white adhesive tape. With a flourish, she set the envelope across her legs.

"This," she said excitedly, tapping the adhesive tape across the top. "This is different. I didn't have to rip open the envelope to pull out the clue. This envelope was never sealed."

Gasping, Ron reached for the adhesive tape, but then retracted his hand at the last second. "Go ahead. You do it."

With trembling fingers, Lexi gripped a corner of the seal and peeled off the tape.

GO HERE

"You have got to be kidding me!" she said.

"Oh my gosh!" Ron whispered.

"The Eiffel Tower!" Lexi added with a laugh. A few seconds later, she added, "Mal's gonna be mad."

"Nice going!" Ron said, holding the envelope up to his eyes. He held out his fist for a congratulatory pound. "Now you don't have to spend the night plotting points!"

True. Lexi fell back on her cot and covered her face with her hands as relief flooded over her. She'd get some rest after all.

Uncovering her face, she stared at Ron, who was still mesmerized by the tiny Eiffel Tower drawing. She sat up and nudged his arm. "You know, it's a good thing you guys started the clue. I totally would have gone straight to plotting points on the map."

Ron tilted his head to the side. "Well, I don't know about that. We already screwed up one puzzle by not reading the whole clue. I'm sure you would have caught it."

Lexi glanced at the picture again. Ron's castle screwup was entirely different from this. She had been in a hurry to solve the clue. There's no way she would have taken the time to notice that the word *Destination* was missing. Her teammates saved her. Big-time.

Ron rose and gawked at the dining area. "Aw, man, they're cleaning up. I'm gonna get a final plate. Want anything?"

"No," Lexi said, pointing to her plate. "I'm good. Thanks."

As Ron left for the buffet, Lexi sneaked a peek at Haley. She wondered if Haley had plotted all the points or if she had found the hidden picture. It seemed weird she would have told Lexi to work on the coordinates if she knew there was a shortcut.

"They said they're closing the computer station down in a half hour," Mal said, interrupting Lexi's thoughts. She returned her camera to her purse. "You should go now before everyone rushes over."

"Yeah, okay," Lexi said. She started walking toward the computers, but stopped. "Oh, hey. Ron and I figured out where we're going in France."

"Where?" Mal asked, eyes wide.

"Eiffel Tower."

"What?!" Mal groaned and flailed onto her cot. "Yuck."

Giggling, Lexi left a grumbling Mal and walked to an open computer station. She logged into her e-mail account, wondering if her parents had checked in. They were spending the weekend at her grandmother's farm in upstate Wisconsin, where Internet service was spotty.

She had one new message and clicked on it.

Dear Rental Customer:

We have detected a modification to Tel-Med No. 610116271. Per the rental agreement, no alterations may be made to any rental Tel-Med without permission. At this time, we have no reason to believe the Tel-Med is not functioning properly, but we at Wren Tech take our customers' safety seriously.

Please report to the nearest Wren Tech store or facility with Tel-Med No. 610116271 so that it may be inspected for defects. If necessary, a substitute Tel-Med will be supplied to you at that time. Please also note that, if at any time, the Tel-Med's warning features are triggered, the Tel-Med will enter our Critical Protocol, potentially leading to deactivation. Thank you for your cooperation.

Sincerely,
John Hardek
Wren Technologies

Lexi stared at the screen, her hands twitching.

It had to be the installation of the tracking and disabling chip.

That was the only possible modification. Well, other than the ugly blue RENTAL stamp. Lexi set a finger to her chin. But, like the e-mail said, the Tel-Med was still working. She slid her finger to the Delete key, but hovered over the e-mail for a moment.

Wren Tech stores *were* everywhere. She undoubtedly could find one—either in Poland or Paris—and have the Tel-Med checked out to be sure. Problem was, if the tournament chip *was* at fault and they removed it—she'd be out of the tournament. Even worse, Wren Tech could charge her for damaging the medallion! And when she couldn't pay, they might refuse to replace it. Then, not only would she be out of the tournament, she'd also have to find a way to get back to Wisconsin. Lexi clicked her tongue as she imagined the phone call. "Uh, Mom. I'm stuck in Poland. Can I have airfare home?" She'd be grounded for life for sure.

Lexi deleted the message. No way was she going to let any of that happen. She'd teleported three times since the chip was installed. She'd be fine. She logged off. As she backed from the computer, her chair nicked Dr. Harrison as he'd been walking past. "Oops. Sorry."

He laughed. "No problem." Lexi rose, and Dr. Harrison patted her elbow. "So, how's it going?"

"Great!" Lexi said.

"Good," Dr. Harrison said. "Glad to hear it." He tapped Lexi's cap. "You know, the scientists are very impressed with you—leading racers who don't have the standard science background. It definitely caught their attention."

Lexi's jaw dropped. "You mean you talked to the scientists . . . to Dr. Vogt . . . about me?"

"Of course." Dr. Harrison stepped away.

"Even though we're so far behind?" Lexi called after him.

Dr. Harrison paused and glanced over his shoulder. "Just keep racing, Lexi. Anything can happen."

Lexi watched Dr. Harrison exit, barely able to keep it together. As soon as he left, she raised her hands to her chest and clapped softly, but excitedly. The scientists—Dr. Vogt—knew who she was!

Yeah, on the team in 25th place.

Lexi halted her celebration. If she had any shot of winning, she had to get her team together. She slid into her cot, stretched out, and gazed at the ceiling. Tomorrow would be different. No misread clues, lost Tel-Meds, or goofing around with swag or photos. It was time for Team RAM to make its move.

CHAPTER
TEN

After breakfast the next morning, Team RAM took its place in line to teleport to Paris. Due to overbooking of the telepods at the station, the start of the race had been postponed to 9:00 a.m. so the teams could leave one right after the other.

As they waited their turn, Lexi rubbed the logo on her Brewers cap for luck and turned to her teammates. "You know, this is already a good sign. If they had let some of the teams leave at seven a.m. and then made us wait for traffic to clear, we'd be really behind. Now, we'll all be together—for a little bit, at least."

"Yeah . . . at the Eiffel Tower." Ron groaned. "With tons of American tourists. I'm not going to sell anything."

Mal flipped her ponytail and adjusted the addition to her wardrobe—a steel-gray, fringed poncho. At least jeans (with decent pockets) had replaced the skirt and leggings. "Tell me about it. I'm not going to even bother with photos."

Lexi smiled at her gloomy teammates. This was exactly what she needed to hear. Things were already looking up!

Ron stretched. "I wonder if I have time to run back and grab another bagel. My energy is seriously low this morning."

Mal yawned. "Me too."

Lexi couldn't help it. She yawned, too. "Yeah, I know. It's because of the time change." She checked her watch. "Right now it's around nine a.m. here, so it's two a.m. back home."

"No wonder I had a hard time sleeping," Ron said. "It was like I was tired, but couldn't get comfy."

"What time is it in Paris?" Mal asked.

"Same as here."

"Good. Maybe our bodies will get used to it," Ron said. He backed out of line and did a few jumping jacks. "I'll get the blood flowing. I'm sure once we get started, we'll feel better."

The line moved, and Team RAM reached the telepod. They landed in France and let Mal loose at the counter to impress everyone with her fluent French. Sure enough, they checked in quickly.

Mal ripped open the envelope and slid out the clue. "Holy cow! We get to skip the Eiffel Tower!"

"What?" Ron said. "Awesome, but why?"

Mal tipped her head toward Lexi. "Because of *you*." She flashed a piece of paper to her teammates.

Congratulations!
You solved the Madame Curie worksheet correctly. You may skip the Eiffel Tower puzzle and proceed directly to:

VERSAILLES

"Wait. Is that right?" Ron wondered. He shuffled through his pack and pulled out the Kraków clue.

> Did you choose the correct answer? MAYBE YES, MAYBE NO. If not, you'll be told at your next destination and given another chance to get it right along with another puzzle to solve. If your answer was correct, you'll proceed directly to the next stop.

"Hey, yeah," he said. "It says right here that if you get the right answer, you'll be able to skip this stop." He gave Lexi's shoulder a light fist pound. "Way to go, Magill."

Lexi thought back to her worksheet. It seemed like she had completed it ages ago. She glanced at the check-in counter. A tournament monitor had shooed the Stargazers to the side and was handing them a blank copy of the worksheet. Their calculation must have been wrong.

"I wonder how many other teams got it right," Lexi said. *Probably a lot.* It was a science problem after all. But at least they vaulted over one team.

Mal nudged her teammates to the exit.

Lexi halted. "Wait. What are you doing? Should we ask someone how to get there?"

Mal didn't slow. "I already know. We take the train. I was on it a few times with my parents. It's right across the bridge."

As Team RAM waited on the platform for the train, Ron tapped the clue. "The city on here, this Ver-sail-es—it's pronounced

Ver-sigh? Have you been there?"

"Yep. It's King Louis the Fourteenth's palace."

"Great," Ron said. "Another puzzle involving a king and a castle."

Lexi and Mal laughed. "Don't worry," Mal said. "I think we're experts by now!"

Twenty minutes later, Team RAM exited the train at Versailles with a horde of teams and tourists. Signs everywhere identified how to get to the palace, and they followed the massive group down the tree-lined corridor of shops and residences.

"Hey, hey!" Ron shouted. "Another McDonald's!"

"Later," Mal said, yanking Ron's elbow before he could cross the street.

"Yeah, look!" Lexi said, pointing to a white stone barrier at the end of the road. "That must be it. Everyone's going in."

Team RAM scurried forward and through a tall golden gate topped with a crown and elaborate swirls. The palace before her was immense—the size of several city blocks. Made of red brick and stone columns with gold embellishments decorating the roof and balconies, there were so many arched windows, rectangular windows, yellow-framed windows that Lexi couldn't count. It was like nothing she had seen before. She couldn't imagine how the interior looked. This thing was huge—it had to be larger than the castles in Germany.

They hustled to the tournament booth and grabbed the clue.

DESTINATION NO. 5

Welcome to the Château de Versailles!

Proceed to the back of the palace to the gardens of Versailles, where the Labyrinthe de Versailles, also known as the Versailles Fable Maze, awaits!

The original hedge maze contained over three hundred animal statues and thirty-nine fountains, which portrayed fables as told by Aesop. This reconstructed maze follows a similar design, but is much smaller in scale. The goal is not to find a way out, but to assemble clues located among thirty-nine statues to figure out your next destination.

YES! You may find yourselves going in circles!

YES! You may feel frustrated!

But remember, success often comes after many failures.

Now for a hint:

You don't have to visit all thirty-nine statues in the labyrinth! Thirteen of the thirty-nine statues have all the information you need to determine your next destination. But which thirteen should you visit? We think you can figure it out. You've collected all of the information you need to do so! Good luck, and enjoy your time in the gardens!

*** YOU ARE REQUIRED TO STAY WITH YOUR TEAMMATES WHEN YOU ARE IN THE MAZE. YOU MUST VISIT THE STATUES TOGETHER AS A TEAM. **IF YOU SPLIT UP, YOU WILL BE DISQUALIFIED.**

"Hmph," Ron said, sticking his hand into the envelope. "Let's see what else they gave us." He slid the rest of the envelope's contents into his hand. A Trek Tracker sticker with a picture of a mouse fluttered to the ground, and Lexi snatched it up.

"There's a map in here. And some kind of list," he said as Lexi slid the sticker into her notebook.

"Wow," Mal said, finishing the clue. "We have to visit thirty-nine statues and then decode all the clues? This is going to take a while."

Ron raised his eyes from the clue and sighed. "For sure."

Mal glanced at their surroundings and fiddled with her camera. "At least it's a beautiful garden." She snapped a photo.

Nodding, Ron turned in a circle and shifted his backpack.

Lexi held her breath. A lot of people were coming through the gate. She couldn't let Ron drop everything and start selling. They had to stay focused.

"They've done this before," she said.

"Huh?" Ron spinned to face her.

Lexi swallowed hard. "On Day Two—usually a Sunday—they make a longer, weirder puzzle. One time it was in a zoo."

"A zoo?" Mal laughed. "Really?"

"Yeah. But at least it's different, and if you look at it, it's not science-y. I bet it'll throw a bunch of teams offtrack. If we figure it out fast, we can probably make up some time."

Ron rubbed his jaw. "You don't say?"

"I do like fairy tales," Mal said. "And fables. Or folk tales." She giggled. "Well, you know what I mean."

"Yeah, me too," Lexi said.

"Okay," Ron said. "Let's go."

Team RAM followed the stone path, maneuvering through

fountains, ornamental statues, and pruned greenery on the way to the maze's entrance. Mal stopped for a few seconds once or twice to snap a photo, but Ron didn't make a move to sell swag, so Lexi held her tongue and marched forward.

As they turned a corner, a plaza came into view. Several teams huddled around benches at its borders, seemingly working on the puzzle. The hedge maze stood straight ahead, and Lexi glimpsed three black shirts running toward the entrance, which was guarded by tournament monitors.

"Over here," Ron said, pointing to a shady area under a tree. "Let's take a look at what we're supposed to do."

Starting with the map of the maze, Ron placed the papers on the ground. Right away, Lexi could see why the clue said that the goal wasn't to find a way out of the maze. There were hardly any dead ends. Instead, a path would fork into two, with each path going for some distance before forking again or rejoining a previous trail. Any path taken would, for the most part, eventually twist its way to the exit.

Mal picked up the map. "There are spots on here numbered one through thirty-nine. I guess each of these numbers marks a statue, huh?"

"That's my take," Ron said. "Maybe it'll make more sense when we look at this." Ron set another piece of paper on the ground.

"Holy swiss cheese," Mal said. "What's that?"

"I think it's a list of the fables that are in the maze," Ron said. "The clue mentioned the maze was designed after Aesop's Fables, right?"

"Right," Lexi said, scooping up the clue. She read aloud, *"The statues and fountains portrayed fables by Aesop."* Lexi returned the clue to the ground and reviewed the fable list and then the map. "Since there are thirty-nine fables listed, my guess is that fable number 1 probably relates to statue number 1 on the map."

"That makes sense." Ron said. "So then all we have to do is figure out which thirteen statues we need to visit, and we can plan a route."

"How are we supposed to do that?" Mal asked. "I have no idea what the clue means."

"Me neither," Ron agreed.

Lexi read it again, hoping there was a teleport-science connection she had missed, but nothing clicked to mind. Unless . . . "Well, the clue uses the word 'figure.'" Ron craned his neck, and Mal leaned forward as Lexi explained, "It says 'figure out.' I wonder if we have to calculate something."

Ron stretched out on the lawn. "Let me think," he said, closing his eyes.

"Hm," Mal said, sidling next to Lexi to read. "The clue uses the numbers 300, 39, and 13. Are there any fables with those numbers in the title?"

"I don't know," Lexi said. "Good idea, though. I'll look." Lexi reviewed the titles. "No, nothing."

"Are those numbers significant to teleportation somehow?" Ron said, still on his back. "You know, like was it the three hundredth try before it worked, or there's thirty-nine elements in a Tel-Med or something?"

"No. *But* that's another good thought." She reviewed the papers again, scouring for some kind of scientific connection she had overlooked.

Ron shifted to a seated position. Elbows on his knees, he rubbed his temples. "Someone read it again," he mumbled. "Just the part about the thirteen. There was something there.... It's ... I can't get my mind around it."

Mal read the clue, *"You don't have to visit all thirty-nine statues in the labyrinth! Thirteen of the thirty-nine statues have all the information you need to determine your next destination. But which thirteen should you visit? We think you can figure it out. You've collected all of the information you need to do so!"*

After a few minutes of complete quiet, a long and loud "Arrrrrr-rrrrgh" sounded from Ron's mouth. "I have no idea," he said, ripping out a handful of grass. "Come on, think! What're we missing?"

Lexi frowned in frustration. Not only did she not have any ideas how to solve it, but since their arrival, she had seen more teams enter the maze. She checked her watch. Already eleven a.m. "Do you think we should get started—just plan on visiting all the statues?" she asked. "If something comes to us while we're inside, we can always switch it up then. So many teams are running in. I can't believe they figured out which thirteen to visit."

"I don't know," Mal said. "The Versailles gardens are ginormous. If the maze is as big as it looks, it could take hours."

"It's here," Ron said. "I know it is. Just . . . read it again."

Mal huffed. "Reall—"

"Just give it to me," Ron interrupted, snatching the paper out of Mal's hand. "Maybe it'll help if I see the words."

"Fine," Mal replied with a flip of her ponytail. She took out her tablet. "I'm going to research the maze and Aesop to see if there's a connection with thirteen, thirty-nine, or three hundred."

Team RAM worked silently for the next several minutes—Ron with the clue, Mal with the tablet, and Lexi with the list of fables. The "figure" terminology of the clue still tugged at her. She tapped the pen to her lips. Maybe the answer was *inside* the list, like the word *Otto* had been inside the word *Grotto*. She grabbed a pen and flipped to a fresh page in her notebook. Deciding to look for a connection with the number thirteen first, she started with Fable No. One and counted words in titles until she reached the thirteenth word. She wrote it down.

The

Okay, not earth-shattering, but a start. She continued through the list, pausing only to write down every thirteenth word she encountered. When she reached Fable No. 39 and there weren't enough words left to reach another thirteenth word, she looked at what she had written.

The The Pig Mouse Monkey The The The Porcupine And And The The Weasels Kits A

Gibberish. If there was a clue in there about figuring out which statues they needed to visit, it escaped her. She'd have to try something else.

Restarting from the top of the page, Lexi counted every thirty-ninth word:

Pig The Porcupine The Kites

Strike two. Maybe she was supposed to count every thirteenth letter? Or three-hundredth letter? She rubbed her eyes. She didn't feel like counting anymore.

"Find anything?" Lexi asked, lifting her eyes to Mal and Ron. "I'm getting nowhere."

Mal answered first, "Well, I sort-of found a science connection. Dr. Bressler's son is named Aesop, and he's published books known for their modern take on fables."

Lexi sagged. "Not really helpful," she said. "Anything else?"

"*Nada.* There's a bunch of stuff in here about the history of the Versailles gardens, all of the years they were remodeled, which king remodeled them, the architects. It's all really interesting—I'm totally going to ask my parents if we could spend some time here one day—but nothing helpful for the clue."

Mal bumped Ron's heel with her shoe. "How 'bout you?"

Ron kept his eyes on the clue—actually an assortment of clues. He had taken out the previous puzzles and set them side by side. Not wanting to disturb her teammate, Lexi kept quiet, clapping her notebook closed. The mouse sticker they had received with the map escaped and glided to the ground. Lexi picked it up and reached for the team's Trek Tracker.

"Here's the thing that I keep going back to," Ron said. He moved in closer and lowered his voice as he referred his teammates to the instructions. "*Collected.* The clue says we've collected everything we need to figure out which statues to visit."

"Hm," Lexi said as she peeled off the sticker.

"Collected to me means stuff they've given us," Ron continued. "I've been going over the other clues, looking at what we've collected so far."

"And?" Mal said.

"I'm not seeing it. Do you want to take a look?"

Mal bent over to read the clues as Lexi hurriedly stuck the fourth sticker in place. She pressed down her palm, flattening the sticker's edges to ensure it wouldn't peel off, and scooted toward her teammates.

"Nothing's coming to mind," Mal said as she read.

Ron kicked the papers, which floated into the air before settling on the grass. "Well, what else is there?" he growled. "What else could we have collected?"

"Maybe it's not physical," Lexi offered. "Maybe it's metaphorical, like collecting knowledge—you know, knowledge of Da Vinci's flying machines or that King Ludwig liked black swans."

Swans. The word poked Lexi's mind.

"Yeah," Mal added. "Or like how we know that the animal the woman in the painting was holding wasn't a lamb or a sheep." Mal chuckled.

Stoat. The animal was a stoat.

"That's it," Lexi said, clutching Mal's arm.

Ron and Mal stared at Lexi as she thrust the Trek Tracker toward them. She opened her notebook to the first page, showing where she had written "COLLECT NINE STICKERS" during the rules explanation. Then she pointed to each of the stickers.

"Swan, Stoat, Eagle, Mouse. Right?"

"Yeah?" Mal said.

Lexi placed the list of fables on top of the stickers. "These fables. Look at them."

"Oh my gosh," Ron blared.

"Shhhh!!" Lexi and Mal hushed.

"That's it!" Ron whispered. "Look! There's a bunch of fables with the words 'swan,' 'eagle,' and 'mouse' in the title. Let's underline them!"

"Eleven," Lexi said after Ron finished. "Two short."

"I didn't count Fable Number Fifteen, *The Mice in Council*," Ron said. "If I count that one, then we have twelve."

"I don't think we can count it," Mal said. "The sticker shows a single mouse. Not mice. If it made it thirteen, I'd say let's go for it, but it still leaves us one short."

"Are you sure there's no stoat?" Lexi asked. "It seems weird they'd skip one of the animals entirely."

"Hang on," Mal said, reaching for the tablet.

"Well, we can plot a course for these statues, and if we see a statue with the stoat thing along the way, we can stop," Ron offered.

"Ha!" Mal cried. "Weasel. Look for fables with the word 'weasel.'"

"Huh?" Ron said.

Mal flipped the tablet so it faced her teammates. "Meet the stoat, everyone. It's a short-tailed weasel."

"Got it," Lexi said, bouncing on her knees. "There are two with weasels. Well, three, actually, but one of the fables is *The Mouse and the Weasel* so we already had it marked." Lexi placed the list on the ground, and the team counted the underlined words again. Thirteen.

"Perfect," Ron said. "Now give me that map of the maze, and I'll plot a course so we can get started."

CHAPTER
ELEVEN

Ron studied the map for less than a minute before suggesting he should track their path through the maze in private. "Like you said, teams are running inside with no idea where to go. If they see us all huddled over a map plotting, they'll know we know which thirteen statues to visit, and they'll follow for sure. But if I'm by myself, they won't even give me a second look."

As if to prove Ron's point, the Solar Flares paused and studied Team RAM before darting into the hedges.

Lexi blew out a breath. "It's not that I disagree," she said. "Working on it in private is a great idea, but look around. There's nowhere to go."

Ron gestured toward the path leading to the front gate and smiled. "Sure there is. How about that McDonald's?"

Mal threw up her hands. "*Right.* Like we're gonna fall for *that.*"

Ron's jaw jutted out. "I'm serious. I can eat and plot at the same time. I'm a maze expert."

Lexi guffawed. "A maze expert? Really?" She crossed her arms. "Give us a break."

"No, I'm serious. You know how science is your thing? Well, mazes are mine. I go to at *least* three corn mazes a year, and I even helped diagram this year's big one in Mukwonago. I'll have our route in no time."

Lexi exhaled, trying to maintain her composure. She checked the time. Nearly 11:30 a.m. They were wasting time, which is specifically what she promised herself *wouldn't* happen today. But as another team zipped into the plaza, Lexi couldn't shake the feeling that, like it or not, Ron was right. If anyone got wind they solved the fable list, they'd lose their advantage.

"Okay," Lexi said.

"Okay?" Mal gasped, whirling toward her.

"For real?" Ron asked, his face contorted into a dubious expression.

Lexi waved him off. "Yeah, go." She paused and pointed. "But on two conditions: one, you go fast, and two . . ." She eyed his behemoth of a backpack. "Your swag stays here."

Ron arched an eyebrow. "Wow, Magill. That hurts. You really think I'd set up shop while you're waiting for me? Where's the trust?"

"I trust you, but I also *know* you, and this way you won't be tempted."

Ron cocked his other eyebrow. "All right, deal. But, as long as you're going to be hanging out here . . ."

Lexi crossed her arms. "Yeah?"

"*You* can sell."

"What? No way!"

Ron dragged his pack to her. "Why not? What's the big deal? You have to wait for me, anyway. Besides, I really need to sell this stuff. Otherwise I won't have enough for camp, and I'll have completely wasted my weekend."

Lexi sucked in a breath. She'd been so annoyed with Ron's swag she'd forgotten his reason for selling it. Football camp probably meant as much to him as the academy meant to her.

Mal raised her camera. "He has a point. I'll take some photos, too. That way we won't have to use up a lot of race time later."

"Yeah," Lexi said, remembering Mal's photo exhibit. While Lexi didn't know anything about photography, she could understand how photos of the garden would be impressive. "I guess that makes sense. But—"

"Awesome! You're the best, Magill!" Ron said, emptying his pack.

Lexi closed her eyes and pinched her nose. It's not that she minded selling, it was more like *where* she was selling. If any of her former classmates saw her, she'd die of embarrassment. If Dr. Harrison spotted her, well, she could only wonder what he'd think. She could just picture the scientists asking for an update and all he could say is that she was standing in the middle of the plaza selling swag. Not solving science problems, not discussing the tournament with other teams, not reviewing teleport principles . . . *selling swag.*

She opened her eyes. The only good thing was that the tree they were under was a little out of the way. Teams running straight into the maze would have no reason to look in her direction.

"Oh, and move up some, too," Ron directed. "You need a prime location. Customers will miss you back here." He picked up the souvenirs and moved closer to the entrance.

Fan-tastic.

Lexi followed Ron as Mal ran ahead and disappeared down a path. "All right, I got it—just go," Lexi said. "And hurry."

Ron left as a family of four entered the plaza.

Don't look. Don't look. Keep walking.

Nope.

"*Bonjour!*" the man said as he approached.

"Hi," Lexi said. "Would you like to buy anything? It's all from the Green Bay Packers."

"Sure. My brother's in America right now. Boy, will he be surprised when he gets back." The man picked up a cap and placed it on his head. "Twenty euros."

Lexi didn't think twice. "Sold!" The man handed over the money, and Lexi took it with a smile. *That wasn't so bad.*

More people came, and within ten minutes, Lexi was getting into it. A cap there, a shirt here. Maybe if she sold enough, Ron wouldn't have to sell the rest of the trip. *Heck yeah.*

"GET YOUR GREEN BAY PACKERS GEAR HERE!"

For an added effect, Lexi waved her arms over her head. It

worked. Bunches of would-be customers wandered her way. She made a few sales, and as she stuffed the cash into the side of Ron's pack, a shrill laugh rang out.

"O.M.G!"

Oh no. Lexi jerked. Haley approached, laughing like a hyena. "What in the world are you doing?"

Lexi relaxed. Haley she could handle. Haley at least would understand. She waved her friend over. "Hey, Hale. Just watching Ron's stuff while he's plotting a course through the maze."

"Plotting a course?"

"Yeah, he's into corn mazes, so he said he could track the fastest path."

Haley laughed. "Ohhhh, that's an interesting idea. It *is* twisty in there. Andre didn't want to waste any time, though. We've been zig-zagging all around. I think we've gotten to about twelve statues so far." She tightened her ponytail. "They're setting up a food tent, so we thought we'd take a quick break before diving back in."

Twelve statues? Lexi swallowed hard. Haley was a third done and Team RAM hadn't even started. Hopefully by visiting only the statutes they needed to, they'd make up some time.

Before Lexi could respond, Haley sprung toward Lexi and gripped her elbow. "Guess what? I talked to Dr. Harrison this morning, and he mentioned me to Dr. Vogt!"

Lexi startled. "Really?"

"Yep! Dr. Harrison said the scientists had asked how the race was going, and he mentioned the top teams. Isn't that awesome? I'm totally getting that internship!"

Lexi sucked in a gasp. First, Haley was a third done with the maze, and now Dr. Vogt knew about her. Lexi tried smiling to show she was happy for her friend, but her body suddenly felt very heavy.

"That's great, Hale," Lexi finally squeaked. "*Dr. Vogt*, I mean—"

Haley clapped a hand over her mouth. "Oh, Lex. I'm sorry. I know you like her, too, but . . ." Haley softly shook her head and gave Lexi's hand a small squeeze. "You weren't thinking you had a shot, were you? You guys are *so* far behind. You might not even survive today's elimination."

Lexi pulled her hand away from Haley's. Her friend had always been blunt, but this was too much to hear.

"It's early," Lexi stated with an edge to her voice. "We still have all day."

Haley stepped back. "Oh, of course!" she said brightly. She nudged Lexi's elbow and winked. "Hey, you know what might help? Working with another team."

Lexi's heart skipped. This was more like it. If Team RAM formed an alliance with Haley's Comets, not only would they leap to the front of the pack, but she'd be racing with her best friend. It'd be like old times.

"Thanks," Lexi said with a grin. "That's a great idea. We—"

"Sure," Haley interrupted. "We're working with the Phenoms and Tesla's Techies. For now, anyway. We agreed once we're in the top five, it's every team for themselves." Haley adjusted her pack. "It was a good move, too. Kwame from our summer camp last year is on the Techies, and he's got all these programs on his computer for translation, European museums, maps with transportation stuff. . . . With the way this year's race isn't focusing a lot on science, we'd be in serious trouble if it weren't for him."

Lexi pressed her lips together. Haley wasn't interested in teaming up *with* her. She already had formed her alliance and, like the practice tournaments, had skipped asking Lexi. Lexi's stomach roiled. It was like Haley had completely forgotten she existed since she wasn't at the academy anymore.

"Oh, hey." Haley pointed. "There's Edison's Excellencies. Arturo's smart. Maybe you can ask him."

Arturo and his Excellencies darted into the maze.

"Or how about Kacey and the Rambunctious Robots?"

Lexi gritted her teeth. Haley had never had a nice word to say about Kacey in her entire life. Now Haley was recommending her? Did Haley really think Lexi had forgotten that?

Rubbing her forehead, Lexi sidestepped Haley and knelt to straighten Ron's swag. "Nah, that's okay."

Haley flecked loose specks of glitter off her T-shirt. "Just trying to help."

Lexi stared at Haley. If her friend were really trying to help, she'd have offered to let Team RAM join her alliance. She swallowed hard. It couldn't hurt to ask.

"Why don't we join your alliance? We always said we wanted to race together. This would be the next best thing."

Haley froze, then tapped her lips, and then let out a sigh. "Yeah, I know, but that was before. Emma and I have the physics covered, and Andre has been great with the teleport station locator programs. Besides, I'm not sure the other teams would go for it. We're in the lead, and it's not like you have anything to offer to help us, you know?"

Lexi frowned. She had hoped Haley would want to race together to *be* together, to hang out and have fun like they used to, not just to win. But with Emma and her other classmates around, Haley apparently wasn't interested in keeping Lexi as a friend.

Breathe. Lexi's mind told her as her heart walloped against her chest. She glanced at Haley, who had turned and was gazing into the plaza as if nothing had happened, as if she hadn't just dumped all over her best friend. Scratch that. *Former* best friend.

Lexi stretched her fingers and blinked away tears. Team RAM had nothing to offer? She was a science whiz and teleport expert, Mal spoke a bunch of different languages, and Ron solved codes in his sleep.

Shaking her head, she opened her mouth to give her friend a good, hard dose of the truth, but stopped short. Let Haley think Team RAM couldn't win. It didn't matter what she thought about the internship. The only thing that mattered was what the scientists thought.

The scientists. Lexi's lips curled into a smile as she remembered what Dr. Harrison had said. *He* had been encouraging. She'd almost forgotten.

She straightened. "Yeah, you're right," Lexi said. "Now that you mention it, it probably *is* better we race on our own. After all, Dr. Harrison said Dr. Vogt was impressed with me because I was leading a team that didn't have a science background. If we joined you guys, that wouldn't be the case anymore."

Haley spun, narrowing her eyes. "What? He said that? When?"

Lexi hid a smirk. Haley's sudden concern felt deliciously good. "Last night after we checked in."

"Huh. And he mentioned Dr. Vogt specifically?"

"Yep. He said to keep racing and anything can happen."

"Hm," Haley murmured, fiddling with her necklace. "Well, that's . . . that's great, Lex. I, uh, I guess—"

Incoming hoots and hollers sounded from the plaza's entrance. Lexi peered past Haley and smiled. "That must be my teammates. See ya."

As Haley walked away, Ron ran toward Lexi, excitedly waving the map over his head.

"Got it!" he screamed.

"Shh!" Lexi said as she trotted to meet him. "What happened to playing it cool?"

"Sorry," Ron replied. "But relax, no one's around."

Lexi whirled. Haley was making her way to the food tent, clearly out of earshot.

"I'm here!" Mal shouted, running to join them.

Team RAM huddled. "You won't believe what I found!" Ron

whispered excitedly. "One of the gardeners was at Mickey D's. He spoke pretty good English and told me that the maze has, like, over seven miles of paths. Those teams that are running to all of the statues have a *lot* of ground to cover."

"Good," Lexi said, reaching for the map. "But all the more reason not to be running around screaming your head off. Now, what's the route?"

Ron held out the map. "It's actually better to use this entrance, grab most of the clues, and then head on down to the exit." He tapped the exit on the far side of the map. "We can reenter the maze there and then visit the last few statues on that side." He directed them to a spot in the top-middle portion of the maze. "This is the only statue that's going to be a pain—number twenty. There's no quick way of getting there, and it's at one of the few dead ends."

"Okay," Lexi said. "Sounds good."

Ron repacked his swag and heaved the backpack onto his shoulders. "Hey, it's a little lighter."

"Yep," Lexi said. "I did pretty well. Money's in the side pocket."

"All right, but once we're done with the maze, I want about ten minutes out front."

Mal gave a small wave. "And I'd really like to get a pic of the *Grotte des Bains d'Apollon*. It's a rock structure with water and statues. I'm figuring I can do a contrast/compare with the Venus Grotto we saw in Germany."

Lexi scratched her nose, not sure how she could refuse when it was two against one. Plus, they should be able to make up time now with Ron's secret route. "How about we do this part of the maze and then take a quick lunch break? Maybe you guys can sell or take photos while we eat?"

Mal and Ron looked at each other.

Ron nodded first. "Definitely doable."

"Yeah," Mal said. "That'll work."

Lexi pushed up her glasses and gave a firm nod. While she preferred they grab their food and continue straight away into the maze, this was probably the best compromise. Besides, given their bodies were still adjusting to the time change, taking a break would do them good.

Team RAM jogged through the maze's entrance. Almost immediately, the gravel path forked to the left and right. Without hesitation, Ron veered right, and Lexi and Mal followed. Trotting down the trail, Lexi was more grateful than ever that Ron had plotted a course *and* was leading. The leafy hedge rows bordering the paths were over six feet tall and impeccably trimmed. No matter how many turns they made, their surroundings didn't change: gravel path lined with tall bushes. Lexi knew she'd have already gotten twisted around and lost.

"The first statue should be up here," Ron eventually whispered. "Even though it's not one of the ones we marked, let's stop anyway in case someone's watching."

Lexi considered the path ahead. The trail extended at least fifty feet, and there wasn't a soul in sight. She peeked over her shoulder. No one there, either. But, if this was the closest statue to the entrance, another team could come jogging down at any moment.

They traveled around another bend, and Ron halted. A five-foot statue of a coiled snake stood before them. Sitting atop a white stone column, the snake had its mouth open wide, fangs bared. *The Viper and the File*, the name of the first fable, was etched into the column's side.

"Yikes," Mal said. "Creepy."

Lexi studied the snake, marveling at the intricate detail of the stone carving. Except for its white color, the snake looked lifelike, as if it had been frozen in time. As Mal turned away and shuddered, Ron stooped to the ground. A blue-and-gold framed plaque leaned against the column's base. He pointed at the word etched into it: STREET.

"I'll write it down," Lexi said, grabbing her notebook. "But I'll keep these clues on a separate page so we won't get confused."

As Lexi finished writing, another team raced through, pausing long enough to record the clue and move on. Team RAM faced each other. "Well, that's good," Mal said. "If everyone goes as fast as that, we won't have to worry about being followed."

"For sure," Ron said. "Come on, the first *real* clue is up ahead."

By the time Team RAM reached the next statue, the other team was on its way. This statue had two animals. A weasel on all fours faced a fat fox staring into a crack at the base of the column. A stream of water projected out of the crack, rainbowing over the column and into a small cement plate on the ground. The tournament plaque rested against the plate.

"A fountain," Mal whispered.

"Hmm?" Ron said, swiveling to face her.

"A fountain," she repeated, smiling. "Remember how the clue said that, in the original maze, there were thirty-nine fountains among the three hundred statues? One of the things I read was that, when the maze was first built, there was a sort-of challenge for people to run through the maze and cross all thirty-nine fountains as fast as they could."

"Yeah? So?" Ron answered.

Mal exhaled deeply. "*Think* about it. I bet each of the statues *we're* supposed to visit is going to have a fountain, kind of like how it was in the original maze—the fountains were important."

"Wow, so this means we're on the right track!" Lexi said.

"Yeah!" Ron agreed, giving Mal a high five.

Lexi stooped to record the clue.

FOR

Mal sneaked a look over Lexi's shoulder. "That's it?"

Lexi shrugged. "I guess. Come on, let's keep moving."

With Ron leading the charge, Team RAM navigated the maze. By the time they reached the eighth statue on their list, Lexi knew Mal had been right. So far, each statue with a swan, eagle, weasel, or mouse, also contained a fountain. Lexi wrote each fountain's clue next to the fable's number. Her list was taking shape.

Fable #3: FOR
Fable #6: YOUR
Fable #8: NEXT
Fable #11: LOCATION
Fable #15:
Fable #16: THE
Fable #20
Fable #22: OF
Fable #24: THE
Fable #25:
Fable #28:
Fable #31:
Fable #37: SCIENCE

"Jeez," she muttered as they curved around a bend. "It's a good start, but this can turn out to be anything."

Ron stopped at an intersection and unshouldered his pack. He pointed to a grass path that darkened in the distance. "I'm thinking we rest a couple minutes and then head up there. It leads to that out-of-the-way statue—number twenty—that's at the dead end at the top of the maze. This is the closest we'll be to it."

"Okay," Mal said as she retied her ponytail. "Then we can eat."

Lexi checked her watch. "Wow. It's almost three p.m. We've been inside for a while." She fumbled in her pack for a few granola bars to tide them over. The thud of footsteps off to her side made her pause. Trotting from the dead-end trail, the Comets and Phenoms approached, ultimately stopping at the intersection. Hands on their knees, the Phenoms leaned over to catch their breath. Haley stuck out her lip and blew her bangs out of her eyes while her teammates slumped against the hedgerow.

"Wow," Ron said. "I guess it really is far, huh?"

Phenom Simon swigged from a water bottle. "Yeah. Dark, too. Lots of overhanging branches."

"Kinda spooky," Comet Emma added. "You guys going down?"

"Yeah," Lexi answered. "We're about to. Just resting for a sec."

Simon took another drink and then replied, "Good idea." He nodded to Haley. "Let's meet up with the Techies and see how many they found. Maybe we can start solving while we eat."

The Phenoms walked away, and Haley's teammates followed. Haley stayed behind a second, patting her stomach.

"Hey, Lex," Haley said, walking to her. "Can I talk to you for a sec?" Haley didn't wait for a response. "I want to say that I'm sorry about before. I was way out of line."

Lexi jerked her head. "Huh?"

Haley gave a half shrug. "I shouldn't have said what I said. You're smart and have as much chance as anyone to win." She leaned in. "I also want you to know that I asked the others if you could join our alliance."

Lexi's shoulders eased. She studied her friend's face and saw the person she had known forever staring back at her. "Really?"

Haley smiled. "Yeah. I had a chance to think about what you said. It *would* be good to race together." She paused. "But they said no, that three teams were enough since the race was already half over."

Lexi squeezed Haley's hand. She didn't really care about joining the alliance anymore. The important thing was her friend was back. "That's okay, Hale. Thanks, anyway."

Haley started to turn, but paused. Lightly tugging her necklace, she faced Lexi. "But that's no reason we can't hang out. Why don't you guys take a break and come eat with us?"

Lexi's heart nearly burst through her chest. This was the Haley she had been looking for. *This* was the Haley she had missed. But her stomach tightened as she realized the offer came at the worst possible time. They had to get to the statue.

"I'd love a break," Mal said as she stretched out on the lawn in a yoga pose. "I'm really getting stiff."

Ron picked up his backpack. "Not yet. We gotta get number twenty done while we're in this section of the maze."

Lexi tossed the granola bars to her teammates. "Here, these will help."

Ron tore the wrapper off with his teeth. "Trust me. We'll be taking a nice long rest with a nice long meal as soon as we finish this one."

Haley winced. "Oh yikes. You do know that the food tent might be down by then?"

"What?" Lexi asked.

"Yeah," Mal said, stepping toward Haley. "What do you mean?"

Haley fidgeted with her pack's straps. "They can't keep it up all day. I heard one of the officials say it was a temporary thing."

"Still, I can't see it closing before four," Lexi said. "We'll be quick."

Haley stared down the path leading to the statue. "I don't know. That statue's pretty far, and then you still have to go all the way to the beginning to get out, remember?"

Ron and Mal looked longingly toward the maze's entrance. "Shoot," Ron said. He looked at Lexi. "We really need to eat, and how are we going to work in time for my swag?" He gestured to Mal. "And for Mal to visit that other grotto thing?"

Lexi set her hands on her hips. "But we'd waste too much time coming all the way back here. Like you said, it's at a dead end."

"Well," Haley said. "I guess . . . I mean if you *promise* not to say anything . . ."

"What?" Lexi asked.

Haley bobbed her head as if considering her options. "It's only *one* word. I don't really see the harm." She smiled at Lexi. "Besides, what are friends for, right?"

Lexi stayed quiet, not sure what to say.

"Last," Haley said. "The word on that statue is 'last.'"

Lexi exchanged glances with her teammates. Ron and Mal's eyes were practically bulging out of their heads.

"Thanks," Mal said first, followed a second later by Ron. They looked toward Lexi.

"Last?" Lexi repeated.

Haley backpedaled to the path. "Yep, but remember, you didn't hear it from me! Come on, let's eat!"

147

Haley disappeared into the maze. Within seconds, Mal skipped after her, and an instant later the Filipino Flyer bolted past both.

Lexi filled the blank in her notebook, not sure how to feel about Haley's help. Haley no doubt felt bad about their earlier conversation and was trying to make it up to her, but a part of Lexi really wanted to prove to everyone that she could lead Ron and Mal on her own.

Lexi slid the notebook into her backpack and took the last sip of water from her bottle. Her head throbbed, and her stomach rumbled. Swinging her backpack over her shoulder, she headed down the trail. Accepting Haley's help was the right thing to do. They could eat, Mal and Ron could do their stuff, and then they'd have more energy to finish the rest of the maze.

Smiling, Lexi sped her walk, anxious to catch up. Haley had definitely saved them a lot of time. She'd have to find a way to return the favor, and, at the very least, remember to thank her when the race was over.

CHAPTER TWELVE

Lexi and Mal waited at the maze's exit as Ron stuffed another slice of pizza into his mouth.

"Where does he put it all?" Mal asked as Ron started toward them. "I'd weigh three hundred pounds if I ate what he did."

Lexi laughed. "I know, but at least he eats fast. You guys were really quick—it was hardly thirty minutes."

"The *Grotte* wasn't far." Mal curled strands of hair behind her ears. "How many statues do we have left?"

"Four," Lexi answered. "And I don't have the map, so I have no idea how far they are."

Mal motioned toward the opposite side of the plaza, where the Solar Flares and Powerful Protons were running out of the garden. "So many teams are leaving. I'm kind of surprised. I don't think we've been that slow."

"I know," Lexi said. "I'm hoping that they don't know where they're going yet, though. If they have thirty-nine words to sift through, it might take a while. We'll have only the thirteen we need."

"I hope so," Mal replied, bouncing on her toes. "France has been great, but I want to see where they send us next."

Mal tightened her purse straps, and she and Lexi entered the maze as Ron, map in hand, flew by. For the next hour, Team RAM scurried through. This side was twistier than the other, and even Ron had to backtrack at one point after realizing he had led them down a wrong path. Finally, only one word remained.

"The last one should be only a few turns ahead," Ron said.

"Good," Mal puffed. "I'm so ready for a rest. I hope we have to take a train a long way to our next location so I can take a mega long nap."

The tip of a white pillar came into view. Statues of a mouse and a frog stood atop two columns. A stream of water arched between them with the water ultimately trickling into a goldfish's mouth at the base of the pillars.

The Mouse and the Frog

Ron leaned over to the tournament plaque. "Father," he said. "The clue for fable number twenty-five is 'father.'"

Lexi wrote it down and reviewed the list.

Fable #3: FOR
Fable #6: YOUR
Fable #8: NEXT
Fable #11: LOCATION
Fable #15: VISIT
Fable #16: THE
Fable #20 LAST
Fable #22: OF

Fable #24: THE
Fable #25: FATHER
Fable #28: OF
Fable #31: COMPUTER
Fable #37: SCIENCE

"Something's wrong," Lexi said. "This doesn't make sense." She read the clues aloud, "For your next location visit the last of the father of computer science."

Mal and Ron gave quizzical looks.

"Huh?" Ron asked.

"Yeah, I know," Lexi said. She tilted the notebook so Ron could see, too. "Here, take a look."

As Ron and Lexi reviewed the list, Mal retrieved her tablet. "Has anyone ever heard of an Alan Turing?" she asked after a minute. "According to these websites, everyone seems to agree he's the father of computer science. He created a machine that translated words into numbers, so in a way he invented the first computer."

"You know what?" Ron said. "That name *is* familiar."

"Yeah," Lexi agreed. "It is. I don't know from where, though."

Ron snapped his fingers. "I know. It's from a movie my dad likes. Alan Turing built a machine that helped Britain decipher encrypted messages in World War II."

"Yep, that makes sense," Mal said. "From what I'm reading, Turing was born in London and cracked codes at a place called Bletchley Park in England. He died in England, too."

Lexi punched a fist into her hand. "Great. So we know it's something to do with Alan Turing and we'll be going somewhere in England. We just have to figure out exactly where." She glanced at Ron and gestured to her notebook. "Did you figure anything out?"

He tapped the page. "Yeah. It's the word 'last' for statue twenty that screws everything up. It doesn't make any sense."

Lexi hiccupped over the word. *"Last?"* Her voice trailed and she shifted her eyes between Mal and Ron as her stomach sank. "That's the one Haley gave us. Do you think—"

"She lied to us!" Mal yelled as she stomped over and snatched the notebook out of Ron's hands. "But why?"

Ron shook off his backpack and tossed it to the ground. "I thought you were friends?"

Lexi didn't move. *Haley lied?* She flipped off her baseball cap and ran a hand through her hair, jostling her glasses in the process. They fell to the ground with her cap, and she let them be. Her heart pounded. Haley couldn't have lied. It had to have been a mistake. Her head spinning, she extended her arms, trying to stay upright.

"Lexi! Sit down," Mal said, lightly pressing her against the hedge. "You look terrible."

Panting hard, Lexi slid to the ground. She set an elbow on her knee and wiped her forehead as she wracked her brain for a reason Haley would have lied. She had apologized for her earlier comments and said how awesome it would be to hang out—Lexi caught herself. The lunch invite. It had been part of her scheme to lure them away from visiting the statue so she could give them the wrong answer. The whole apology was a sham.

Lexi shook her head, her tired brain unable to figure out Haley's motive. Why sabotage them when it was obvious they were so far behind, as Haley herself kept pointing out?

"I don't get it," Lexi said. "We've been best friends for years."

"What was she talking about?" Ron asked. "You know, before— when she said she asked the others, but they said no?"

Lexi rose to her feet. "While you were plotting the course through the maze, she came over and said we should think about working with another team. I asked to join her alliance, and she said she didn't see how we could help given we were so far behind. She was telling me she had checked with the other teams, and they said no."

Ron guffawed. "Couldn't help? Really?" He reared back and kicked the grass.

"Oh, I get it," Mal said with a sneer. "She thinks we're stupid. I'll have her know that I've won *five* statewide art exhibitions, I speak four languages, and both my parents have PhDs. Plus, I've been all over Europe. That's *real* world experience—not sitting behind a desk at an academy."

Ron jumped in. "And I'm being recruited by high school teams *and* college coaches for football and basketball. I also get all As and Bs. I'd like to see her read and memorize a football playbook if she thinks she's so smart."

Lexi picked up her glasses and cap. She hadn't known any of these things about her teammates, either. Though she liked to believe she had given them more credit than Haley had, she had to admit that, in reality, she had thought she'd have been the one leading the team. Thinking about it now, she had no idea where she'd be without Mal or Ron. She put on her glasses and cap and faced her teammates.

"Tell me something." Ron motioned to the exit. "Is that why you wanted to join her alliance—because you don't think we can win on our own?"

"Yeah," Mal added, turning to face her. "Do you think we can't win because we're not super smart science students?"

Lexi flinched. "Of course not. I asked you to be on my team, didn't I?"

"That's not saying much," Ron muttered. He set his hands on his hips. "You've only been in school this semester, and it's not like you have tons of friends."

"I have friends," Lexi said. "They're just . . . at the academy . . ." *Or so she thought.* She blew out a breath. "Look, I admit that I thought there was going to be tons of science puzzles and I might be—okay *would be*—doing most of the work, but I asked you guys because I *know* you're smart, too. You both rocked our Egypt project." She tapped Ron's shoulder. "You're Hieroglyphics Man, remember? I figured if you could create your own fake language, you'd have a knack for puzzles, and I was right."

She looked at Mal. "And you are so freaking fast on a computer, Mal. Yeah, I didn't know about all the languages you speak, but every tournament requires us to research things." She crossed her arms. "So, no, I'm not like Haley. In fact, I told her it was better if we didn't join her stupid alliance because—"

Lexi gasped as she put the final pieces together. Dr. Vogt. She had told Haley that the scientists were impressed with her because she was leading a team that didn't have a science background. Of course Haley became threatened, and her solution was sabotaging Team RAM so they'd be eliminated today. Lexi shook her head. This whole time she'd been trying to get back to the academy to save her friendship with Haley, and Haley . . . Lexi slumped as the truth hit her. Haley didn't care about their friendship at all.

"What is it?" Mal asked.

Lexi shook her head. "I figured out why Haley lied. We were talking about the internship. Haley really wants it, too. If we don't make the elimination today, she figures it'll be hers."

Ron and Mal didn't move.

"I'm sorry," Lexi said. "I should have kept my mouth shut, but she kept saying how we were so far behind and she was on one of the top teams and Dr. Vogt knew about her. . . . I got upset and wanted her to know we still had a chance, too."

Ron arched an eyebrow. "Well, if she thinks she's so smart . . ." He grabbed Lexi's notebook. "Give me that."

"Yeah," Mal said, stepping to his side. "We'll show her."

Ron flipped to the list of words. "You know," he said. "We might be able to figure this out without going back to that statue. It's really just a fill-in-the-blank puzzle—*Wheel of Fortune* style. All we have to do is pretend the word *last* isn't there. What word can we insert that makes sense?"

With renewed energy, Lexi advanced toward her teammates. "Hey, yeah. That's a great idea." She turned to Mal. "You've read a little about Turing. Is there a word we can plug in that works?"

"Other than England?" Mal chortled. She retrieved her tablet. "Hmm," she said after a few swipes of the screen. "How about 'hometown'—as in *For your next location, visit the hometown of the father of computer science.*"

"But where in his hometown?" Ron said. "The hospital where he was born? His childhood home?"

Lexi tapped her lips. "Yeah, 'hometown' might be too vague."

Mal kept reading. "That Bletchley Park place is a well-known tourist attraction. They call it the home of the Codebreakers, and there's a bunch of exhibits on codebreaking."

"But that wouldn't be one word," Lexi said. "And it's real specific. If the clue was 'Bletchley Park' everyone would know where to go after visiting that one statue."

"True," Ron said.

Mal hopped in place, and her eyes got wide. "Okay, how about 'memorial'? As in, *For your next clue, visit the memorial of the father of computer science?*"

Ron tilted his head to the side. "Before I answer, *is* there a memorial?"

Mal shifted her weight and eyed Ron. "Duh. And get this, it's in a place near Manchester University called Sackville *Gardens*, and the memorial is actually a *statue* of him. It makes perfect sense—so far the clues have sort of related to one another."

"Yeah, you're right," Ron said. "We'd be going from one place with gardens and statues to another place with gardens and a statue. It's kind of like how the Hall of Mirrors at King Ludwig's Linderhof Castle was connected to the clue on Da Vinci's mirror writing."

Lexi hurriedly retrieved her tableau and unfolded it so she could see what teleport stations she had listed for England. "Oh wow. The teleport station for Manchester is at the university!"

Mal and Ron beamed.

"Well?" Ron asked. "Retracing our steps all the way to the statue would take another hour, and then we'd have to walk all the way back to the entrance. This is riskier, but if we're right, we can make up some time and . . ."

". . . shove Haley's stupid 'last' clue right in her face," Mal avowed, pulling the ribbon on her ponytail tight.

"Mal!" Ron and Lexi cried.

Ron burst into laughter as Lexi stared at Mal's tight jaw and steely eyes.

"I say we go for it," Mal added.

Ron turned to Lexi. "What do you say, Magill?"

Lexi remained still, stunned at the sight of her teammates, her *two excited and totally invested teammates*. Grinning, she punched a fist into her hand. "Manchester it is. Let's do it."

Team RAM rushed to the maze's exit. An orange team and a lime green team mingled at the food tent, but no other teams were around. Lexi turned to exit the plaza.

"Hold up," Ron said. He marched to the food tent.

"Why am I not surprised?" Mal murmured.

Lexi chuckled. "Actually, I can go for another baguette." She opened her mouth to call, but Ron was already returning—empty-handed.

"Wow," Mal said. "That was fast—even for you."

Ron removed his backpack. "Just wanted to check with the official on something," he said. "By the way, the food tent didn't close and isn't closing. Haley lied about that, too."

Lexi met Ron's eyes. She had no idea what to say. Facts were facts, and the ones she had proved Haley had tried to sabotage them. She remembered Haley's comments about plotting the coordinates to France and wondered if that was a trick to slow them down, too.

"Well, we were dumb enough—and lazy enough—to believe her," Mal said, kicking the ground. "We said we were worried about missing our chance to take photos and sell stuff. She knew we'd trust her answer instead of going to the statue ourselves."

"I know," Ron said, unzipping his pack. He started pulling out his gear and setting it on the ground.

"What are you doing?" Mal asked. "You know we're behind. You're not really going to sell stuff now, are you?"

Lexi shot Mal a look and wondered if Mal had read her thoughts. Ron waved at the tournament official at the booth, and the official came over. "This is it," Ron said. "Whatever you don't sell, if you can bring it back with you, that'd be great."

"No problem," the official answered, stacking the swag into his arms. Lexi's mouth hung open as the official left. Ron folded in his backpack, snapping and attaching clasps to make it smaller. When it was reduced to the size of a large—but not extraordinarily large pack—he unzipped a small pouch and pulled out . . . lipstick?

Ron screwed off the cap and twisted the bottom of the tube. A black stick peeked out. He raised the stick to his face and drew two black lines under his eyes. Swinging his pack across his shoulders, he faced his teammates.

"It's Game Time."

CHAPTER
THIRTEEN

Back in the Paris teleport station, Team RAM waited in line for the telepod engineer to wave them forward. Lexi kept turning around to peer at the curtain behind the tournament booth. Teams inside were working, but which teams and how many remained a mystery.

Even though the tournament officials said they could enter, Team RAM decided not to waste the time. If they hadn't guessed right and *memorial* was the wrong word, they'd have to come back to Versailles and check the statue themselves. The better move was getting to England as soon as possible.

The engineer motioned to Lexi, and she stepped to the telepod. The e-mail from Wren Tech flashed to her, and she shuddered. What she had brushed off last night without too much thought poked at her now. To be safe, maybe she *should* visit a Wren Tech store. She placed the Tel-Med into the slot, and the shield closed.

Moments later, Lexi opened her eyes in Manchester. She exhaled.

After the crowds in Florence, Kraków, and Paris, the nearly

empty university station was a welcome sight. But was it too empty? Lexi looked for another team or a tournament booth as Ron and Mal joined her.

"Well?" Ron said.

"I don't see anyone, but I haven't really moved."

Team RAM took a collective breath. "All right. Let's go," Ron said, and he led the charge into the next room.

"Good afternoon!" a tournament official called from the corner.

Team RAM ran over, and the official proceeded to check them in. Lexi inspected the official's face, looking for a sign they were in the right place. Like Dr. Harrison had explained in the beginning, the tournament had set up booths in cities off course because they had anticipated some mistakes.

"You can have these back," the official said, returning their passports and badges.

Lexi held her breath, waiting for the official to reach under the counter and pull out an envelope.

He didn't.

"Okay," the official said. Lexi, Ron, and Mal leaned in. "For this puzzle, you're limited to Sackville Gardens and the university grounds. Once you've figured out the next clue and where you want to go next, come back here. There's a special Travel Request Form to fill out during this round."

Lexi excitedly beat her hand against the counter and jumped off the ground. They'd guessed correctly!

"Yeah!" Ron whooped.

Mal leaped into the air, clapping. "We did it! *Without* the word. Guess we're not so stupid, huh?"

Still celebrating, Team RAM made its way to the exit when Lexi halted and checked the time. She reset her watch from 6:45 to 5:45. They'd gained an hour coming to England, but the time also meant they'd spent over seven hours running around the maze in Versailles. If the tournament kept up with its three-puzzles-a-day schedule, Team RAM would have to solve two more before the next travel cutoff at 10:00 p.m. or risk falling behind.

Surging ahead, Lexi exited the building, where an asphalt path wound its way through rows of green leafy trees. Benches bordered the path, and a few students mingled about. "Anyone have any ideas?" she asked.

"It's either to the left or the right," Mal said, glancing at her tablet. "Pick a direction."

"Okay," Ron said. "I choose right," and he hurried to the path.

Lexi rushed after him, with Mal only a step behind. A short stretch down the path, a blue-and-gold streamer waved in the wind, beckoning them forward. The ribbon was tied to a bench, where a bronze statue of Alan Turing sat.

"Alan Turing, father of computer science," Lexi read from a plaque near the statue.

Ron lightly slapped a pedestal next to the memorial. "This must be the clue. There's a video screen embedded in the top."

Lexi retrieved her notebook and Mal readied her tablet. Ron pressed Play.

Dr. Kent flashed into the frame. Lexi hopped in anticipation, knowing there was a good chance the next puzzle was physics-related. Born in Nigeria and educated at various universities around the world, Dr. Kent served as the teleport team's critical thinker and great quantum theorist. If it hadn't been for him, quantum computers capable of storing the data needed to teleport living matter never would have been invented.

Dressed in beige khakis and a colorful Hawaiian shirt, Dr. Kent waved. "Welcome! Congratulations for finding our friend Alan Turing, the father of computer science, and a very important person in the development of teleport travel!"

He spread his arms out wide. "All of the developments in physics and chemistry utilized in teleport science would be useless without quantum computers. But it's not as though we snapped our fingers and a quantum computer appeared. No sirreee! Before quantum computers, we had digital computers." He held up a finger. "And before digital computers, there were machines like our Mr. Turing invented, which were programmed to follow a specific set of instructions in order to find an answer or a solution to a problem."

Dr. Kent leaned forward. "But how do you give a machine instructions? What language does it understand? English, French, Chinese?" He clapped his hands together. "That's where you come in. We need you to find a computer scientist who invented a way to talk to computers—the person credited for developing the first high-level computer programming language."

Dr. Kent straightened. "Ready for a couple of hints?" He held up a finger. "First, *she* was quite the officer in her day. And second . . ." He paused and raised a second finger. "She has a bridge named after her." He clapped again. "Okay, that's it. Hop to it!" Dr. Kent winked and then the screen went dark.

"Well," Ron said. "That was . . . interesting."

Lexi pounded the pedestal. "Ugh. I was really hoping for another worksheet." Shaking her head, she added, "Either of you know anything about computer programming?"

"I'm looking," Mal said. She walked to the bench and slid next to the statue of Turing as Ron and Lexi took positions behind her. Within seconds, Mal was scrolling, swiping, and tapping away. She needed only a second on a website before deciding to move on or zoom in. She switched so fast between pages, Lexi's eyes blurred, and she had to look away.

"Woo-hoo, here it is!" voices called. Lexi and Ron swiveled. The Mighty Sanbornes and Physics Phenoms advanced to the pedestal.

"Awesome," David Sanborne said. "I knew our telepod line was shorter. We beat the Comets and Techies!"

"First place!" Daniel Sanborne added, skidding across the path.

Ron elbowed Lexi. "First place?" he mouthed, his face twisted into an expression of bewildered excitement.

Lexi opened her mouth, but no words came. *First place?* She adjusted her glasses and tried to think whether it was possible they had overtaken all the other teams.

"Hey!" David Sanborne yelled.

Lexi glanced up. David was pointing at her. "Hey," she said as David stumbled into the pedestal, so focused on Lexi he wasn't paying attention to where he was going.

The Phenoms reeled with laughter as David centered himself. "How?" David questioned, looking at Team RAM and then his brother. "I don't get it. They hadn't even gotten to the rest area when we left."

Phenom Tomoka giggled. "They probably skipped the rest area," he said, pressing the button to start the video. He tipped his head toward Lexi. "Let me guess, you didn't have to go to all thirty-nine statues to solve the clue?"

Before Lexi could answer, Haley's Comets streaked into the garden. Although a part of Lexi wanted to see Haley's reaction at the moment she discovered her sabotage had failed, Lexi knew her heart couldn't take seeing her former friend. Blinking back tears, Lexi quickly averted her eyes and nudged her teammates to an empty bench farther down the path.

"Find anything?" Lexi asked Mal.

Mal flipped the tablet to face Ron and Lexi. "Yep. Meet Rear Admiral Grace Murray Hopper. She did exactly what Dr. Kent said. She helped create the first high-level computer programming language. There's a bridge named after her in South Carolina."

Ron and Lexi stared at the screen.

Mal sighed. "This is it, you guys. Grace *Hopper*. Like Dr. Kent told us to *hop to it*, remember?"

Ron groaned, and Lexi stashed away her notebook. "Yeah," she said. "I forgot about that part, but you're right. It makes sense."

Team RAM ran to the tournament booth, passing Tesla's Techies and the Powerful Protons along the way. Another tournament official had joined the initial worker, and both worked frantically checking in teams. It seemed everyone was arriving from Paris.

The new official signaled Team RAM to the side. Leaning over the counter so the other teams wouldn't hear, Lexi whispered, "We know where we're supposed to go."

He slid a pen and piece of paper to her. Lexi wrote it down.

Grace Hopper Memorial Bridge—South Carolina

The official exchanged the piece of paper for a manila envelope. "Your special Travel Request Form is inside. Come back when you're done, and I'll issue your tickets." He pointed to the lounge. "You can work in there."

"Got it," Lexi said. She snatched the envelope and led Ron and Mal to a pair of plush couches. Once they were seated, Lexi tore open the envelope and pulled out the clue.

PUZZLE TIME!

TEAM NAME:_____

To get to South Carolina, you need to provide the longitude and latitude coordinates (in decimal form) of the teleport station where you wish to travel. The coordinates, in degrees of our temporary telepod station near the Grace Hopper Memorial Bridge, are:

32°55'6"N, 79°57'26"W

To continue, you must convert these coordinates into decimal form. YOU MUST SHOW YOUR WORK. We are fully aware there are websites that do this conversion for you. That will not count. You must show the math you used to change degrees into decimals to continue your trek.

WORKSPACE:

ANSWER: Your coordinates in decimal form: _____

Turn in your completed worksheet to the tournament booth, and you will receive tickets to your destination. (Check your work! Your next destination **WILL BE** based on the coordinates you provide!)

"Well?" Ron prodded.

Lexi considered faking out her teammates and pretending it was hard, but she couldn't contain her excitement. She lowered the page. "Easy-peasy—another science problem." She set the worksheet on the coffee table.

"You know how to do this?" Mal asked.

"Yep. It'll take me ten minutes. Tops."

Lexi paused, thinking about Dr. Harrison's comment that she was leading a team of nonscience students. What better way to show her leadership skills than to teach her teammates how to perform the calculation? "I can show you," she said. "Then you'll know, too."

She took out her notebook.

"Wait," Ron said, referring to the worksheet. "It says to show all your work."

"I know," Lexi replied. "I will. But it's good to do things on scratch paper first in case I make a mistake. I'll copy it over when I'm done." She slid next to Mal. "Okay, let's start with longitude. The degrees stay the same."

Lexi wrote down 32.

"Really?" Mal asked.

Lexi nodded. "And then the second number stands for minutes. You're supposed to read it as 32 degrees, 55 minutes, and 6 seconds. To convert the 55 minutes into a decimal, we divide 55 by 60."

"I'll do it on the tablet," Mal said, opening up the calculator. "55 divided by 60 is zero point nine one six six six six six—"

"Okay," Lexi said, laughing. "You don't have to go that far. Six places is fine." Lexi wrote 0.916667 in her notebook. "Next is the 6 seconds. To get that into decimals, we have to divide 6 by 3,600."

Mal punched the keys on the tablet. "6 divided by 3,600 is zero point zero zero one six six six six six six—"

"Again, you can stop, Mal," Lexi said, giggling as she wrote 0.001667. "Perfect. Now all we have to do is add the new numbers together.

"0.916667 plus 0.001667 is . . ."

Mal didn't respond, and Lexi lifted her eyes. Mal was staring at her. "I-i-i-i-i-is?" Lexi repeated.

Mal jumped. "Oh!" she cried. "I'm supposed to be doing that! Sorry." Mal picked up the tablet. "Say those again."

Lexi repeated the numbers. A second later, Mal answered, "0.918334."

"All right, so then the answer should be 32.918334."

"Wow, that was quick," Ron said.

"It is," Lexi replied. "All you do is divide and then add the numbers together." She confirmed the math was correct. "Okay, let's do the latitude."

The girls followed the same procedure to solve the latitude portion, with Lexi recording the calculations. When she finished, she circled her answer. "The correct location of the temporary telepod station in decimal form is 32.918334 by 79.957222."

"Cool," Ron said, handing Lexi the worksheet. Lexi copied everything over, being extra careful all her numbers were legible. She handed the worksheet to Mal.

"Let's be sure I copied it correctly," Lexi said. She read aloud, "32.918334, 79.957222."

"Right!"

"Great! Let's go so we can get out of here still in first place."

Ron tugged Lexi's shirt. "Hang on—the clue said there are websites on the Internet that will do the conversion for us. Should we check to be sure we got it right?"

Mal retrieved her tablet. "Right."

Lexi stood silent, searching for a nice way to tell her teammates this was the easiest math problem she had done all semester and that there was no doubt in her mind she had the correct answer. They had even used Mal's computer for a calculator! But as she opened her mouth to explain, the Sanbornes advanced to the counter.

"We're ready!" Daniel said.

Papers rustled from the other end of the room, and a chair squeaked. Haley's team was packing their things. Lexi's chest tingled. She could beat Haley to South Carolina if she hurried. They'd be mere minutes behind the leaders, despite Haley's sabotage.

"There's no time, you guys. We fell to second, and Haley's nearly finished." She made a move toward the counter. "Come on, let's snag our place in line. You can check from there."

"Good idea," Ron said.

Lexi sidled next to Daniel. The official handed tickets to the Mighty Sanbornes, and Lexi slid Team RAM's worksheet to him.

"Wait!" Mal said. "I'm not done checking."

The official paused. "If you're not ready, you'll have to get out of line."

Haley bounded to the counter, the Phenoms right behind her.

Lexi swallowed hard. Given Haley's alliance, Tesla's Techies would be joining them soon. If Team RAM stalled now, they'd lose the lead they'd gained.

Lexi turned to Mal. "There's no time," she whispered. "Not if we want to keep our lead. I'm sure this is the right answer." Not waiting for her teammate's response, Lexi turned back to the official. "Go ahead. We're ready."

The official typed in the information and slid three tickets across the counter. "Here you go." He handed Lexi a sticker. "This goes on circle 5 of your Trek Tracker."

Lexi stuck the sticker of the Turing computer to the Tracker, and Team RAM ran to the telepods. As the telepod operator scanned the tickets into the quantum computer, Ron jumped atop the platform. Mal went next, and Lexi hopped up last. She gave the thumbs-up sign, and a light flashed.

Seconds later, Lexi reopened her eyes to a scowling Mal and an arms-crossed Ron. Confused, she grabbed the Tel-Med and picked up her backpack.

"What's the prob—"

Lexi slammed her mouth shut. The sign on the wall told her exactly what the problem was:

WELCOME TO TIBET

CHAPTER
FOURTEEN

Lexi dropped her backpack. "Tibet? That's impossible."

A tournament worker swooped in from the side. "Ah, so unfortunate!" he said, setting his hands on Mal's and Ron's shoulders. "But don't worry. I'm sure many others will make the same mistake. I'm Liu Yang. I'll be your chaperone. Come along."

"Wait," Lexi said. "What happened? We're supposed to be in South Carolina."

Mr. Yang indicated for Lexi to step off the telepod. "I'm sorry, but you must have entered the wrong coordinates."

No way. No freaking way.

Lexi shook her head, refusing to move.

"In here, in here," he said, shuffling Ron and Mal out of the room. In a huff, Lexi stormed off the telepod and followed. Mr. Yang led them into a larger room containing rows of cots.

No, no, no! We are so not spending the night.

"Mr. Yang," Lexi said, trying to speak as calmly as possible. "There's been a mistake. I know I gave the correct coordinates.

We're supposed to be in South Carolina."

Mr. Yang took a seat behind a small desk. "I need your badges and passports, please."

Team RAM handed everything over.

"What's going on?" Mal demanded. Lexi shooed Mal away. She needed to focus on Mr. Yang, who couldn't be checking them in any slower if he tried.

"Mr. Yang," Lexi repeated. "I'm telling you there's been a mistake. I know my math was right."

"Show him your scratch work," Ron said to Lexi. He faced Mr. Yang. "She did all the work in her notebook first and then copied the answer to the worksheet."

Lexi gasped. "Good idea." She dug into her pack and lifted out the notebook. She flipped to the right page. "Here," she said, thrusting it in front of Mr. Yang's eyes. "See?"

With a small smile across his lips, Mr. Yang rose, walked to a small side table, poured a cup of tea, and then returned to his seat. He put on his glasses. "Let's see," he said, adjusting the notebook so he could see through his bifocals.

Lexi gripped the edge of the desk to keep upright. Mr. Yang clearly did not understand the need to move with any urgency whatsoever. *Come on!* The Physics Phenoms, Mighty Sanbornes, Haley's Comets, Techies, Protons—there could be five teams in front of them by now.

A minute later, Mr. Yang set the notebook on the table. "You're positive you copied *this* work over to the worksheet?"

"Yes," Lexi answered. "100 percent."

Mr. Yang fingered the corner of the page and tapped the circled answer. "And these coordinates, 32.918334, 79.957222. You're positive these are the same coordinates you entered on the worksheet?"

"Yes," Lexi said, joined by Mal, who shifted her weight.

Mr. Yang pushed the notebook toward them. "Then that's why you're in Tibet. These are the coordinates to the exact spot where you're standing."

Flipping off her baseball cap, Lexi tugged at her hair. *This man is impossible!*

Dr. Yang held up his palm. "You have a tablet, yes?"

"Yes," Mal said, quickly retrieving it from her backpack.

"Good. I'm going to check on a few things. Why don't you enter these coordinates into a longitude/latitude website and see what happens?" Mr. Yang rose and pushed in his chair. "I'll be back in a bit—once you've had a chance to sort it all out."

"This is ridiculous," Lexi said as soon as Mr. Yang left. "There's no way this is wrong." She edged next to Mal, and Ron did the same. "Go ahead, type it in."

Mal loaded a longitude/latitude site and keyed in the coordinates. A red dot flashed on the screen.

In Tibet.

"What?" Lexi grabbed the tablet out of Mal's hands. "That's impossible!"

"Great," Ron whispered, plopping into a chair. "So much for super easy."

"Lexi?" Mal whispered, voice shaking.

Lexi gulped. "No," she squeaked. "This isn't right. You guys, something's wro—" Lexi glimpsed the screen, which displayed the coordinates in degree *and* decimal form. Her breath caught in her throat, and she closed her eyes and sank to the floor. Pulling her knees to her chest, she clutched her head as her stomach churned. "Oh no."

Mal scooted beside her. "Lexi?"

Lexi put her head in her hands. "I can't believe I was so stupid."

"Whaddya do?" Ron called as he tossed a pen into the air and caught it. "Mix up the order of the numbers or something?"

Sniffling, Lexi wiped her eyes. "No. I forgot the negative sign."

"The what?" Mal replied.

"The coordinates for the bridge were 32 degrees north and 79 degrees west. When you convert degrees to decimals, all south and west coordinates get a negative sign in front of them." Lexi pointed to the tablet. "Look. It says Tibet is 32.918334, 79.957222. Go on and type a negative sign in front of the 79 coordinate."

Mal picked up the tablet and typed -79.957222. A new red dot flashed on the map, with "Charleston, South Carolina" appearing alongside. Mal slumped. "Yeah, I see what you mean. Oops." She handed the tablet to Ron, who gave it a quick scan. Mal patted Lexi on the back. "Well, at least we know what happened."

"Yeah," Ron agreed. "It's okay. We'll wait for Dr. Yang and give him the right coordinates. Like Dr. Harrison said, if we end up off course, we get a chance to fix our mistake."

Mal walked to the desk. "I wonder if there's another worksheet to fill out." She sifted through papers on the desk. "I don't see anything."

"I'll check by the telepods," Ron said, leaving the room.

Still on the floor, Lexi watched, mouth open and eyes wide, as her teammates pretended nothing horrible had happened—as if she, their teleport science expert—had not made a humungous blunder that had sent them wildly off course. Talk about striking out with the bases loaded. She tried forcing herself up, knowing she should be helping, but the boulders in her stomach weighed her down.

Ron reentered the room. "I couldn't find anything," he said. "But I ran into someone who said he'd let Mr. Yang know we needed him." Ron walked by, nudging Lexi with his toe. "Get up, Magill. Think of it this way: at least you didn't send us to Antarctica."

Lexi got to her feet and dusted off her pants. "Ha ha. I know. It's just that you guys were counting on me to do the science stuff."

Ron and Mal stood still. "It's okay," Mal said after what seemed like an eternity, though Lexi guessed was probably only a few seconds. "You're not the *first* person to send us to the wrong place."

"Hey!" Ron said. "At least I didn't drop my Tel-Med in the toilet!"

"Well, I didn't, either," Mal said with a laugh. She tipped her head toward to Lexi. "See, we all made mistakes."

Lexi lowered her eyes to the ground. While she appreciated the kind words, she still felt crummy. They'd been so close to being in first place! To catch up so much . . . Lexi paused. Team RAM *had* been the second team to leave Manchester. Even though a few others had been right behind them, it wasn't like there had been *twenty* other teams ready to travel to the Hopper Bridge. Team RAM could very well still make the top fifteen. They hadn't been in Tibet that long.

"Okay," she said. "Good pep talk. You're right."

"Exactly," Mal said. "All we need is our new tickets, and we're back in it."

"Unfortunately, it's not that simple," Mr. Yang said from the doorway. Team RAM turned, and Mr. Yang entered the room and poured another cup of tea. "You *do* get a second chance to calculate the correct coordinates, and after that you can teleport to the bridge, but . . ."

"But what?" Ron asked with an edge to his voice Lexi hadn't heard before.

Mr. Yang pointed to the cots. "That's why these beds are set up. I know it doesn't feel like it, but when you came to Tibet, you crossed quite a few time zones. While it was near seven p.m. in England, it's almost two a.m. here. Your Tel-Meds deactivated as soon as you landed. I'm sorry, but you're going to have to wait until morning to leave."

Ron's eyes widened. He grabbed Lexi's backpack. "You said you had a chart of the time zones, right?"

Lexi reached for it, but Ron was quicker. He set the Time-Zone Cheat Sheet on the table.

LEXI MAGILL'S TIME-ZONE CHEAT SHEET

HOME	EAST COAST	ENGLAND, SPAIN, PORTUGAL	FRANCE, ITALY, GERMANY, POLAND, SWEDEN	INDIA/ TIBET/ THAILAND	FAR EAST/ AUSTRALIA
MIDNIGHT	1:00 A.M.	6:00 A.M.	7:00 A.M.	1:00 P.M.	2:00 P.M.
1:00 A.M.	2:00 A.M.	7:00 A.M.	8:00 A.M.	2:00 P.M.	3:00 P.M.
2:00 A.M.	3:00 A.M.	8:00 A.M.	9:00 A.M.	3:00 P.M.	4:00 P.M.
3:00 A.M.	4:00 A.M.	9:00 A.M.	10:00 A.M.	4:00 P.M.	5:00 P.M.
4:00 A.M.	5:00 A.M.	10:00 A.M.	11:00 A.M.	5:00 P.M.	6:00 P.M.
5:00 A.M.	6:00 A.M.	11:00 A.M.	12:00 P.M.	6:00 P.M.	7:00 P.M.
6:00 A.M.	7:00 A.M.	12:00 P.M.	1:00 P.M.	7:00 P.M.	8:00 P.M.
7:00 A.M.	8:00 A.M.	1:00 P.M.	2:00 P.M.	8:00 P.M.	9:00 P.M.
8:00 A.M.	9:00 A.M.	2:00 P.M.	3:00 P.M.	9:00 P.M.	10:00 P.M.
9:00 A.M.	10:00 A.M.	3:00 P.M.	4:00 P.M.	10:00 P.M.	11:00 P.M.
10:00 A.M.	11:00 A.M.	4:00 P.M.	5:00 P.M.	11:00 P.M.	MIDNIGHT
11:00 A.M.	12:00 P.M.	5:00 P.M.	6:00 P.M.	MIDNIGHT	1:00 P.M.
12:00 P.M.	1:00 P.M.	6:00 P.M.	7:00 P.M.	1:00 A.M.	2:00 P.M.
1:00 P.M.	2:00 P.M.	7:00 P.M.	8:00 P.M.	2:00 A.M.	3:00 P.M.
2:00 P.M.	3:00 P.M.	8:00 P.M.	9:00 P.M.	3:00 A.M.	4:00 P.M.
3:00 P.M.	4:00 P.M.	9:00 P.M.	10:00 P.M.	4:00 A.M.	5:00 P.M.
4:00 P.M.	5:00 P.M.	10:00 P.M.	11:00 P.M.	5:00 A.M.	6:00 P.M.
5:00 P.M.	6:00 P.M.	11:00 P.M.	MIDNIGHT	6:00 A.M.	7:00 P.M.
6:00 P.M.	7:00 P.M.	MIDNIGHT	1:00 A.M.	7:00 A.M.	8:00 P.M.
7:00 P.M.	8:00 P.M.	1:00 A.M.	2:00 A.M.	8:00 A.M.	9:00 P.M.
8:00 P.M.	9:00 P.M.	2:00 A.M.	3:00 A.M.	9:00 A.M.	10:00 P.M.
9:00 P.M.	10:00 P.M.	3:00 A.M.	4:00 A.M.	10:00 A.M.	11:00 P.M.
10:00 P.M.	11:00 P.M.	4:00 A.M.	5:00 A.M.	11:00 A.M.	MIDNIGHT
11:00 P.M.	MIDNIGHT	5:00 A.M.	6:00 A.M.	MIDNIGHT	1:00 A.M.

Ron slid his finger over the various times. "Okay, so it's almost two a.m. here." He slid his finger down the India/Tibet/Thailand column to 7:00 a.m. and then to his left until he was under the East Coast column. "So according to the chart, if we leave here at seven a.m. tomorrow morning, we'll arrive at the Hopper Bridge in Charleston at seven p.m. Sunday night?"

Lexi nodded. "Looks right to me."

"It's really not that bad," Mr. Yang interjected, sipping his tea. "You can hang out here, take a nap if you wish, and then at seven a.m. teleport to the Hopper Bridge. You'll spend the night in the South Carolina rest area. All teams are being held there, and then the race will start tomorrow morning with the top fifteen teams."

Team RAM stared at Mr. Yang, who frowned upon seeing their less than enthused response.

"Well, I guess I'll leave you. There's a kitchen through the door to your right, and a sitting room beyond it. Eat, rest, and be ready to teleport at seven a.m. sharp. I'm sure other teams will make the same mistake, but you'll be first to travel since you're here first. Good night."

As soon as Mr. Yang left, Lexi turned to her teammates, who quickly looked down, avoiding her eyes. Their reactions told Lexi all she needed to know: Ron and Mal were perfectly aware that her mistake had cost them the tournament.

CHAPTER FIFTEEN

"Five hours," Ron muttered. "We can't leave for five hours." He walked to the other side of the room as Mal and Lexi sat on their cots.

Lexi let him pace, too sick to her stomach to respond. Forgetting the negative sign was such a stupid thing to do, and so unlike her. She never made careless mistakes. She fell back onto the cot. Equally ridiculous was that her mistake had landed them in a time-zone trap. So many teams in previous tournaments were eliminated due to time-zone mishaps. It was why she created the Time-Zone Cheat Sheet and reset her watch every time they teleported somewhere new. She had taken so many precautions to avoid this type of thing from happening.

She shifted to a seated position. "I'm so sorry," she repeated. "You have every right to be mad. I should have been more careful. It probably was all the time-zone changes and running around all day. I'm not thinking straight."

"No," Ron said, halting. "That's not the problem."

"Huh?"

"You should have let us double-check the coordinates."

"What?"

"If you had let Mal check the coordinates, none of this would have happened. We would have found your mistake."

"Ron's right," Mal said. "We told you we wanted to double-check, and you went ahead and turned in the sheet, anyway. We could have totally fixed it, and everything would have been fine."

Lexi looked from Mal to Ron, confused how they could possibly think that checking would have been the right thing to do. "But you saw the line of teams. We didn't have time."

"Says *you*," Ron yelled. "But we're a team, remember? I gave up my swag, and Mal hasn't taken a single photo since we left the maze. We've been 100 percent focused, trying to prove we're smart enough to win on our own, but no—super-science-girl, you overruled us and did what you wanted to, anyway."

Mal crossed her arms. "Exactly. You even said at the beginning of the race that it never hurts to double-check. You made me *prove* to you and Ron that the Neuschwanstein Castle was the right one. But when it came to double-checking *your* answer, you totally blew us off."

Lexi shook her head. Her teammates were totally missing the point. "But Haley was right there! You heard the official—we would have had to go to the end of the line. She would have passed us. You really wanted to let her back in the lead after she lied?"

"Yes!" Ron and Mal shouted at the same time.

Lexi flinched. "But—"

"No," Ron said. "No *but*. That's what we're trying to say. We're supposed to be doing this together. You have to listen to us. This isn't *your* team."

"And now we're stuck," Mal said.

Ron threw his hands in the air. "Completely stuck—which makes what you did a thousand times worse than anything Mal and I ever did."

Lexi tightened her jaw. Her mistake *was* the worst of them all, but that's not what was eating her insides. The truth was that she had dismissed their suggestion to double-check the answer because she thought there was no way she'd make a mistake on a science problem. She also had made the unilateral decision to hand in the worksheet, even though they both had asked her to wait. She *had* completely ignored them, even after they'd made it clear in the maze that they were going to go all out to win the tournament. She'd finally gotten them to care about the tournament, and then she went ahead and ruined it.

"Right through here," Dr. Yang said from behind.

Lexi turned. The Doppler Daredevils entered the room.

"Hey, Lexi," Doppler Chris said. "Tough one, huh?"

Lexi nodded. "Yeah."

Chris tossed his backpack on an empty cot. "Well, don't feel too bad. From what I overheard in the lounge, I think the Perfect Plancks will be joining us, too." Chris flailed his body onto the cot and covered his head with a pillow. As he crunched it over his face, he screamed, "Arrrrgh! Stupid negative sign!"

Despite how Lexi's stomach was roiling from her fight with Ron and Mal, a laugh escaped her lips. She turned to share it with her teammates.

They were gone.

The rest of the Plancks entered the room. After a short nod in their direction, Lexi walked to the kitchen. Ron and Mal sat at a small table in the far corner, plates of food in front of them. Lexi paused at the door.

"What we need is a McDonald's," Ron muttered to Mal.

Mal picked up her chopsticks. "Don't start that again," she said, slowly picking at the rice.

Ron attempted to trap rice between his chopsticks, but they slipped out of his fingers.

"Here," Mal said, showing him her grip. "Hold them like this."

He tried mimicking Mal's hold. "I wouldn't need them if I had a burger and fries."

Lexi's stomach lurched. Every ounce of her wanted to be over there with Ron and Mal, eating and joking around. But her feet wouldn't move. She couldn't get it out of her mind that they had been totally right about how she had treated them. In trying to beat Haley, she had turned into Haley, letting her obsession with winning destroy true friendship. She couldn't blame them for not wanting anything to do with her.

Ron blew out a long breath. "I still can't believe this. I really thought we had a shot once we caught up at that Turing dude."

Mal chuckled. "I know. Seeing Europe again and getting photos for my exhibit was awesome, but I have to admit the tournament was a lot more fun than I expected. I was really hoping we'd make it to the finals."

"Finals, schminals. I wanted to win and prove to Ms. Smarty-Pants and her alliance we're as smart as they are."

Lexi cringed and turned away. Ron wasn't wrong. Team RAM *was* just as smart as Haley's team. Problem was, no one would believe it unless they crossed the finish line ahead of the other teams.

Fists clenched, she strode to her cot, grabbed her backpack and Time-Zone Cheat Sheet, and hunkered down in the far corner. Pulling out her Teleport Tableau, Trek Tracker, and all the notes she had made from her review of previous tournaments, she organized a work station. Somehow, some way, she was going to figure out a way to get Team RAM back in the race.

* * *

An hour later, Lexi gathered her papers and set off to find her teammates. She found them at the same corner table huddled over Mal's tablet playing a game.

Lexi cleared her throat. Neither turned her way. "Ahem," she repeated. "Ron? Mal?"

Two sets of eyes shot dirty looks her way.

Swallowing hard, Lexi pressed onward, clutching her papers to her chest. "Can I talk to you for a second? I had an idea, but before I tell you what it is, I want you to know that I'll only go along with it if you both want to."

Ron cocked an eyebrow, and Mal narrowed her eyes.

Lexi tapped the stack of papers. "I've been thinking about it, and if we were out of it, why wouldn't they teleport us home instead of to South Carolina? Mr. Yang specifically said we'd be going to the bridge and spending the night there with the rest of the teams and that the race would begin from there the next morning, right?"

Ron and Mal glanced at each other. Since neither of them told her to get lost, Lexi took another step forward and slid into a chair at a nearby table. She set her papers on her lap and faced her teammates.

"I decided to investigate, and before the tournament, I reviewed a bunch of previous tournaments, newspaper articles about them, and even interviews with some of the teams. I looked at my notes, and, sure enough, whenever teams were eliminated, they were sent straight home. They didn't teleport to the other locations."

Mal put her tablet aside. "But we were what, the second team to leave Manchester? They might not know to eliminate us yet."

Lexi smiled. "Exactly." She plucked out the Time-Zone Cheat Sheet, scooched her chair closer to Ron and Mal, and set the sheet on her lap so they could see. "Look. We left England around seven p.m. While there, we saw the Comets, Techies, Phenoms, and San-bornes. Anyone else?"

185

"I'm not sure," Ron said, scratching the back of his neck. "Maybe one more?"

"Okay, so that would be five. They still need ten more teams for the top fifteen, and we know the Dopplers and Plancks are here."

"So are the Isaac Fig Newtons, Awesome Einsteins, and the Gravity Gurus," Mal said. "They're back in the lounge."

Lexi caught her breath. She totally missed the other teams' entrance. "Really?"

Ron waved her off. "I don't see how that matters. There are plenty of other teams unaccounted for. Surely, ten of them made it to the bridge by now to be part of the top fifteen."

"Not if you consider how much time was left," Lexi said. She tapped the Time-Zone Cheat Sheet. "When we left the maze in Versailles, there were still several teams in the plaza who hadn't finished. They still had to figure out where the next destination was, walk back to the Versailles train station, take the train back to Paris, teleport to England, find Turing, listen to the clue, and solve the longitude and latitude problem." She pointed to the column with England's time zone. "With all of that, it's entirely possible teams wouldn't finish by ten p.m."

Mal gasped. "Meaning they'd be stuck in England while we're stuck here."

Ron arched an eyebrow. "Hang on. Let me see that sheet." He shook his head as he read. "But they'd still have a head start on us. If they get trapped in England, they'll leave at seven a.m. England time—"

"—and arrive in South Carolina at two a.m., *seven hours* after we get there at seven p.m." Lexi finished.

"Wait—what?"

Lexi sprung from her seat and stood next to Ron. "See?" She pointed to the row of times indicating it was 7:00 a.m. "When we leave at seven a.m., it will be midnight in England. We'll be teleporting while they're still trapped. We'll beat them to South Carolina."

Ron tapped his fingers against his chin. "What time did we leave England again?"

"A little before seven p.m."

"Huh. So the other teams only had three more hours to figure it out before they were trapped, too."

Lexi plopped into her chair. "Right." She adjusted her glasses. "I know three hours is a long time, but the maze *was* hard, and teams were tired. I think it might be possible." After not seeing any reaction from her teammates, Lexi added, "*Or*, we can ask Mr. Yang if we can hang out here tomorrow morning before teleporting back."

"What?" Mal asked.

Lexi explained, "So you can take some photos for your exhibit. I can't imagine anyone will have photos of Europe *and* Tibet." She nodded at Ron. "And I know your swag isn't here, but after we *do* get to South Carolina, I bet we can track it down. You can sell some of your stuff before we teleport back to Wisconsin."

Ron and Mal looked at Lexi as though she had suggested they swim across the Atlantic Ocean to get home.

Lexi averted her eyes from her teammates and kicked the floor with the toe of her gym shoe. "Like you said, if you don't sell enough, you'll have wasted the whole weekend." She nodded to Mal. "You too, Mal. More photos will help."

Ron rubbed his chin. "I shouldn't have said that. That's not what I meant—not exactly, anyway." He let loose a breath. "Truth is, I'm glad I came. It's different from what I expected, but I like to compete . . . and I'm not a quitter."

Lexi offered a small smile. "There's no guarantee we'll get to keep racing. And with all the time-zone changes, our bodies are *really* going to be messed up. We might fall asleep before we get to the finish line."

"Nah," Ron replied. "We'll have all of Sunday night in South Carolina to sleep. That shouldn't be a problem." He glanced at Mal. "What do you think?"

Mal leaned over and met Lexi's eyes. "You'd really quit now if we wanted to?"

Lexi nodded. "You were right, you know, before. We should be making decisions as a team. I'm sorry."

Ron crossed his arms. "It wasn't just you."

"Huh?"

He blew out a breath. "I'm sorry I didn't wear blue and gold. You told us we should all wear Brewers colors so we looked like a team, and I completely blew you off."

"Oh," Lexi replied. "That's no big deal."

"No," Mal said. "He's right. We were each interested in doing our own thing—swag, photos, and science. We didn't even look like a team."

A few moments of awkward silence followed. Finally, Lexi bit the bullet and asked, "So, do we want to keep racing?"

Ron looked at Mal and then Lexi. "Down two touchdowns with less than two minutes on the clock?" he joked. "That's my specialty." He threw out his hand, palm down. "I'm in."

Mal slammed her hand on top of Ron's. "Me too."

They looked at Lexi.

Smiling, she leaped forward. "Bottom of the ninth, two outs, bases loaded, full count?" She added her hand atop Mal's. "Heck yeah."

Ron set his other hand on top of Lexi's. "Ready? On the count of three, it's Team RAM." He pushed their hands down. "One, two . . ."

"TEAM RAM!" Ron, Mal, and Lexi shouted.

"What? Who is that?" Mr. Yang called from the other room. "Is something wrong?"

Oops, Lexi thought. But as Team RAM burst into laughter and quickly scattered to their cots, she couldn't stop smiling. It wasn't over yet.

CHAPTER
SIXTEEN

After waking from a short nap, Lexi grabbed something to eat and was readying her pack for their 7:00 a.m. departure time when Mal bounded over. She dangled two long, bright red plastic strips in front of Lexi's face. "Here you go. I just gave Ron his."

Lexi accepted the strips and side-eyed Ron as he stepped to her side. He stretched the strips in front of his chest with what she was sure was the same *what-the-heck-are-we-supposed-to-do-with-these* look on his face that she had on hers.

With a huge grin, Mal nodded in her teammates' direction. "I couldn't sleep, and I kept thinking about what we were talking about earlier—how we don't look like a team." Mal motioned to the kitchen. "Mr. Yang was already up, and he said I could use one of the tablecloths." She plucked a red strip off her cot and wrapped it around her wrist. "We can wear one on our arm and use the other as a headband."

Mal secured her new wristband and then tied the other strip around her forehead, making a knot in the back. When she finished, she adjusted the front so it didn't cover her eyebrows. She tapped the knot and faced her teammates.

Lexi eyed Mal. If fashionista Mal could wear them, she supposed she could, too. She secured her strips like Mal had, all the while noticing Ron wasn't moving a muscle.

"Ron?" Lexi called. "Hurry up. It's six forty-five a.m. We have to get in line."

He flipped the red band and scowled. "Seriously? We're wearing these?"

Mal set her hands on her hips. "It's called *improvising*. What, it doesn't match the baggy shorts and too-big T-shirt look you have going on?"

Ron rolled his eyes. "All right, fine." He tied the headband. "Maybe we'll be able to distract the other teams with the bright red."

Lexi giggled. "Yeah, we'll definitely be able to find one another in a crowd."

Mal clapped excitedly as Ron finished securing his bands. "Perfect. Let's go."

Team RAM took their place at the head of the line. As the clock neared 7:00 a.m., Mr. Yang invited Lexi to the telepod. She inserted her Tel-Med, set her backpack on its spot, and waited for the thumbs-up.

Ding! The clock chimed.

Moments later, Lexi opened her eyes. She stood in the middle of . . . a tent? Wrinkling her nose, she stepped off the telepod, waving her arm to clear the dusty air and get a better look. Wood beams holding white canvas sheets surrounded her. Definitely a tent. Ron and Mal joined her.

"Where the heck is this?" Ron wondered aloud. "Are we joining a circus?"

"Over here!" a woman called, rushing through a flap of canvas. "Check-in's through here!"

Team RAM darted to the official, who stood in an adjacent tent, just as sparse, and with the same white canvas serving as the walls and ceiling.

"It's seven p.m.," the official said as she checked them in. "Please note the time."

Lexi didn't flinch. She had changed her watch before teleporting.

"As you can see, this is a temporary teleport station. To reach the Grace Hopper Memorial Bridge, walk straight out this tent." The official pointed to an opening in the canvas on the opposite side of the flap they had entered. "Cross the bridge—please stay in the designated walkway marked by police tape—and on the other side you'll see another tent. That's where you'll find your next instructions. Good luck!"

"Thanks," Lexi said.

The Doppler Daredevils joined Team RAM at the counter and tossed their badges to the official.

"Let's go," Ron said. "Everyone's coming."

About halfway across the bridge, Lexi noticed a row of tents on the other side. Lights streamed from opened flaps, but the angle prevented her from seeing how many teams were inside. Her chest tightened. *Please not fifteen. Please not fifteen.*

When they reached the end of the bridge, Mal paused. She gripped Lexi's and Ron's arms and linked them with hers. "This is it," she squeaked.

Lexi squeezed Mal's hand as Ron slapped the canvas out of their way.

Tables were scattered throughout the tent, all unoccupied except for one in the far corner around which the Solar Flares huddled. Lexi swallowed hard. She'd hoped to see several teams still working on a puzzle.

As Team RAM reached the tournament booth, an official slid an envelope across the counter. "Welcome to South Carolina. As you know, only the top fifteen teams will be racing tomorrow. Here is your next clue."

The worker turned away. No one from Team RAM moved.

"Oh, wait!" the worker said, whirling around to face them. "I need your electronic devices." Team RAM remained still. "You'll get them back after you solve the puzzles associated with the clue."

Lexi inched forward and tried to make sense of what was going on. He was confiscating their electronics, so did that mean—

The official shoved the bin toward them. "In here, please. All electronics—tablets, phones, etc. Don't worry, we'll keep them secure."

A fuzzy feeling filled Lexi's head. *This had to mean . . .*

Mal leaned in. "Are you saying we're still in it?"

"Ahhhh!" the official said. "That's why you're all looking at me as if I have two heads!" He laughed. "Yes, you're still in it. You're the twelfth team to arrive."

"What?" Lexi said.

"For real?" Ron added.

The official nodded. "We had eleven teams arrive between two p.m. and five p.m. The last of those is completing the clue now. Five other teams are arriving with you from Tibet, and the other thirteen are in England or didn't make it past the maze."

Lexi looked at the envelope, then the official, then the envelope, and then back at the official. "I can't believe it!" she cried.

Shrieking with delight, Mal twirled and wrapped her arm around Lexi's shoulders. "Holy baloney! We did it!"

Ron punched one fist into the air, then the other. "Yes!"

The Doppler Daredevils ran into the tent.

Team RAM immediately halted their celebration and dug out their phones. "Hurry up," Lexi said. "There are only four slots left, and six teams trying to make it."

Ron and Mal tossed their electronics into the bin. As Lexi pulled out her phone, she saw the blank screen. "The battery died. Is there a place to charge it?"

"Sure thing. I have a power strip back here."

"Thanks."

Team RAM picked a table, and Ron tore open the envelope and slid out its contents, including a bridge sticker for their Trek Tracker. Lexi scooped up the sticker as her teammates filtered through the other papers.

"Wow," Mal said.

"Uh, yeah," Ron replied.

"What?" Lexi asked, putting the bridge sticker over circle No. 6. *Three to go.* She lifted her eyes to the table, where Ron was stacking worksheets. "Oh my gosh. Please tell me some of those are duplicates."

"Doesn't look like it," Ron said. "Hang on. I'm organizing them by type." When he finished, he had three piles. Lexi picked up the stack closest to her.

TEAM NAME: _____

WORD SEARCH # 1

ELEMENTS

```
W Y M E P L A T I N U M A M F E R Z S W G M J K U
W U S K N L D A Z J R E R Q R D M V T I U B D B U
J E C K T P H U D E O R E O I Z N Z W N N W F T J
U F M P F H T X W A Y C D U F H K Z I J Y K M B Y
C Q U U V C P A B B C U L Y J X H M Q R E C U J H
E Z M W I E Z U H A W R O B C W U S D O U J I A K
W V Y N A D J M R U G Y G J L L H X M D F X N L V
R D Z L E C O B G U B Q Y L A G U M U X U O O C J
Q L M P D G O S S P K K I X J B P M I A I J L S Y
N O N E X N O A M E H B K P R F B F D C D A O M F
J V R W Y U E R W A Q P Y X W O C D A B M D P C N
N F O C Z E T N D Z P M P E I S W U R J C P D T A
Y A W W D O N E G Y X O Z I J K C F M A S J G D I
X S S W P S V A L R H H V L Q K C W E R O N A Y P
G M U O U Y Z Q X L C W A A R A R N L N Y Y R E M
G D P L X E C R Y N Y W L E U W A Y I H O B H K Z
V F F H R E J O S N Z Y V D V V J G P Z S O F T C
A U H P W B I J Z J K L Z S X H J Z B T X N C N N
R M B N H M M Z R D I I K Y Z Z H Z U C O M O D T
H A N N U T A M G S N G F V S G U H P C M N P K L
Y W O P V C S G M J M K R Z H L P M E F O Y P W F
L E V U C I Y E R D T I N Y F O V D E L P H E F W
N D E N G C C N G R E F R Y N I C K E L I Q R F W
A U V Y F H L V N O E H O M S G K H N H Y U W G Q
J G I E Z D T R C A N N N H R L T S F R B F M U D
```

ALUMINUM	MERCURY	SILVER
CARBON	NEON	SODIUM
COPPER	NICKEL	SULFUR
GOLD	OXYGEN	TIN
HELIUM	PLATINUM	XENON
HYDROGEN	POLONIUM	ZINC
KRYPTON	RADIUM	

Lexi flipped through the stack. Four different word searches, all with a science theme. Mal leaned over and looked, too.

"Well," Mal said. "I can do word searches. I mean, yeah it'll take some time, but it shouldn't be too bad. Busy work, really. What else is there?"

"These," Ron said.

Lexi looked at the top page.

TEAM NAME:_____

WORD SCRAMBLES

PHYSICS

1. TOERCCALRAE _____
2. NCVCIEOTON _____
3. MTOA _____
4. DCORLILE _____
5. UNNRTEO _____
6. ROLTCEEN _____
7. SEPOOTI _____
8. SMSA _____
9. TMPSUCRE _____
10. AURQK _____

11. WHEGLNETVA _____
12. JUOEL _____
13. EOITYVCL _____
14. TZHER _____
15. YRGVATI _____
16. PWEOR _____
17. TOHPON _____
18. NYEGER _____
19. TCSNDAIE _____
20. CNINUTODCO _____

"There are four sheets of these, too," Lexi said. "Physics, general science, chemistry—yeah, I should be able to do these, though it would be quicker if we had Mal's tablet. There are programs that can unscramble words for you. My mom uses them when she plays hangman against my dad on their phones."

Ron chuckled. "Nice."

Lexi stared at the remaining stack on the table. "That one's a lot thinner. What're those?"

Ron fingered the pages. "There are only two pages, but these are the hardest. Ciphers."

"Ciphers?" Lexi repeated.

"Yep." Ron slid the first page to her and Mal.

CIPHERS

GREAT SCIENTIFIC MINDS

1. WEH'B PT KLCKRW EL XKCW DECZ. HEBXRHY
DECBXDXRGT JEATU TKURGS. WEH'B GTB EBXTCU
WRUJEOCKYT SEO EC BTGG SEO BXKB SEO JKH'B
WE RB. –YTCBCOWT TGREH

Hint: W=D

2. QNU QADU KEIM TJ EMQUXXEIUMPU EK MTQ LMTFXUWIU
HDQ ESBIEMBQETM.–BXHUAQ UEMKQUEM

Hint: H=B

3. VL MOWRI YBQJLGWOA CRQ WGWO SRYW CBINLPI R
ULHY MPWQQ.–BQRRJ VWCILV

Hint: O=R

4. THPK XLBSKHUOH YC GB XLBS GJH HMGHLG BN BLH'C
YOLBTPLEH.–EBLNZEYZC

Hint: N=F

5. PBMFDTDH DBKBF BJIMSXVX VIB OTDU.–PBADMFUA UM
KTDYT

Hint: O=M

Lexi slumped in the seat. "Ugh. I hate ciphers."

"I've never done one," Mal said. "But at least they give you a hint. That should help."

Ron tapped the stack. "I actually like ciphers. My grandma and I do them together on the weekend. But this is a lot."

Mal plopped into her chair. "It's all a lot."

The Isaac Fig Newtons stormed into the tent.

"That's three teams so far," Lexi said. "We should get started." She nodded to Ron. "You start with ciphers, I'll start unscrambling, and Mal can do the word searches." Lexi distributed the stacks, but then paused. "Wait a second. So, let's say we do all of this. Then what? Is there anything that tells us how to figure out where we're teleporting next?"

Ron nodded. "Yeah, I saw something. I set it aside." He placed the paper in the middle of the table.

DESTINATION NO. 7

Quantum physics is critical to teleportation. Many scientists have contributed to the development of quantum theory. Your next destination will introduce you to a scientist who invented instruments to measure magnetic and electric properties and was one of the first individuals whose work validated quantum theory.

To determine his identity, complete **ALL** of the worksheets in this folder. Then, bring them to the tournament official, who will give you the key you will need to complete the second part of the clue.

"Shoot," Lexi said. "I was hoping that maybe we'd only have to solve the relevant words, but it looks like we're going to have to do them all."

"Pizza's here," an official shouted from the back of the room. "Help yourselves."

Ron spun out of his seat, his ciphers sliding across the table in the breeze. Lexi caught them before they hit the floor.

"No. Wait," Ron said, returning to his chair. "No pizza until I solve the first cipher."

"What?" Mal and Lexi were shocked.

Ron straightened the page of ciphers in front of him. "It'll motivate me."

Mal and Lexi continued to stare at him, not believing what he'd just said, but when Ron didn't look up, they shared a smile and got busy with their own worksheets. They were still in it, but with six teams and only four slots, Team RAM had to get to work if they wanted to be racing tomorrow.

CHAPTER
SEVENTEEN

Team RAM worked diligently on its puzzles over the next few hours, with Ron holding his trips for pizza to a minimum, even after he completed the first cipher. By ten-thirty p.m., Ron's hair stuck straight up from all the times he'd pulled at it in frustration, Mal's exquisite braid had unraveled, and Lexi wore her cap backward, the snap barely above her eyes as she placed her hands over the top of her head and pressed down in an attempt to push the answers out of her brain.

Around the same time Lexi unscrambled her hundredth word, Mal slid her sheets across the table.

"Done," Mal said. "Finally."

Lexi glanced around the room. While the Solar Flares had finished shortly after Team RAM had arrived, none of the teams from Tibet had received the second part of the clue.

"Argh," Ron said, not taking his eyes off his paper. "I need a break. This last one's next-to-impossible."

Mal fingered one of Ron's worksheets. "Yours are the hardest, that's for sure."

Ron yawned.

"Do you want me to take a look?" Lexi said. I might be able to recognize the scientist's name.

Ron slid the sheet her way. "Be my guest. I rewrote what I figured out so far underneath."

8. TD PVWK ULQD ADCWDQDCLFXD LFO LSZQD LHH
XZFERODFXD RF ZVCWDHQDW.–PLCRD XVCRD

Hint: H=L

WE PVWK HAVE AECWEVECANXE AND ASZVE ALL
XZNEIDENXE IN ZVCWELVEW.–PACIE XVCIE

Lexi stared at the puzzle. *"We blank have blank and blank all blank in blank."*

Mal laughed. "Nice. I'm sure that's helpful."

"Wait." Lexi pressed her fingertip onto the last two words. "Marie Curie," she whispered. "I don't know what the quote is, but I bet you anything that the scientist is Marie Curie. Look at the *i-e* at the end of the first and last names. What other scientist's name is like that?"

"Let me see," Ron said, taking the page. A second later, he nodded. "Yeah, that'll work. Give me a minute. I'll switch all of the *C*s to *R*s and *P*s to *M*s and see what's left."

Lexi and Mal leaned over, watching Ron work. A scratch here, a mark there, and a few scribbles later, he showed them:

WE MUST HAVE PERSEVERANCE AND ABOVE ALL CONFIDENCE IN OURSELVES.—MARIE CURIE

"That's it! We're done," Lexi said as they all traded fist pounds. "Way to go, Ron!"

Mal nudged Lexi. "Let's see what's next."

Team RAM brought their completed sheets to the tournament monitor amid a few gasps from the other teams.

"Stay here," the official said. "I'll check the answers and be right back."

Screech.

Doppler Daredevil Chris shot out of his chair, and his team bounded to the counter. "I think we got it, too," he said.

Lexi pursed her lips. If other teams were about to finish, it would come down to how quickly everyone solved the second part of the clue. Team RAM's slight lead would mean nothing if they stumbled.

"Here you go," the official said, returning. He noticed Chris. "Please stand back with your team. I'll be right with you." The official slid another envelope across the counter. "This is the second part of the clue. Since you don't have electronics, we're not going to ask you to find the teleport station. Simply note your destination location at the bottom of the sheet."

"Got it," Lexi said, and Team RAM darted to their table.

Ron made quick work of the envelope and set the clue in front of them.

DESTINATION No. 7 (Part Two)

To determine the identity of the mystery physicist, use your answers to the worksheets to find:

1. The last letter in Word Scramble word #12: _____
2. The last letter in the seventeenth word in the solved quotation of Cipher No. 1. _____
3. The letter in the 6th row, 3rd column of Word Search #1: _____
4. The second letter in Word Scramble word #14: _____
5. The third letter in the fourth word in the solved quotation of Cipher #8: _____
6. The letter in the 6th row, 23rd column of Word Search #1: _____
7. The last letter in Word Scramble word #3: _____
8. The most popular letter in the scientist's name in Cipher #7: _____
9. The letter that appears twice in Word Scramble word #8: _____

ANSWER: _____

Now, to determine your next destination, which is where this scientist taught physics, use your answers to the worksheets to find:

1. The letter in the 20th row, 13th column of Word Search #1: _____
2. The eighth letter in Word Scramble word #2: _____
3. The last letter in the thirteenth word in the solved quotation of Cipher No. 1: _____
4. The letter in the 1st row, 24th column of Word Search #1: _____
5. The third letter in Word Scramble word #5: _____
6. The letter in the 23rd row, 4th column of Word Search #1: _____
7. The most popular vowel in the solved quotation of Cipher No. 2: _____
8. The third letter in Word Scramble word #11: _____
9. The first letter in the 6th row of Word Search #1: _____
10. The first letter in the first word in the solved quotation of Cipher #4: _____
11. The letter that repeats itself in the same word in the solved quotation of Cipher #3: _____
12. The first letter in Word Scramble word #7: _____
13. The second-to-last letter in the third word in Cipher #5: _____
14. The last letter in Word Scramble word #13: _____

ANSWER: _____

"All right," Ron said. "At least all we have to do is plug in the letters."

"I'll read the sentence, and then you guys can look at the worksheets and let me know the answer," Lexi said. "If it seems tricky or weird, we can all look at it."

Mal distributed the worksheets. She leaned over the table and whispered, "Don't say the letters too loud. We don't want the other teams to hear."

Ron slid his chair closer to Lexi, and Mal did the same.

Team RAM worked their way through the first half.

"Hold up!" Ron said as Lexi reached the second to last question. "Read that one again."

Lexi reread number 8, "The most popular letter in the scientist's name in Cipher Number Seven." She peered over Ron's arm at his worksheet. "What's Cipher Number Seven?"

Ron showed her.

Imagination is more important than knowledge.—Albert Einstein

"Oh," Ron said. "It's *E*. I was looking at his last name and saw a tie between *E* and *N*. Never mind."

Lexi wrote, *E* and moved to the next clue. After all the letters were completed, Lexi wrote:

E-L-M-E-R-I-M-E-S

"Elmer Imes," she said. "Let's move on." Team RAM continued with the second half clues. When they were done, Lexi wrote:

"So it's Elmer Imes at Fisk University," she murmured. "Let's get to the booth!" She slid her chair back from the table, then caught herself. She set the paper on the table. "Here. You guys take a look to make sure I wrote everything down right."

Ron scanned the answers and pushed the page to Mal, who nodded after a glance.

Team RAM ran to the booth, where the Powerful Protons and Isaac Fig Newtons were receiving the second part of their clue. Lexi peered over her shoulder. The Doppler Daredevils were packing up, apparently having completed the second part of the clue as well. Lexi checked the time—it was nearly midnight. She exhaled, relieved Team RAM wouldn't be battling for one of the last two spots in the middle of the night.

The tournament official approached, and after a quick check of Team RAM's worksheet, declared, "Congratulations. You're team twelve." He punched keys on the computer and printed their teleport tickets. "Start time tomorrow is nine a.m. The sleeping area and computers are in the back tent." He pointed to an opening in the canvas on the opposite side of the room. "Right through there."

Team RAM grabbed their tickets and turned to one another to exchange high fives. With the teleport ticket in her hand, Lexi let it sink in. They had made it!

"Here are your electronics," the official said, placing the bin on the counter. He reached behind him to the power strip and unplugged Lexi's phone. "And here's the phone that was charging."

Electronics in hand, Team RAM headed to the rest area. Lexi turned on her phone, and a barrage of sounds proved it had come to life.

Ding. Chirp. Ding.

One voice mail, one e-mail, and one text. Lexi dropped to an empty cot and opened the e-mail first.

Dear Rental Customer:

*****ATTENTION*****ATTENTION*****ATTENTION*****

This is your second notice. We have detected unusual activity in Tel-Med No. 610116271. Please report to the nearest Wren Tech store or facility with Tel-Med No. 610116271 so that it may be inspected.

Please be advised that further use of the Tel-Med may trigger the Critical Protocol, where problematic features will be disabled, potentially resulting in complete deactivation. We strongly advise you to visit our facility so that TEL-MED NO. 610116271 can be cleared for use.

We at Wren Tech take the safety of our customers very seriously, and these measures are put in place for your protection. Please contact us for additional details.

Thank you for your cooperation.

Sincerely,
John Hardek
Wren Technologies

Lexi closed the message and checked the text and voice mail. They were from Wren Tech, too, and they said the same thing—"irregular activity" had been detected and her Tel-Med could enter the critical protocol—whatever that was (though Lexi admitted it didn't sound good)—at any time. Worse, her Tel-Med could eventually deactivate.

Her phone slipped between her trembling fingers and fell to the floor. Team RAM might not get to finish the race.

"What's wrong?" Ron said, dropping to the cot across the aisle. "You should be celebrating. We made it."

"Yeah," Mal added as she unwrapped her wrist and headbands and set them on the table beside her cot. "We're top fifteen!"

Lexi blinked and dug the Tel-Med out of her cargo pants. She turned it over in her palm so the bright blue RENTAL stamp was visible. It was time Ron and Mal knew the truth.

She held it out to Ron. "I rented it."

"So?" Ron said.

Lexi passed her phone to Ron. His eyes grew wide as he read the e-mail.

"I'm guessing it's the tracking and disabling chip," Lexi explained as Mal stood and read alongside Ron.

Mal grabbed the Tel-Med and rubbed it between her fingers before holding it up to the light. "It looks okay to me."

"Me too," Lexi said. "But the company probably detected installation of the chip and thinks there's a glitch."

Ron furrowed his brow and flashed the e-mail to Lexi. "What does this mean, *second notice*?"

Lexi blew out a breath. "They sent an e-mail yesterday saying basically the same thing, that irregular activity had been detected." She shrugged. "But it was working, and it's not like I could do anything about it."

"Sure you could. You could do exactly what it tells you to do—bring it to Wren Tech and have them check it."

Lexi rose to her feet. "Yeah, but what if they had made me take out the chip? Or said it's been damaged and confiscated it? I wouldn't have been able to race."

Ron shook his head. "You don't know that. It's equally likely Wren Tech wouldn't have even cared as long as the Tel-Med wasn't damaged—*you just had to tell them.*"

Mal nodded. "He's right, and even if Wren Tech had wanted its Tel-Med back, we could have told Dr. Harrison or asked for help." She gestured to their surroundings. "Now it *is* too late. It's near midnight, and we're in a tent in the middle of nowhere."

Lexi slumped. "I . . . I never thought of all that. I don't know. I just didn't want to risk it." She looked at her teammates. "I should have told you. I'm sorry." She read the e-mail again. "What should we do? The way I read this, they can shut it off at any time. We might not even make it to the university."

"We can't think of it like that," Ron said. "We can't think about the fourth quarter when we're in the first half. It won't help. The only thing we can do now is keep going."

Mal handed the Tel-Med back to Lexi. Lexi eyed the blue RENTAL stamp again as she stuffed it back into her pocket. "Stupid rental."

"I can't believe you rented one," Mal said. "That must have been expensive."

"It was—my birthday and allowance money for a year, but . . ."

"Aw, man, I wish you would have said something," Ron said. "My mom might have been able to loan one to you. They have a few for their office." He held up his Tel-Med. "That's where I got mine."

"Yeah," Mal said. "My parents got mine from the university's history department. I totally could have asked if they had another."

Lexi rubbed her forehead. "I used to have one," she said. "But we had to sell it when my dad lost his job. I didn't want you guys to know."

Ron and Mal stared at her with blank expressions.

"I thought you'd think it was weird, you know, how I'm really into science and wanted to race in a teleportation tournament, but didn't have a Tel-Med. It's embarrassing."

"It's not embarrassing," Mal said. "It's . . . inspiring. A total make-it-work moment. You did what you had to do."

Lexi cocked an eyebrow. "What?"

"Moreno's right," Ron said. "Knowing you spent all your money on a Tel-Med to race with us is super motivating. It also explains why you want to win so badly. I bet your family can really use the money."

"Yeah," Mal said.

No, Lexi thought as guilt pulsed through her veins. The prize money wasn't for her family—well, except for tickets to a Brewers game for her dad—it was for her to attend the academy. With a slight groan, she hung her head. She didn't deserve her teammates' respect. She glanced at their still-beaming faces. There was no way she couldn't tell them the truth.

"Actually," Lexi said. "I've been planning to use the money to re-enroll at the science academy."

"What?" Mal asked.

"For real?" Ron added.

Lexi nodded. "I've been going there for years, and there are all these classes and clubs that West Elm doesn't have, like robotics, inventions, and teleport science." She tipped her head toward Ron. "Plus, like you said, it's not like I have tons of friends here. But over there, even without Haley, there are kids that like the same things I do."

Mal tapped her lips. "Hm. Well, I'd be interested in an inventions club. I can help people draw their designs, maybe build models, too?"

Lexi scrunched her nose. "Really?"

Ron slid his hands together. "And I might go for a physics club, but it'd have to be geared toward useful stuff—like how you figured out Moreno didn't flush her Tel-Med down the toilet."

Mal lightly punched Ron in the shoulder.

"No, I'm serious," Ron continued. "Football is all about force and motion and acceleration and stuff, and I'm wondering if you could be a special consultant to the team and figure out the best positions to place our feet or hands or move our body to make more of an impact."

Lexi's eyes widened. Special consultant to the team?

Mal turned toward her cot. "I think if you asked around, there would be other kids who might be interested in this stuff, too."

"Definitely," Ron said, dropping to his cot. "I can talk to Coach when we get back, if you want."

"Wow," Lexi said, her mind racing faster than the speed of light thinking of all the ways she could help the football team. Torque, center of mass, axis of rotation, velocity . . . the possibilities were endless. Forget programming a grasshopper to jump over a can. She'd be doing meaningful science—stuff to help Ron and her classmates win games.

And there were tons of ways physics interacted with photography and fashion, too. There was luminance and motion blur's effect on photos—and magnetic nail polish totally involved physics! She swallowed hard. Her teammates' suggestions were brilliant. She didn't have to be at the academy to do science.

Lexi slid into her cot. She hadn't been this excited about science since before she left the academy. And it was all because of Ron and Mal, two classmates who didn't even necessarily like science.

Lexi turned on her side. Now more than ever, she wanted Team RAM to win. She crossed her fingers. *Just one more day*, she whispered as she drifted off to sleep. *Please let the Tel-Med work one more day.*

CHAPTER EIGHTEEN

"Next!" called the telepod engineer.

Mal nudged Lexi forward. "You go first. If you can't travel, we're out."

Lexi set down her backpack and locked the Tel-Med in place. Straightening, she rubbed the Brewers logos on her shirt *and* her cap for luck and then flashed a thumbs-up.

Lights blinked, and Lexi opened her eyes. A large sign suspended from the ceiling said "Welcome to Fisk University, Tennessee." Her knees buckled, and she gripped the Tel-Med shelf to steady herself before bounding off. *Whew!*

Seconds later, Mal arrived, placing a palm over her heart upon seeing Lexi. Ron teleported in a minute after that, heaving a breath as he caught Lexi's eyes. He ran to his teammates . . . and then kept running past them.

Mal and Lexi watched, confused.

"Blue arrows!" he called, pointing to the blue arrows taped to the floor. "Quit lollygagging. Let's go!"

Mal dashed to catch up to the Filipino Flyer. A second later, Lexi followed. She had to hand it to her teammates. They didn't waste even a moment dwelling on her Tel-Med fiasco. They were already thinking about the next puzzle. As she chased after them, Lexi tried to do the same. It was like what her dad said whenever she made an error in a softball game. *Forget about it and focus on the next play.* If her teammates could do it, she could, too.

The arrows led to the school's gymnasium, where pennants hung from rafters and banners adorned the walls. They checked in at the tournament booth, and Ron opened the envelope for the next clue.

PUZZLE TIME!

Use the directory to find Elmer Samuel Imes
(or, as he's known to us, E-S-I) on campus.

"Well, that's short and sweet," Mal said.

"We should try the physics department," Lexi suggested.

Ron nodded. "Let's find the directory."

Team RAM left the gym and entered a courtyard framed by older brick buildings. A track and field stood to their right. Ron tapped Lexi's arm and pointed to a sidewalk, where the Phenoms, Techies, and Comets crowded around a campus directory.

Lexi bit her lip as they approached, not sure what to say if Haley tried talking to her. While part of her wanted to confront Haley about the lie, another part wanted to ignore Haley completely. Ron and Mal deserved her undivided attention.

Team RAM reached the directory as the alliance backed away. Ron nudged Lexi and Mal forward to take their places. As Lexi side-stepped Tomoka, she brushed against Haley.

"Oops. Sorry," Lexi said.

Haley didn't respond. In fact, although Lexi could have sworn they made eye contact, Haley acted as if she didn't even recognize her. Seconds later, the Comets scattered across campus.

Lexi watched for only a second before advancing to the directory. Time to focus.

"Well," Ron said. "Is it me or is there no physics building on this map?"

Lexi shook her head. "I don't see one, either." She looked again. "In fact, I don't even see a reference to Imes."

Mal whipped out her tablet. "I'm going to research the university. Maybe the school's site has something."

Lexi glanced past the directory, where other teams raced in and out of buildings. Even the Doppler Daredevils and Awesome Einsteins, the two teams that had teleported after Team RAM, had begun their search. Team RAM had to be missing something obvious. She pressed her nose against the glass and studied the map.

"Hey, did you guys see the numbers in the center of each of these buildings?"

Ron joined her. "No, but I see them now. What do you think they mean?"

Lexi retrieved her notebook. "I'll write them down."

"You two ready for a summary of Dr. Imes?" Mal asked as Lexi wrote.

"Yeah," Lexi replied, finishing the list. She showed it to Ron.

Park-Johnson Hall: A-18-83
Biology Labs: B-19-41
Harris Music Building: C-19-03
Talley-Brady Hall: D-00-04
Dubois Hall: E-16-53
Adam K. Spence Hall: F-19-18
Crosthwaite Hall: G-19-30
New Livingston Hall: H-24-27

"Okay," Mal started. "Dr. Elmer Samuel Imes was the second African American to earn a PhD in physics. He developed the physics department at Fisk University. He had four patents, all having to do with instruments that measured magnetic and electronic properties." Mal paused. "Whatever that means."

Lexi laughed. "Go on."

"He published a bunch of articles in physics journals. Do you want to know the titles?"

"Not right now."

Mal continued, "Okay, it looks like he was one of the first scientists to show that quantum theory could be applied to all . . . regions of the electromagnetic spectrum? Something about infrared spec . . . spectr—"

"Spectroscopy," Lexi finished. "Interesting."

Ron arched an eyebrow. "Verrrrrry interesting."

Lexi tapped his elbow "Fine. Not interesting to *you*, but *I* think—"

"Enough," Mal scolded. She looked at Lexi. "So is any of that useful, 'cuz to me, um, *nada*."

"No," Lexi said. "At least I don't think so." She tilted her notebook so Mal could read the list of buildings. "Do any of these mean anything to you?"

Mal read the list. "Yeah, maybe." Her fingers danced across the screen. "Oh my gosh. These numbers. Look." Mal referred to a paragraph of background information on Imes. "Imes was born in 1883 and died in 1941. The first two buildings have 1883 and 1941 in their . . . whatevers."

Lexi gasped. "You're right."

"It also says that Imes received his physics degree in 1903 and got his masters in 1918. He started teaching in 1930 . . ."

"Those numbers are all on here," Lexi said.

"Cross out those buildings," Ron offered. "Maybe it's the building that's left."

"There are three left," Lexi said. "Maybe we can go to these buildings first?"

Ron stepped away, mumbling to himself, "Use the directory to find him. Use the directory to find him."

"E-S-I!" Lexi cried. She slapped a hand to her mouth as the Fig Newtons and Daredevils returned to the directory. She lowered her voice. "We're looking at it wrong. The clue says they know him as 'E-S-I.' I bet *that's* who we're supposed to find—not Elmer Imes." She pointed to the three remaining buildings:

Talley-Brady Hall: D-00-04
Dubois Hall—E-16-53
New Livingston Hall: H-24-27

"Well, if it's E-S-I, maybe it's Dubois Hall since it starts with an *E*," Mal said.

Ron agreed. "Makes sense, but how is a 16 an *S* and a 53 an *I*?"

Lexi couldn't contain her excitement. "Sixteen is the atomic number of sulfur, which is the symbol *S* on the periodic table, and 53 is the atomic number for iodine, which has *I* for its symbol. So if we're looking for E-S-I, it—"

"Would be E-16-53," Ron finished. "It *is* Dubois Hall!"

Mal advanced to the directory. "You have to be kidding me," she grumbled. "Dubois Hall is right on the other side of the gymnasium. We could have been there already."

"Shoot!" Lexi motioned her teammates to follow her. "C'mon!"

Minutes later, Team RAM entered Dubois Hall. A bulletin board near the doors contained class schedules, and a quick skim revealed the physics laboratory was on the second floor. Team RAM pounded its way up the stairs and around a corner. They skidded to a stop as they entered the lab. Six teams, including the Comets, were already there.

"Check out the posters," Mal said, pointing to the far wall where most of the other teams congregated.

Team RAM maneuvered around the lab tables and toward the wall, where several photos of Dr. Imes hung over a table containing miniature rockets, journal articles, and computer equipment. A tablet encased in a clear plastic case stood atop a table in the corner. The Mighty Sanbornes, Solar Flares, and Edison's Excellencies surrounded it, notebooks in hand, while the Comets, Phenoms, and Techies waited behind them. Lexi peeked between two heads to catch a glimpse.

"It's another video clue," Lexi said out of the corner of her mouth. "We'll have to wait our turn."

"I don't hear any—"

The teams removed their earbuds.

"Ohhhhhhh," Ron said. "Never mind."

Lexi fidgeted. Six teams would see the clue before Team RAM, and since they had to wait for the video station, there was nothing she could do about—

"Lexi?" Haley's voice called. Haley left her teammates and stepped toward Lexi. She looked her up and down before finally pointing at Lexi's red headband. Giggling, she shook her head. "What in the world?"

Lexi fumbled for a response as Emma tapped Haley's shoulder.

"Let's go, Haley. We're up."

Ignoring Emma, Haley gave Lexi another once-over. "Seriously," Haley said. "What are you doing? You look ridiculous!"

Lexi told herself to stay calm. "I think it's awesome. *Different.* Anyone can wear matching T-shirts."

Haley guffawed.

"Haley, come on. It's our turn," Emma repeated.

Lexi watched as the Comets, Phenoms, and Techies moved into position at the video station. One spot remained—the spot that belonged to Haley. Lexi opened her mouth to tell Haley, but closed it just as quickly. Mal had slinked from Lexi's side and was now creeping toward the last spot. If Haley didn't turn around soon, she was going to miss the video and Mal would see it instead!

Lexi returned her attention toward Haley, who flicked the end of the red band around Lexi's wrist.

Lexi pulled her hand away. "I don't get it, Hale," she said. "Why'd you do it?"

Haley shrunk back. "Do what?"

"The maze," Lexi said. "You told us the wrong word."

Haley narrowed her eyes. "What are you talking about? I tried to *help* you guys. It was hot and I was tired. Maybe I made a mistake. Don't take it personally, Lexi. We all want to win."

We all want to win. The words pierced through Lexi, hitting her at her core. Haley had chosen winning over their friendship. No doubt about it.

Lexi peered past Haley at the clue station. "You're right. We all *do* want to win. Now if you'll excuse us, we have a clue to solve."

Haley smirked. "Not yet you don't. We got here first. You have to—" She whirled to the video station, where the Phenoms, Techies, Haley's teammates, and Mal were listening to the clue. Haley spun to Lexi. "You cut in line!"

"No, we didn't. Emma called you, but you ignored her. Mal took your spot. Nothing illegal about that."

Doppler Chris laughed from the back of the room. "She's right, Haley. I saw the whole thing. Other teams shouldn't have to wait while you chitchat."

Haley walked away in a huff, and Lexi stepped back toward Ron.

He offered her a quiet fist pound. "Go, Mal. That. Was. Tremendous." He bumped his shoulder into hers. "She squeezed right in."

Lexi smiled. "I know. I looked up and all of a sudden she was there!" Lexi recalled the look on Haley's face when Haley learned she had missed her turn. If Team RAM could solve the clue based on Mal's report, they'd be right with the top teams. Making it to the top five for the final puzzle was totally within their grasp.

CHAPTER
NINETEEN

As the video clue ended, Mal removed her earbuds and joined her teammates. "Quick," she said. "Over here. I want to tell you everything real fast before I forget."

Lexi retrieved her notebook as Team RAM grouped around a table.

"Okay," Mal said. "This one showed all three teleport scientists and, first of all, I have to say that they were all wearing these bright red Wisconsin T-shirts that had a weird animal on them. I'm not sure what they were thinking with those or whose idea it was, but it wasn't a good look. But *anyway*, first they congratulated us. Then one of them said it was time to 'implement your invention.' The American scientist then said our destination is where teleportation had its start. All three then did this jokey thing where they were winking at the camera and smiling. A lot. It ended with one of them telling us not to badger them for more clues." Mal took a deep breath. "And that was it."

"That was it?" Ron asked incredulously. "You were up there for, like, three minutes."

Mal scowled. "I'm giving you the important stuff. There was a lot of mumbo jumbo about dreams becoming reality and inventing and—"

Laughing, Lexi stuffed her notebook into her backpack and sprung from the desk. "It's enough, you guys. I know where we're going. Come on. You know the drill. Let's get back to the telepods. I'll explain while we're in line."

"I'll save us spots," Ron said, and the Filipino Flyer tore out of the building. By the time Mal and Lexi caught up to him, he had secured a place in front of the Phenoms and Techies.

Joining the line, Lexi pulled out her Teleport Tableau.

"So, where are we going?" Mal asked.

"The National Teleport Museum," Lexi answered. "Madison, Wisconsin." She filled out a Travel Request Form. Three of the last five tournaments had included a stop at the museum, and she had made sure to include Madison's station code on the tableau.

"How do you know?" Ron asked.

"The museum was built on the site of Dr. Vogt, Dr. Bressler, and Dr. Kent's original lab, which is where they made the first telepod. It has to be what they meant by where teleportation got its start. It's the museum's most popular exhibit. I've been there almost every summer for science camp, too."

"Hm," Ron said. "But I remember something about a baboon teleporting from San Diego to L.A."

Lexi nodded. "You're right. They teleported with baboons first, but I think the clue's asking about the lab and the site of the first human teleportation because A, the tournament's nearly over and we have to get back to Wisconsin, and . . ." She put an arm around Mal. "B, our wonderful fashionista had the brains to tell us they were wearing Wisconsin sweatshirts with a 'weird animal.'"

Ron gave her a puzzled look. "Otherwise known as a *badger*? The University of Wisconsin's mascot? That cinches it."

Mal snapped her fingers. "Hey! I bet that's why he said that thing about badgering him for clues, too. It was really awkward, but also so weird I figured it had to mean something."

Ron laughed and shook his head. "I can't believe it. Badger. Who knew knowing teams' mascots would be helpful in a teleportation tournament?"

Team RAM reached the telepod engineer and handed in their Travel Request Form. After receiving a sticker of a rocket for their Trek Tracker (*seven!*), they took their positions on the telepod. Three flashes later, they stood at a tournament booth at the University of Wisconsin-Madison campus.

In a matter of minutes, the line contained the Sanbornes, Excellencies, Flares, Team RAM, Phenoms, Techies, Comets, Fig Newtons, and Daredevils. Lexi's heart pounded. With the teams so close, any mistake could oust them from the top five.

She peered down the road toward the administration building. Trams left the building every ten minutes to transport passengers to the museum, which stood on a small island in the middle of Lake Mendota. Lexi scratched her head, thinking back to when she had attended science camp at the museum last summer. At this time of day—after the opening rush, there would only be a couple cars on the tram. Maybe four to five teams would fit, but if museum visitors were in line, it'd be even less. The teams that didn't make the first tram would fall at least ten minutes behind as they waited for the next.

Lexi had no doubt Team RAM would be one of them. While Ron and Mal would undoubtedly keep pace with the fastest teams, there was no way she would. She had barely made it up the trail to Castle Neuschwanstein.

With a sigh, she pointed to the museum. "It's going to be a race to that building to catch the first tram."

"Oh, really?" Ron stretched his arms over his head and bent sideways. "I need to loosen up."

"For sure," Mal said as she started lunging.

Lexi watched her teammates in silence. A little stretching wasn't going to make her faster. An idea struck, and she tapped Ron's elbow. "Hey, do you have your eye black?"

Ron arched an eyebrow and handed it over.

Straightening, Lexi marked her cheeks with resolve. She was about to run the fastest she'd ever run in her life. "It's Game Time," she said with a stiff nod as she returned the stick to Ron.

Smiling, Ron applied it to his face, too. Before he could put the stick away, Mal grabbed it out of his hand and stroked it on her cheeks. Lexi laughed, imagining how the three of them must look with their red head and arm bands and marked cheeks. *Definitely like teammates.*

As Ron dropped the stick into his pack, the tournament monitors arrived. Teams jostled for position at the counter, elbows poking and jabbing. Everyone realized a few seconds could make all the difference in the world.

"Okay," a monitor said, peering at the nine teams huddled at the counter. "We've counted heads, and you're all checked in. You're free to go."

A flurry of colored shirts darted down the block. Lexi ran, too, but as four teams increased their lead, her mind whirled. Unless the eye black was a high energy wave like a gamma ray that could instill her with supernatural powers, she was not going to catch up to the leaders. Her peripheral vision caught sight of the lake, and an idea zapped to mind.

Keeping an eye on her teammates, Lexi kept pace as best she could. As Ron and Mal reached the entrance, she shouted, "Wait! Ron! Mal! Hold up!" Her teammates skidded to a halt. Lexi caught up and diverted her path to a nearby water fountain.

"You okay?" Ron asked.

Lexi heaved a breath. "Yeah."

The Dopplers passed by, and Ron whirled to dart after them.

"Wait!" Lexi shouted. She let the Dopplers disappear into the building before leaning in and whispering, "I have an idea." She gestured to the building. "The tram's that way, but there's no way it's going to hold all of us. Some teams are bound to be left behind waiting for the next one."

"Which is why we should hurry and get our place in line," Ron said.

"No, look." Lexi dug deep into a side pocket of her backpack and pulled out her junior scientist badge. "I got this last summer when volunteering at camp. It lets me use the employee ferry, which sails straight across the lake to the museum. When we went on field trips at the academy, he'd let those of us with badges use it. This should be the same thing, right?"

Mal tapped the badge.

"Oh wow," Ron said. "Really?"

Lexi nodded. "It *is* a risk, though. We have to follow the dirt path down to the docks, and if he won't let us board, we'll have to backtrack up here."

Ron glanced toward the tram entrance.

Mal shook her head. "Do you think he'd let all of us on?"

Lexi pursed her lips, then nodded. "I think he will. My parents have gone with me."

"I vote yes," Ron said. "It's a trick play—like when the running back passes to the quarterback for a touchdown. Sure, there could be a fumble or other disaster, but if it works, it's *huge*. High risk equals high reward."

He threw his hand into the middle, and Lexi and Mal added theirs. After a quick Team RAM cheer, they trekked down the hill.

Stepping off the trail and onto the dock, Lexi craned her neck to see inside the boathouse. She'd met several ferry captains, but Captain Peter had been the nicest. Their chances were best with him. She opened the door.

The Mighty Sanbornes and Physics Phenoms spun to face her.

Lexi froze, then sighed. She should have expected other science camp volunteers would have remembered the ferry. Still, she'd rather be with two teams on the ferry than stuck waiting for a tram.

Daniel Sanborne flashed his volunteer badge. "Great minds think alike, huh, Lexi?" he joked.

Lexi laughed. "I guess so. Is the captain letting us board?"

"Yep," Tomoka said. "He told us he'd be right—"

"All aboard!" Captain Peter's voice echoed through the boathouse.

The teams bolted through the door and onto the ferry. As Captain Peter pushed off from the dock, Lexi peered up the trail. She was too far away to make out how many teams had made it onto the first tram. They were in front of at least a few of them, though.

Ron offered Lexi a high five. "Good call, Magill!"

A short time later, the ferry bumped into the museum's dock, and the teams disembarked. As they ran to the museum, the Comets, Techies, and Solar Flares joined from the tram's driveway.

The teams crossed into the courtyard, where a bevy of oak and elm trees surrounded bronze statues of Dr. Kent, Dr. Bressler, and Dr. Vogt. The statues pointed to an elegant white stone building atop the small hill.

A blue-and-gold sign hung above the building's entrance.

PUZZLE TIME!

You know what to do—find the location
where teleportation began!

"The lab," Lexi whispered. "Follow me."

Lexi raced into the museum and across the foyer to the far staircase. Grabbing the railing as she skidded to a halt, she checked over her shoulder for her teammates. Ron and Mal were right behind her, not missing a step.

She jumped down the last couple stairs and turned. "This way! Hurry!"

Riiiiiiiing! Riiiiiiiing! Ringity Ring!

Lexi skidded to a stop. Her cargo pocket was glowing. Her phone. But it wasn't her parents' ringtone, or, actually, *any* of the personalized ringtones she had programmed for her friends and family. This had to be an unknown caller.

Wren Tech.

Her stomach plummeted at the thought, and she slowed as she felt for the zipper on her cargoes to retrieve her phone.

"It's up ahead!" a Sanborne shouted.

The elevator's doors opened and teams hustled inside.

Lexi let her phone be. They had fallen behind while she had been trying to get the pocket unzipped. Now other teams were closing in. Darting around a corner and through the cafeteria, Lexi wound a path through the various exhibits to the auditorium.

"Here it is," Lexi said, and she bolted through the doors . . .

. . . and smack dab into a tournament official talking to the Phenoms. Lexi glanced at the stage at the front of the auditorium. The Mighty Sanbornes were taking their seats in the front row.

Oof.

The Solar Flares bumped her from behind.

The tournament official directed the teams to seats in the front of the auditorium. A second after Team RAM settled in, Haley's Comets emerged at the door. The official placed them in seats behind the Flares, and the auditorium doors thudded closed.

Dr. Harrison took the stage. "Congratulations. You're our top five!"

Silence, then gasps, and finally excited screams echoed through the auditorium. Lexi remained quiet, trying to absorb Dr. Harrison's words. She placed her hands over her head, closed her eyes, and hunched forward in her chair. *Top five? Top five!* Tears pricked her eyes as her stomach bounced. The events of the last three days flashed through her mind, from traveling to the wrong castle, to almost fishing Mal's Tel-Med out of the toilet, to Haley's attempted sabotage, and, of course, to her blunder that had led the team to Tibet. Despite it all, Team RAM had battled through and made it into the finals.

She shook her head in disbelief. Before the tournament, she had often dreamed of being in this position, but now that she was here, it was ten times more exhilarating than she had ever imagined. She glanced at her teammates. She couldn't picture being here without them. She turned to them to celebrate.

Ding!

Lexi flinched as her cargo pocket vibrated. The light, fuzzy feeling coursing through her body instantly drifted away, replaced by a heaviness that weighed her into her seat. Their top-five finish was about to be wiped out. She fumbled for the phone, wishing she had a reason to ignore it. But she'd put it off long enough. She pulled out her phone and squinted warily at the screen.

*** CRITICAL PROTOCOL HAS BEEN ACTIVATED ***

Tears welled in Lexi's eyes. The exact thing she'd been dreading had become a reality. Their race was over, and all because she'd ignored the messages. If only she would have shared them with her teammates. Together, they might have been able to come up with a solution. Now, it was too late.

As teams around her continued to cheer, Lexi slid low in her seat. She glanced at Mal and Ron, trying to figure out how to tell their laughing and smiling faces that their tournament had come to an end.

The auditorium lights flickered, and Dr. Harrison approached the stage. Photos of King Ludwig's castle, the art museum, and other tournament locations flashed on a screen behind him. Lexi straightened in her seat. At almost every location, Team RAM had overcome some sort of problem. No matter how bad things had gotten, they hadn't given up.

A speck of hope surged through Lexi. Maybe this was no different. *Maybe* if she solved the clue real fast, she could be the first one to teleport and get to the final destination before Wren Tech completed the protocol and her Tel-Med deactivated.

In a flurry, Lexi took out her notebook and readied herself for the next clue one last time.

CHAPTER
TWENTY

"Attention everyone!" Dr. Harrison said. "One of our officials is passing out your stickers for this stop. Then we'll begin."

Lexi stuck the sticker on the Tracker and refocused on Dr. Harrison.

Ding!

Her phone beeped again. Irritated, Lexi zipped her pocket closed, hoping to muffle any more dings. She knew what she had to do, and the incessant chiming would be a distraction.

The lights dimmed, and Dr. Harrison left the stage. A projection of Dr. Kent, Dr. Bressler, and Dr. Vogt zapped onto the screen.

Dr. Kent moved to the front and peered into the auditorium. "Well, they found us," he said. "Now what?"

Dr. Vogt playfully tapped his shoulder. "Oh, quit teasing." Straightening, she addressed the camera, "In developing teleport travel, Dr. Kent, Dr. Bressler, and I worked as a team. Each of us brought a different way of thinking, a special set of skills that the others didn't have, that made us successful. I venture to say the same is true with you—that each of you has made valuable contributions to your teams. True advancements in technology are always a team effort. Remember that when the race is over. It will serve you well in life."

Dr. Bressler advanced to the camera next, and Lexi leaned forward, still waiting for the scientists to say something about the next clue.

"What, I ask, is the purpose of technology?" Dr. Bressler started. "Why do we invent things? What prompted Da Vinci, an outstanding artist, to pursue science and invention? Why did Marie Curie study radioactivity? Why did Alan Turing build a computer? Simple. It was an effort to make our lives better, to end suffering in some respect." He held up a finger. "Teleport travel started no differently. Yes, of course the science of it, the dream of it, was enchanting. But to make it a reality, to make it possible for people to see loved ones, to travel to far off places in a split second"—Dr. Bressler snapped his fingers—"Remember that as you go forward. Whatever you decide to do, do it with the intention to make the world a better place, and you will live a happy life, indeed."

Dr. Bressler returned to his colleagues. Lexi craned her neck and looked around the auditorium, curious whether any of her competitors had heard something worth writing down, but it was too dark to see. As Dr. Kent took the stage, she hoped she hadn't missed anything.

"Home," Dr. Kent said calmly. "No matter where we travel, no matter what we do, in the end we share the same thing—a desire to get back home. It's where we feel safe. Teleportation travel allows us to make those trips home quicker, but even if we take our time, we get there. I hope you all have safe and happy homes."

Dr. Kent stepped back as Dr. Vogt joined him. "Dr. Kent is right. There's nothing like going home after a long day."

Buzz.

Lexi's phone vibrated. She stared at her pocket, willing it to stop. Dr. Vogt's voice shook her out of her trance and Lexi refocused.

". . . we do it on the count of three? One. Two. Thr—"

"Wait!" Dr. Bressler called. "I want to help! Now, where were you? One, three, two?"

Lexi rubbed her forehead, confused. She'd missed something. None of this made sense. Her pocket vibrated again. With one eye on the scientists, she undid the zipper. She should have shut it off.

"Oh, come on," Dr. Kent said, placing his hands on his hips. "Next thing you'll say is Germany, Italy, Poland, when you know the correct order was Germany, Poland, and Italy all the way *to the finish line.*"

The scientists laughed. After a few awkward seconds, Dr. Vogt winked and whispered, "Why are you still here? You know what you must do. Be safe at home. After all, that's where the first successful human teleportation ended, isn't it?"

The screen went black, and the auditorium's lights blinked on. Dr. Harrison reemerged at the end of Team RAM's row. A set of double doors opened behind him. "When you're ready, you can exit through here. The scientists' private telepod station is behind me. Hand in your final Travel Request Form, and you'll be on your way."

Laptops and tablets buzzed into action as teams got to work. Lexi pulled her hand back from her pocket and yanked out a Travel Request Form from her backpack.

"Do you know where we're going?" Mal whispered. "'Cuz I gotta say, that was all gibberish to me."

Lexi nodded, scribbling as fast as she could. The part she had missed hadn't been important after all. Dr. Vogt had made it perfectly clear where they had to go.

"Where?" Ron asked.

"Home," Lexi said. "Exactly like Dr. Vogt said."

Mal and Ron stared at her. "Huh?"

Lexi stood and revealed the form and their final destination. "Miller Park," she whispered. "The first successful teleportation was from here to Miller Park. The Brewers were on a road trip, so the stadium was empty. The scientists thought it'd be cool to have a stadium filled with people watching the first human teleport to his destination. That way there'd be thousands of witnesses." Lexi pointed through the double doors at the scientists' telepod. "They showed this telepod on the JumboTron, and the telepod at the stadium was positioned on home plate." Lexi chuckled. "It's perfect. We're going to run *home*."

Mal and Ron shrieked, and moments later Team RAM raced through the doors into the private teleport area. The Mighty Sanbornes and Haley's Comets followed, leaving the Physics Phenoms and the Solar Flares still working on the clue. Lexi handed in the form to the first official she saw.

Her thigh tingled, and Lexi glared at her pocket. Not waiting for approval, she advanced up a small flight of stairs to the telepod and clicked in her Tel-Med. She flashed a thumbs-up sign.

The telepod operator punched a few keys, and the glass doors closed. "Ready. Three, two, one . . ."

Lexi stiffened and closed her eyes, anticipating the flash. When she opened her eyes, she'd be at Miller Park. All of Wren Tech's warnings would be behind her.

Lexi opened her eyes. She hadn't gone anywhere, and now, Haley's Comets and The Mighty Sanbornes were shifting anxiously behind Mal and Ron, ready to board. Lexi eyed the telepod operator again. He gave the signal, and Lexi thrust a thumbs-up forward. Okay, he hadn't been ready. No problem. *Now* she'd go.

Nope.

The telepod operator scowled and punched a few keys. A few seconds later, he addressed Lexi. "Can you reinsert your Tel-Med, please?"

Lexi lowered her thumb as the reality of the situation took hold. Her hand shook as a sudden chill coursed through her fingers.

"Miss?" The operator said, gesturing to the shelf. "Can you please reinsert your Tel-Med?"

Feeling like she was moving in slow motion, Lexi inched forward and tried to pry the Tel-Med out of its slot. Her twitchy fingers refused to cooperate.

The Tel-Med dropped to the platform. Lexi bent to retrieve it, striking the top of her head against the shield. Straightening, she inserted it again, careful to avoid meeting her teammates' eyes. She couldn't risk a peek at their disappointed faces.

"Take your position, please," the operator said.

Lexi tried to think positive thoughts. Maybe it had been a glitch. Things like this *had* to happen every once in a while. Perhaps the inventors' old telepod was rusty. It wasn't like it got a lot of use anymore. She rubbed the Brewers logo on her cap and then on her shirt. Courage mustered, she closed her eyes. *Please. Third time's the charm.*

The operator repeated, "Ready. Three, two, one . . ."

Nothing.

Lexi slumped. The shield released, and she grabbed the Tel-Med and shuffled toward Ron and Mal, fumbling for a way to apologize.

Bump.

"Excuse me," a female tournament official said as she hurried past.

Lexi lifted the chain dividing the telepod from the waiting area so she could duck under and join her teammates.

The official blocked her effort. "A moment, please." Then, to everyone else, she explained, "Sorry about the holdup. We had to shut down the telepod."

Lexi gulped. Shut down? As in, on purpose? She squeezed the Tel-Med, willing herself to keep upright.

"From our observations," the official continued, "these three teams completed the Travel Request Forms at about the same time. But, since Team RAM was seated closest to the exit doors, they made it here first."

"What?" Mal balked. "Are you kidding?"

"Yeah," Ron added. "You're punishing us for sitting by the door where we were told to sit?"

"No, no, not at all," the official said. "What I'm saying is that, to negate any random advantage, we're not going to teleport a full team first. Instead, we're going to teleport one member from each team, then do that again, and then a third time. This way, the third members of each team will arrive pretty close in time. After your teams are complete, you can continue."

The official tapped Lexi on the shoulder. "You can head up now. I didn't want you waiting by yourself at Miller Park wondering what was going on. We wanted to make sure everyone heard the explanation."

Lexi heaved a breath as the official's words sunk in. She grabbed the edge of the control panel and placed a hand to her forehead.

The official chuckled. "I'm sorry. I can see I upset you." She opened the chain. "Why don't you take a minute and let one of your teammates go first."

Lexi pressed her palms to her forehead and stared. The telepod seemed a mile away. She doubted she could get there without stumbling. "Okay," she mumbled.

"I'll go," Mal said, stepping past Lexi and onto the platform.

Ron followed Lexi to the back of the line. "Lex, you okay?"

Exhaling, Lexi met Ron's eyes. "Yeah, I'm fine," she said, swallowing hard. "I thought for a second they deactivated the Tel-Med."

"Yeah," Ron said. "We wondered that for a minute, too." He slapped Lexi on the back. "But it's okay! We're still in it!"

"All right," the official said. "I will leave you to it. Sorry about the delay. We really are trying to make this fair for everyone. . . . Though hopefully with all of you arriving close to the same time, there won't be a tie."

The official left to a chorus of anxious twitters from the other teams, but Lexi lurched, clutching Ron's arm.

A tie.

There couldn't be a tie. During the rules explanation Dr. Harrison said it was impossible—that the tournament was designed specifically to *prevent* a tie. That's why teams couldn't work together. That's why—

"Earth to Lexi," Ron said. He twisted his arm to loosen her grip.

Lexi unclenched. "Sorry." She nudged Ron away from the other teams and retrieved her notebook. There was more to this last clue than simply running to home plate. Unfortunately, they had only a few seconds to figure out what it was. Mal was already gone, and David Sanborne had entered the telepod.

"Something about this clue isn't right," she whispered to Ron. "Dr. Harrison said there was no way there could be a tie, remember? Check your notes from this last clue. I'm going to look at what I wrote during his rules explanation. I think we might have to solve another puzzle before crossing home plate."

As Ron retrieved his notebook, Lexi flipped to the first page.

DON'T LOSE BADGES
DON'T GO TO ANTARCTICA
CHECK IN EVERY STOP
NO TEL—MEDS 10:00 P.M.—7:00 A.M.
NINE PUZZLES
COLLECT NINE STICKERS
ONLY THREE WINNERS, NO TIES

Yep, it was definitely there. *No ties.* She went to circle it and froze as she caught what she wrote above it. *Collect nine stickers.* They had eight.

Lexi pointed to the page as she stood on her tiptoes to whisper into Ron's ear. "Collect *nine* stickers. There definitely has to be another puzzle somewhere."

Ron looked unconvinced. "Unless they give you the sticker at home plate or while running there. There could be a booth set up in between third base and home."

"What, so they throw stickers at the teams while they pass?" She arched an eyebrow.

"Well, I don't know," Ron said.

Comet Andre flashed a thumbs-up from the telepod.

Lexi scanned Ron's notebook. "What did you write about the last clue? I missed part of it."

"Next!" the telepod operator called.

Lexi raised her eyes to Ron's expectantly, but he frowned and closed his notebook. "I don't have anything," he whispered, setting it into his backpack. "It all sounded so mumbo-jumbo-ish. *What is teleportation? We want to go home.*"

"Next!" Haley shouted.

Lexi scowled, irritated she'd allowed herself to become distracted by her phone when Dr. Vogt had been talking. She whispered to Ron, "Fine, go ahead. But, think about it on the way."

Ron took a step, then called over his shoulder. "On the way? That's like two seconds. How's that going to help?"

No idea.

Shaking off Ron, Lexi closed her eyes. *C'mon, Magill! Bottom of the ninth. Two outs. Down by one. You're up to bat. Focus!*

Someone was tapping her arm. Lexi snapped open her eyes. Ashley Sanborne and Comet Emma were staring at her. "You're up," Ashley said.

Stupid telepods. If she had a couple minutes alone with no distractions, Lexi knew she'd get it.

Lexi stepped onto the platform and took her position. Seconds later, she was standing outside of Miller Park, still without a clue of what they were supposed to do.

CHAPTER
TWENTY-ONE

Lexi heard David and Daniel Sanborne first. Their shouts rose louder than the others. She flicked her eyes over the landscape. Those who had teleported before her cheered from the stadium's outfield entrance gate. As Lexi spotted Mal and Ron waving wildly, Ashley Sanborne sped past Lexi. Moments later, Emma did, too.

Lexi took off, irritated that victory was going to come down to an old-fashioned footrace. Not teleport science. Not physics. A race. She tightened her jaw. This was supposed to be a teleportation tournament—not the Olympics.

She glanced ahead. Ashley and Emma greeted their teammates, and the Sanbornes and Comets slowed to a celebratory trot as they entered the stadium. Lexi pumped her legs harder on the off chance she could catch up.

Then it came to her. Physics principles! Gravity, force, acceleration—if she maintained her pace while others decelerated she *would* catch up. Plus, given the amount of energy it took to start up again, there was a chance she could close the gap even more if she ran faster.

Lexi pumped harder, and seconds later she neared Mal and Ron. She opened her mouth to yell for them to join her, but before she could speak, an incoming Tomoka sprinted past. Arms flailing in an effort to keep up, Lexi lost her balance. Her feet jolted, right foot then left, and tripped into each other. A second later, she was on the ground, skidding across the asphalt. After a bump and a thump, she came to a stop.

As Mal and Ron rushed to her, Lexi inspected the damage. Skinned hands and mild bruises—nothing serious. She had suffered worse from falling off her bike. Her legs, however, were a different story. Blood-scraped knees peeked through new holes in her cargo pants, and she winced as the fabric grazed the fresh wounds.

"Magill! You okay?" Ron asked as he approached.

"Yeah, that looked pretty nasty," Mal added, stooping beside Lexi.

Lexi let Mal help her to her feet. "I think so. Tomoka caught me off guard." She squinted toward the stadium's entrance gate, where the other Phenoms had caught up to Tomoka. They disappeared inside, leaving Team RAM in fourth place. "Sorry. I thought maybe we had a chance of catching up if I ran really fast."

Team RAM stood still, watching the stadium entrance. All was quiet.

"Should we go in?" Mal wondered aloud.

"Yeah," Lexi said. "All the teams will be there. Families too."

Mal scowled. "I have no desire to see a trophy presentation to Haley."

"Me neither," Ron said. "But we should be good sports."

Lexi glanced at her dejected teammates. They'd come so close. She hated seeing them so defeated.

"Hey!" she yelled, punching a fist into her palm. "Top five is nothing to sneeze at. We beat forty-five other teams to get here, and none of us has ever raced before. I say that's pretty good."

Mal and Ron smiled.

"Come on," Lexi said, leading her teammates the last fifty feet to the stadium entrance.

A security guard approached. "Hi, I'm Max. I'm here to guide you to your next destination. Where's it gonna be?"

"To the field, I guess," Ron said.

Max paused for an instant before replying, "This way then." Ron and Mal followed a few steps.

"Wait!" Lexi said.

"What?" Ron said.

"Shh," Lexi said. "Listen."

No one spoke. The concourse was quiet.

"I don't hear anything," Mal said.

Lexi gave a firm nod. "Exactly. If someone won, wouldn't we be hearing cheers? Or noise? Or *something*?"

Lexi slung off her backpack, retrieved her notebook, and opened it to the page of notes from the final clue. "They probably crossed home plate without that ninth sticker." Lexi tapped the page. "Come on, you guys. If we figure out where it is and get there first, we can win!"

Mal and Ron huddled around Lexi as the guard stepped away and let them work. Lexi scanned the partially filled page. "My notes aren't very good," she grumbled, recalling how she missed part of Dr. Vogt's speech. "They're incomplete."

"Oh! In that case, try mine," Mal said, opening the cover of a shiny new notebook.

Handwriting covered the crisp page. Lexi's jaw dropped. "Whaa—"

Mal twirled her hair and grinned. "Well, I figured it was time I joined the team and took notes, too."

Lexi shook her head, not believing it. Mal had totally saved them.

"Anyway," Mal said. "From what I have here, I'm thinking it's got to be something with the countries."

DR. VOGT—time for you to run home 1, 2, 3
DR. KENT—1, 3, 2
DR. VOGT—Germany, Italy, Poland / Germany, Poland, Italy
DR. KENT—Germany, Poland, Italy to the finish line

"One, two, three. One, three, two," Lexi said, thinking it through. "Wait! The stickers for the Trek Tracker. Remember how they weren't in order? We went to Germany first, and that sticker was placed over the number one, but then even though we went to Italy second, we had to place that sticker over the number three."

"Right," Mal said. "And even though we went to Poland third, the instructions had us put the Polish sticker over the number two."

Lexi gasped. "Oh my gosh!" She hopped excitedly. "I know what we have to do."

Lexi removed her cap and pointed out the Brewers logo to her teammates. The final clue came down to her knowledge of baseball, and, more specifically, her beloved Brewers. All those games she'd attended with her family had paid off. In a weird way, she probably should have figured it out earlier. Brewers *colors* had been at every location throughout the race. From the navy blue–and–golden ribbon necklaces, to the streamers decorating the tournament booths, to the plaques at the fable maze, the—

"Hey, Magill! We're waiting!" Ron said.

Lexi looked at her teammates, who gawked at her expectantly. She opened her mouth to tell them what they had to do, then closed it. They still had to beat the other teams there.

She whirled to the guard. "Max! Can we go to where they keep the costumes?"

Max rushed over and tapped the bill of Lexi's Brewers cap. "Ah-ha!" he said. "Right this way."

Less than a minute later, Team RAM stood in front of a tournament booth outside a green steel door. "Checking in?" the official asked.

Lexi straightened. "Yep." She stared at the door, wishing she had X-ray vision so she could see if any other teams were on the other side. Perhaps Dr. Vogt, Dr. Bressler, and Dr. Kent could invent that next.

Team RAM handed over their badges, and the official slid a manila envelope forward. Ron grabbed it and tore it open. He dumped a sticker of home plate into his palm.

Nine.

Lexi scarfed it up and stuck it on the Trek Tracker.

Ron tipped the envelope over. "That's it? Just the sticker?"

The official signaled the security guard, who knocked on the green door. It opened a moment later. The official motioned for them to go inside. "Not exactly. Go on in."

Team RAM hurried into the room, a small office and changing area by the looks of it. Two college-aged kids stood before them— one male and one female, both wearing blue shorts and yellow shirts with the Brewers logo.

"I'm Jenny, and this is Wade," the girl said. "We're here to help with the last part of your challenge."

Wade and Jenny led Team RAM into a back room. Lexi's heart skipped as she noticed three costumes lining the wall. She quickly inspected the room to confirm they were the only team there. As her eyes reset on her teammates, adrenaline coursed through her body.

She faced her teammates. "Hurry up! Pick a costume!" Lexi reached for the closest one. Memories of attending Brewers games with her family flooded over her. She hoped her parents had made it to the stadium to watch the finish. She couldn't imagine their faces when they saw her running across the field wearing—

"What is it?" Mal asked, eyeing one of the costumes with a tad of disdain.

Ron wrinkled his nose. "I'm so confused. We got the last sticker. What are we doing?"

Lexi stroked the costume closest to her and laughed.

"I can't believe you guys haven't heard of the Brewers' Famous Racing Sausages. They've been around for, like, over twenty-five years. Every sixth inning of every Brewers home game, they race down the left field foul line, around home plate, and past first base. Haven't you seen it on TV?"

Ron stared at her, eyes narrowed. "No, I know who they are, but what do they have to do with us—or the race?"

"Yeah," Mal added, setting her hands on her hips.

Lexi giggled. "Well, for one, they're the *racing* sausages, and we're in a race!" She gestured to the sausage costume beside her. Shaped like a bratwurst, the top of the sausage depicted a mustached face, while the sausage's middle consisted of green lederhosen. A large number 1 crossed its chest. "Look, this one's number one, the Bratwurst, from *Germany*, the first country we visited, and the first sticker we placed."

She motioned to the next costume, a sausage dressed in a blue-and-red-striped rugby shirt with a 2 across its chest. "This is the *Polish* sausage, which wears the number two. Poland was the third country we visited, but remember that the sticker was placed over circle number two?"

Finally, Lexi went to the third costume. All white with a chef's hat and apron, the sausage costume had a 3 across its chest. "And this one is the *Italian* sausage, for Italy, the sticker we placed over number three. It's what Dr. Kent said—Germany, Poland, and Italy *to the finish line.* We're supposed to wear these costumes as we cross home plate!"

"And *then* we win?" Mal asked.

"Then we win!" Lexi said, barely believing the words as they crossed her lips.

A banging echoed from outside the room, and Team RAM jumped. They stared at the door.

"Hurry up!" Ron said, and he grabbed the Polish's sausage head.

Team RAM scurried to put on their costumes. As Lexi stuck her arms through the sausage head's sides, she shifted to find a comfortable position. "Wow, this is big. And heavy."

Jenny laughed. "This is actually a slightly smaller version made especially for you guys, but the effect is the same. It *is* hard to see in there. Wait until you start running."

Lexi eyed Ron and Mal as they fixed the sausage heads over their bodies. It all made sense now. This was why Dr. Harrison had said there couldn't be any ties—there were only three sausage costumes.

Right?

She looked around the room again. Jenny had said they had made special versions for the tournament. Did that also mean they made several costumes? She bit her lip as an uneasy feeling in her stomach took root. Until they crossed home plate, nothing was official. For all she knew, this was only part of the final puzzle and there could be a bunch of sausages sitting around home plate using physics to figure out launch angles of last year's home runs. They had to keep moving.

"Can we go now?" Lexi asked.

Mal reached for her backpack.

"We got your packs," Jenny said. "You just concentrate on navigating in those costumes. We'll be right behind you."

Team RAM hobbled as fast as they could through the stadium tunnels, getting used to their sausage bodies, and headed toward the left field gate. With every turn, Lexi cringed, panicked she'd see evidence they weren't first.

Finally, Wade opened the door leading to the outfield and motioned Team RAM onto the warning track.

Lexi stepped onto the dirt and froze. The stadium's lower deck from first base to third base was filled with family, friends, and other teams. The Mighty Sanbornes, Haley's Comets, and Physics Phenoms stood near the pitching mound. From what Lexi could tell, everyone was staring in their direction.

Most importantly, none of the other teams were dressed as Famous Racing Sausages.

A fuzzy feeling overcame her. Lexi stretched her arms out to both sides, searching for Ron and Mal. She needed to grab on to something to keep upright. The way her knees were trembling, she could crumble to the ground any second.

Her fingers grasped Mal's elbow, and she squeezed. Science was about facts, and all the facts in front of her led to the same conclusion: they'd done it. They were in first place.

"Oh my gosh!" Mal said. "They're waiting for us!"

"That means—" Ron said.

"We won," Lexi whispered as her heart pounded. "We *won*."

Ron slapped Lexi's hand, and Mal squealed.

"Let's go!" Lexi said.

Side by side, Team RAM trotted down the left field foul line, past third base, past the visiting team's dugout, and to home plate.

Bratwurst, Polish, and Italian . . . to the finish line.

As Lexi, then Ron, and then Mal jumped onto the plate, a voice over the PA system thundered, "Your winners of this year's Teleportation Tournament: Alexis Magill, Ronald Quinto, and Malena Moreno!"

CHAPTER
TWENTY-TWO

Alexis Magill.

Lexi's eyes welled with tears as her name sounded through the stadium and the crowd burst into cheers. Halting a few steps beyond home plate, she raised a hand to wipe her eyes, but her large sausage head blocked her effort. Laughing at her unusual predicament, Lexi blinked rapidly to clear her vision as best she could. Who cared that she couldn't see? She'd won the tournament! No science academy, no practice Tel-Med tournaments, no science teammates, *no matter*. She'd done it. They'd won!

"Magill!"

Lexi jolted and turned toward the voice. Ron's Polish Sausage was waving at her from the top of the stairs that led down into the Brewers' dugout. A second later, Mal's Italian Sausage nudged Lexi's side.

"We did it!" Mal said. "Come on!"

Lexi stepped to follow but stopped. After all the work she'd done preparing for the race, from the tableau and time-zone sheet to studying past tournaments—she wanted to, *needed to*, relish the moment.

She scanned the stands. Faces belonging to former classmates, professors, and friends stared back at her. Her chest tingled. Winning proved she was still one of Wisconsin's top junior scientists.

"Lexi, come on," Mal called from the dugout. "It totally stinks inside this sausage head, and I'm hot."

Lexi laughed. Her costume reeked, too, probably a combination of sweat and heat. She descended the stairs and followed her teammates into the clubhouse behind the dugout. A few minutes later, Team RAM faced one another, their costumes now beside them.

"WAHOO!" Ron yelped first.

Waving his arms in the air, he strutted across the locker room doing a touchdown dance. With shouts of joy, Lexi and Mal joined with silly dances of their own. The tension from the race had evaporated.

"Can you believe it? We won!" Lexi cried as they traded high fives and fist pounds.

"Did you hear all those people as we ran in?" Ron asked. "I couldn't believe it. It was so loud. Definitely louder than any football game I've ever been in." He dropped into a chair. "I mean, for so many people to be so excited . . . about science?"

Lexi laughed hard. "Oh, come on," she said. "It was great!"

"I know!" Ron said. "That's what I'm saying. I never imagined it was possible." He shook his head. "This whole race was amazing. I never thought I'd feel like this. I mean, I was hoping we'd win and everything, but to do it like this, in front of everyone, it's . . ."

"Awesome," Mal finished. She clapped excitedly and hopped in place. "It really is. I can't wait for everyone to find out I won a *science* tournament!" She glanced at Lexi. "We actually did it!"

Lexi grinned. "Only because of your awesome notes! I had *no* idea what to do when we got here."

Mal rolled her eyes. "Neither did I, and I *had* my notes."

"Mal's right," Ron said. "I was clueless, too. You're the one who apparently spends her summers with sausages."

A loud laugh burst from Lexi. Unable to stop, she hunched over and wrapped her arms around her aching stomach. She couldn't remember the last time she'd laughed so hard.

"I think this means we make an awesome team," Mal said. She held her arms over her head. "Team RAM!"

"Hey, yeah," Ron said, standing. "Great idea." He looked toward Lexi. "Are there other tournaments we can enter? If we won this one, I bet we can win more."

"Yeah!" Mal said. "Are there?"

A stunned Lexi straightened and looked at her excited teammates. "Sure, there's STEM competitions all the time, but . . ."

". . . but once you return to the academy, we'll be in different schools and won't be able to race together," Ron interrupted.

Mal slumped. "Oh yeah. That's right."

Guilt overwhelmed Lexi as she took in her teammates' dejected faces. But passing up a chance to attend the science academy would be silly.

"Hey down there!" Dr. Harrison's voice called from the field. "Everyone's waiting to meet the winners!" Footsteps pounded down the steps, and Dr. Harrison appeared. "We have a trophy presentation and interviews to get to!"

Ron stood up tall and smoothed his shirt. "Interviews, eh?" He patted down his hair. "I'm kinda gross from that sausage head."

Mal gasped. "Interviews?" She quickly undid her ponytail and reset it. "With photos? I'm not ready for that at all."

Dr. Harrison chuckled. "You all look great. Don't worry! But I'm talking about the interviews for the internship. The scientists are waiting."

"Oh, that," Mal said. "I'm not interested. I'll be traveling with my parents this summer and working on my portfolio."

"Yeah, and I'm doing football camp," Ron said. "You can skip your interviews. The internship's Lexi's."

Lexi beamed. She'd been so focused on whether her Tel-Med would keep working and winning the tournament that she hadn't thought about the internship, but *yeah*, she was going to be an intern to real teleport scientists! *Dr. Vogt!*

"Oh, I'm sorry," Dr. Harrison said, interrupting Lexi's silent celebration. "I think there's been a misunderstanding. The internship doesn't automatically go to someone on the winning team. The scientists selected finalists—and Lexi is one of them, for sure—but that was based on a review of everyone's academic history, background, and preliminary race results. The scientists want to ask the finalists a few questions about the race before making their decision."

Lexi's stomach twisted as mixed emotions enveloped her. Excitement for being named a finalist . . . but dread that her race performance was anything but spectacular. Once the scientists heard about her Tibet miscalculation, she'd be out of the running for sure.

"Lexi? You okay?" Mal said softly.

Lexi shook herself out of it. "What?"

"You had a weird look on your face," Ron said.

She shrugged. "It's nothing . . . just thinking about the race."

"That we *won*," Ron said.

"Yeah," Mal added. "You seem sad."

Lexi smiled. She won! No matter how the interviews went, that was still a fact. "Nah, it's all good. Let's go!"

"Fantastic," Dr. Harrison said. "Follow me!"

Team RAM exited the Brewers' dugout and walked onto the field. Lexi pushed the interview process out of her mind and focused on the cheers and applause.

"We'll get to our trophy presentation in a moment," Dr. Harrison announced from a microphone erected near home plate. "But first, let me introduce our internship finalists, Alexis Magill, Tomoka Seto, and Haley Davis!"

Haley?

Lexi watched as Haley sauntered down the aisle and onto the field. Somehow, Haley had found time to freshen up since the race ended. Her blond curls bounced as she walked, and she had changed into a fresh lilac denim jumpsuit.

As she took a seat in one of the three chairs set up near the pitching mound, Lexi gave herself the once-over. Her cargoes were ripped from her fall, and her shirt was peppered with specks of blood. She pressed a few strands of hair between her fingers. She didn't need a mirror to know that she had hat-hair from wearing her Brewers cap all day. Add to that a half hour in a hot sausage costume, and she could only imagine how she looked. And smelled.

Tomoka slid into the chair next to Lexi. "Congrats! Great race!"

Lexi tried to forget about Haley. "Thanks. You, too!"

With a massive eye roll, Haley took the empty seat. "Sure, great if you think knowing about painters, fables, and baseball is important. Give me a break. Everyone's already saying how much this tournament has changed. It's supposed to be about science. Next thing you know, *anyone* will be able to enter."

"There was plenty of science, Haley," Tomoka said. "It's—"

"Whatever," Haley interrupted. "The internship's all I cared about, anyway. I'm sure the scientists aren't going to be fooled by someone who can do a word search or goes to baseball games."

Lexi gritted her teeth. Haley had tried to sabotage them, lied about it, and now had the nerve to act like Team RAM's victory was meaningless. As excited as Lexi was about winning the tournament, it no longer was enough. Her former friend didn't deserve an internship. Wiping her suddenly sweaty hands on her thighs, Lexi leaned forward to listen to Dr. Harrison's every word.

He announced, "Everyone, please welcome Dr. Bressler, Dr. Kent, and Dr. Vogt!"

The audience cheered, and Lexi diverted her attention to the scientists as they exited the visitors' dugout and assembled near the on-deck circle. Haley turned in her chair and waved excitedly, smiling wide. Dr. Vogt waved back, and Lexi's heart sunk. She shifted uncomfortably. If she waved at the scientists now, it'd look like she was copying Haley.

"First up: Tomoka Seto!" Dr. Harrison said.

Tomoka rose from his chair and strode the sixty feet to the microphone. Lexi's scientific mind clicked in. She would likely get asked similar questions, and she could start preparing her answers now. Haley would be no match for her!

Dr. Bressler nodded in Tomoka's direction. "Hi, Tomoka. For starters, tell us about your approach to the tournament."

Tomoka pulled his phone out of his pocket and flashed it to the audience. "Sure. Since I knew finding telepods in various cities would be key, I created a Telepod Locator App for my phone."

"But aren't there already apps that do that?" Dr. Kent pointed out.

Tomoka nodded. "But my app identifies all modes of transportation at each telepod location, identifies museums and places of interest nearby, *and* offers real-time updates of any significant wait lines."

"Oh my," Dr. Vogt exclaimed. "You coded that yourself?"

Tomoka shrugged. "It was fun. I have to say that coding and rockets are my passion. I belong to both after-school clubs and am a member of the academic pentathlon team."

"Impressive," Dr. Bressler replied. He flipped through a notebook on his lap. "We received a report on your contributions during the race. It appears your team really worked together well."

"We did. Everything was a team decision to make sure one of us didn't overlook anything."

"Teamwork is key in our lab, too," Dr. Kent said. "Everyone has something different to contribute, and no one person is more important than the other."

Lexi's face grew hot, and she diverted her eyes to the ground. She'd approached the race the exact opposite way, acting like she was Team RAM's leader and had the final say.

Dr. Vogt glanced at the notebook. "Yes, very well done, overall, but what do you think was *your* greatest race accomplishment?"

Tomoka took a breath. "Hmmm. It's hard to say. I think the telepod locator program saved us tons of time, but, like you said, that was something I did before the race." He tapped a finger to his lips. "For the race itself, I think it's the work I put in before we arrived at each location. As soon as we knew where we were going, I'd research the city to find out everything about it to get an idea of where we might have to go or what we might have to do. Like for Marie Curie, we studied the periodic table, and for Alan Turing, we pulled up a map of the university gardens."

Dr. Bressler grinned. "Preparation is everything in science."

"Absolutely," Dr. Kent said. "The unexpected will always occur, but it's those who are prepared for the expected that handle those surprises the best. Well done!"

"Thanks," Tomoka replied. "Unfortunately, we ultimately *struck out* with the last puzzle, but overall we did the best we could!"

The stadium groaned at the baseball pun, but as the scientists stood to congratulate Tomoka, the groans morphed into cheers. Lexi clapped along. Tomoka handled every question well, and his answers were spot-on. He was impressive, as always.

"Next, let's talk to Ms. Haley Davis," Dr. Harrison said.

Haley vaulted from her seat and flounced to the microphone. She grabbed it from Dr. Harrison's hand and faced the scientists. "Before we start, I just want to say that I love all of you. I'm not afraid of hard work, I'm ready to learn, and I'll do anything you need."

Lexi fidgeted, itching to announce that she was willing to work hard, too, but she knew it was better to wait her turn.

"Tell us, Haley, how did you prepare for the tournament?" Dr. Vogt asked.

Haley didn't miss a beat. "Practice tournaments. A lot of them. My practice team created puzzles and clues for one another and then we raced around the world solving them. I feel that preparation is very important, and I would prepare just as hard on any assignments for you."

Lexi sighed. She couldn't compete with practice tournaments—

she hadn't done any. Compared to Tomoka and Haley, her answer on how she prepared was really going to sound stupid.

Dr. Kent held up the report on Haley's race performance. "It says here that you were the first team to check in at quite a few locations! How did you manage to keep your lead?"

Haley stood tall. "We *really* paid attention to the details. For example, the blue envelope. It was the only envelope that wasn't sealed *and* it had 'Destination' written on it. We knew right away it'd be the clue to our next location." Haley flipped her hair. "The same was true with the maze. As soon as we saw some statues had water fountains, we knew the pattern."

"Finding patterns amid data and noticing details is so important in our line of work," Dr. Vogt said. "That's very impressive."

Haley clenched the microphone with both hands. "I know. That's one of the things I've always loved about science."

Lexi recalled her struggle with the envelope. If it hadn't been for Ron, she would have spent hours plotting the points on the map. At the maze, Mal had been the one to notice the fountains to confirm they had identified the right statues. Lexi twisted her lips, racking her brain for how she could answer the same question, but nothing came to mind.

Dr. Bressler asked the final question. "What do you think was your biggest contribution to your team's success?"

"Well, all of the math and science, for sure. I wish there had been more. I did the Marie Curie worksheet, the GPS calculation, the word scrambles. I worked fast, but carefully, and I was sure to check my work—two things I know would be useful in your lab. An internship with you is really the prize of the race, and I hope you'll consider me."

Haley handed the microphone to Dr. Harrison and strode toward the scientists. Lexi's hope that she would be rebuffed and told to march straight back to her seat was quickly dashed as Dr. Vogt, then Dr. Kent, and finally Dr. Bressler hugged her and provided gentle taps on the back.

Tomoka grunted. "Do you think that matters? I would have gone over there, too, if I'd known it was allowed." Frowning, he crossed his arms.

"I know," Lexi said. "Don't worry. You did great. Inventing your own app is more amazing than going on practice tournaments."

"Maybe," Tomoka said. "But look at her with Dr. Vogt."

Lexi looked, and she didn't like what she saw. Dr. Vogt still had her arm around Haley, and the two were chatting as if they were at a family picnic.

"I think they already forgot about me," Tomoka said. "It's going to be up to you."

Lexi gripped the sides of her chair. From the looks of it, Tomoka was right. She was going to have to impress the scientists big-time or else Haley was going to win the internship.

CHAPTER
TWENTY-THREE

"Finally, let's welcome Ms. Magill!" Dr. Harrison announced. Lexi joined him at his side. "Congratulations on your win! I bet it feels amazing!"

Lexi smiled. It *did* feel amazing. She tried to hold on to that feeling as Dr. Bressler asked the first question.

"Tell us, Lexi, how did you prepare for the tournament?"

Lexi swallowed hard. She'd been so proud of her Teleport Tableau, but now it sounded so trivial and unscientific. Parents might be impressed, but esteemed teleport scientists? Not likely.

"Well, I didn't have a laptop, so I created my own telepod locator chart. I made a list of cities and codes of the teleport stations so we could find them fast."

Blank stares from the scientists and a hushed crowd followed Lexi's answer. Lexi held her breath, hoping the next question would come quick.

"See, look at this!" Mal's voice called from the dugout.

Everyone's eyes flicked to Mal as she jogged from the dugout toward Lexi. Lexi's unfolded Teleport Tableau waved from Mal's hand. When she reached Lexi, Mal held it toward the scientists.

"Oh my," Dr. Vogt said, putting a hand over her heart. "You wrote all that?"

Lexi stepped to Mal's side as relief flooded over her. "Yes," she said, pointing to the chart. "It took quite a bit of time, but I went by country, then city, then telepod. We relied on it throughout the race."

"How creative!" Dr. Vogt added. "Often in science we have to make do with what's available versus what we might want. What a great example!"

Whew! Lexi relaxed. *So far, so good.*

Dr. Kent took the microphone. "I was reading over the report of your race, and I wanted to commend you on a few things, starting with this note about how much time your team saved at the check-in counters! Looks like you were very efficient, indeed!"

"What do you expect?" Dr. Vogt called. "Someone who spends the time creating a chart like that is someone who would be highly organized! I don't doubt for a second that Ms. Magill had her team prepared accordingly."

Lexi froze. It was Mal's ability to speak different languages that helped them skip over teams. She opened her mouth, but then closed it as Dr. Kent started to speak.

"The same thing happened at the Grace Hopper Memorial Bridge," Dr. Kent said. "No one completed the ciphers as fast as you. Record time, really."

Lexi glanced at her teammates. Dr. Kent had gotten that wrong, too. That was all Ron's doing.

"I'm not surprised," Dr. Vogt said. "A person who locates coordinates for a chart like this is a critical thinker." Dr. Vogt looked Lexi's way and gave her a thumbs-up.

Lexi bit her lip in excitement. *Thumbs-up!* Dr. Vogt was impressed!

But she's impressed with the wrong person. Lexi swallowed hard. She had to set the record straight, didn't she?

"Let's talk about the periodic table for a second," Dr. Bressler said. "It says here that you solved the Marie Curie problem very quickly and then used your knowledge of elements again at Fisk University?"

Lexi remained still. Mal and Ron had helped figure out that clue, too. It couldn't hurt her chances for her to say *something* nice about her teammates. She held up a finger.

"Ms. Magill?" Dr. Vogt asked. "Is something wrong?"

Lexi motioned for her teammates to join her, but they didn't move.

"Ms. Magill?"

She paused, rethinking. If she wanted that internship, she was going to have to do whatever it took to blow the scientists away. She returned her attention to the scientists. "No, never mind. I'm good."

"Moving on," Dr. Kent said. "We'd like to know how you solved the final clue! You were the only team to do so!"

Smiling, Lexi opened her mouth. This was a question she had no problem answering.

"I'm a big Brewers fan. I've been going to games with my dad since I was a kid, so I knew all about the Famous Racing Sausages."

"I see," Dr. Kent said. "We saw some teams get flustered and try to recreate our video presentation, but from what we've seen, I'm sure your notes were impeccable!"

Lexi pursed her lips. *Her* notes had been awful. She glanced toward Mal. Mal slowly shook her head and put a finger across her lips. Lexi's stomach twisted, but if Mal was okay with it . . .

"Last question," Dr. Vogt said. "Of all these accomplishments, which do you consider the most significant in leading your team to victory?"

Lexi closed her eyes and tried to form her answer. As she reopened them, she saw Haley out of her seat, waving toward Dr. Vogt, obviously trying to distract the scientist during Lexi's answer.

Her former best friend's sabotage came back to her. As much as Lexi had tried to forget about it, it still stung that Haley had tried to oust her from the tournament. They'd been friends for years, and Haley knew how crushed Lexi was when she had to leave the academy and how much the tournament meant to her. A true friend never would have chosen the tournament over her.

True friend. Lexi gulped as it hit her. She was blaming Haley for doing the same thing she was doing right now. She was choosing the internship over her friends. A real friend wouldn't stay silent and take all the credit for their win. Everyone had dismissed Ron and Mal as real teammates, putting them down because they didn't have a science background. She had, too, probably most of all. But they had been pivotal in Team RAM's win. They deserved to have everyone know the truth. She didn't lead the team to victory like Dr. Vogt had said. They had done it together.

"My most significant accomplishment," Lexi started. She looked at Mal and Ron again and then toward the scientists. She took a deep breath. "Actually, my most significant accomplishment happened before the race ever began by picking the best two teammates on the planet."

Grinning wide, Lexi gestured to Ron and Mal. "Mal speaks four languages. She was able to push us ahead of other teams at the check-in counters in Italy and France by being able to speak fluently."

Lexi pointed to Ron. "And Ron is a puzzle master. He solved the Venus Grotto clue in Germany, and he's the one who solved all of those ciphers at the Hopper Bridge."

Everyone in the stadium stared at Ron and Mal, the scientists included. Lexi wasn't finished. "If you want to know the truth, I'm the one who messed up. I sent our team to Tibet." Snickers of laughter rumbled through the crowd. "No, seriously. Me, the teleport science whiz totally forgot to add a negative sign in front of the longitude coordinate. Instead of teleporting to South Carolina, we landed in Tibet."

The crowd roared, and Lexi smiled as tension rolled off her shoulders. It felt good getting the truth out. "So, after that fiasco, I knew I had to step up my game. We worked together for those last few puzzles, and I guess the rest . . . is sausage history!"

Amid additional howls, Lexi handed the microphone to Dr. Harrison. She ran to her teammates, and after a quick group hug, they grabbed their trophies off the table and lifted them over their heads.

"Your tournament winners!" Dr. Harrison shouted, pointing in Team RAM's direction. Team RAM waved to the cheering crowd.

Dr. Harrison proceeded to gather with Dr. Bressler, Dr. Kent, and Dr. Vogt, while Team RAM held a huddle of their own.

"Thanks, Lex," Ron said as they set their trophies down. "But you didn't have to say anything. You made us sound fantastic when we screwed up, too."

"Yeah," Mal said. "You didn't even mention all the good things you did. You determined we were at the wrong castle, found my Tel-Med . . . you totally deserve the internship."

Lexi's throat constricted at the mention of the internship, but she shook her head. "No, it wasn't right." She met her teammates' eyes. "We did this together. The internship would have been great, but it's not worth lying about. Coming clean was the right thing to do."

"It's a good way for Team RAM to end," Ron said.

Lexi caught her breath. She didn't want Team RAM to end.

More than that, she didn't want to lose Ron and Mal as friends. She liked hanging out with them, even though they weren't into science as much as she was.

"It doesn't have to be the end," she said. "Like you said, if I stay at West Elm, I can help your football team with physics stuff. And, Mal, maybe you can teach me about photography? Oh, and I bet there's other kinds of teleportation tournaments we can enter. Winning this one proved we're good at a bunch of different things."

"Really?" Mal asked.

"Really," Lexi answered.

"Heck yeah!" Ron yelled. He threw his hand between them. Mal set hers on top, and then Lexi set her hand on top of both. "On the count of three! One, two, three . . ."

"TEAM RAM!" they shouted together.

As Team RAM cheered, the microphone screeched. Lexi jolted. Dr. Harrison had parted from the scientists and was standing by the microphone.

"Here we go," Lexi said.

Mal clenched Lexi's hand. Lexi squeezed back.

"The winner of the internship is . . ."

"You got this, Magill," Ron whispered. "They're gonna reward you for your hones—"

"Mr. Tomoka Seto!" Dr. Harrison exclaimed.

Without hesitation, Lexi roared, "Yay, Tomoka!"

Ron and Mal slumped. "Sorry, Lexi," they said.

Lexi paused her celebration, surprised how much she didn't feel even a speck of sadness over not winning the internship. No rumbles of jealousy, no knot in her stomach. All she felt was pure joy for Tomoka.

"It's all good," she said. "Really. I came here to win a tournament, and that's exactly what *we* did."

Ron and Mal joined Lexi's cheers and clapped excitedly as Tomoka was mobbed by family and friends rushing onto the field. Haley wasn't one of them. She turned on her heel, scowled, and stormed off.

The stands started to empty. "Hey, now we get to eat, right?" Ron said.

Lexi exchanged glances with Mal, and they both laughed. Some things never changed.

"What's so funny?" a voice called from the stands.

Team RAM whirled to the speaker. Lexi's parents walked through the gate and onto the field. Lexi wrapped an arm around each. "You made it!"

Dad set a hand atop Lexi's head. "Of course we did! One of the tournament directors left a message where the finish line was."

Mom cupped Lexi's cheeks. "Congratulations! I suppose this means we'll have to get you re-enrolled at the academy for fall, huh?"

Smiling, Lexi pulled away and shook her head. "Nah, that's okay. I'm going to give West Elm a chance."

Lexi's parents widened their eyes. "What?"

She gave a firm nod. "It's not like I need a special school to study science." She gestured to her teammates. "Besides, we need to keep the team together."

"Really?" Mom asked.

"Yeah, who are you and what have you done with our daughter?" Dad teased.

Lexi hugged them both.

"Oh!" Mal said. "There are my parents!"

Mal ran to greet her family, and Ron did the same after spotting his.

Lexi stepped out of her hug and faced her parents. "So, since I'm not going to the academy, maybe we can use some of the prize money for a summer vacation?"

Her mom and dad looked at each other. "But the new family budget has us staying put this summer, remember?" Mom said.

"But now we don't have to," Lexi replied. She nodded to her dad's Brewers T-shirt. "And I definitely want to use some of the money for Brewers tickets."

Dad squeezed the back of Lexi's neck and kissed the top of her head. "Thanks, sweetie. We'll think on it. Promise."

Ron and Mal approached with their parents, and after quick introductions, everyone headed to the tailgate. Team RAM lagged behind their families.

"Guess what?" Ron said. "My dad told me this is really going to bolster my chances with high schools and colleges. He said a student-athlete is a much better draw than an athlete, and it will do as much for me as any summer football camp would."

"Nice!" Mal said. "My parents were impressed, too. They said we can definitely go back to France this summer and spend more time at Versailles."

"That's awesome, you guys," Lexi said.

Team RAM exited the stadium and stepped into the sun.

"Ms. Magill?" an accented voice called.

Lexi spun. She knew that voice.

Dr. Vogt reached for Lexi's hands. "I found your honesty refreshing, young lady. One of the traits of a good leader is taking responsibility for her actions—*not* blaming others or finding excuses when things go wrong. You made a mistake, and you owned up to it— even when you didn't have to." She motioned to Ron and Mal. "And you stuck up for your teammates and recognized their accomplishments. A good team member gives credit where credit is due." She patted the top of Lexi's hand.

"Thanks, Dr. Vogt."

Dr. Vogt squeezed her hand. "Those are precisely the qualities I look for in putting together *my* team."

Lexi tilted her head to the side. "Your team?"

"Yes. While Dr. Bressler, Dr. Kent, and I share some employees, we also have our own staff. Tell me, Ms. Magill, would you be interested in working as my personal assistant this summer?"

Lexi stared at Dr. Vogt. She heard the words. She really did, but she couldn't formulate a response. *Personal assistant?* She lifted a hand to her head as her body tingled. *Personal assistant?*

"You bet she's interested!" Ron shouted.

"Heck yeah!" Mal added, jumping up and down.

Mal bumped Lexi, and she unfroze. Her head still felt so light it could float away, but she forced out a response. "I, uh, yes, Dr. Vogt. I would love to!"

Dr. Vogt squeezed Lexi's elbow. "Good. We must talk with your parents and get their permission, of course, but good." The scientist turned. "Now, I'm hungry. Where's the food?"

As Dr. Vogt walked ahead and joined her colleagues, Lexi traded fist pounds with her teammates.

Two new friends.

First place in the tournament.

Prize money.

Dr. Vogt's personal assistant.

"I can't believe it. What a perfect weekend!"

Buzz.

"Is that your phone?" Ron asked, pointing to Lexi's pocket.

"Yeah, I think so." Lexi pulled the phone out of her cargo pants. "It's a text."

ALERT. PLEASE BE ADVISED TEL-MED NO. 610116271 HAS COMPLETED THE CRITICAL PROTOCOL AND HAS BEEN DEACTIVATED

Ron and Mal peered over Lexi's shoulder. "Wow," Mal said. "Looks like we made it just in time."

"Yeah," Lexi said, more relieved and happy than anyone would ever know. She tucked the phone safely in her pocket. First thing tomorrow, she'd return that Tel-Med and get it out of her sight for good.

Lexi grabbed Ron and Mal, and the three linked arms. Together, Team RAM entered the food tent to one more roaring round of applause.

The End

ANSWER KEY

MARIE CURIE PUZZLE

1. Take the year Madame Curie was born: 1867

2. Multiply it by the number of Nobel Prizes she won in Physics: 1

3. Subtract the atomic number of Radium: 1867-88=1779

4. Add the melting point of Radium (Celsius), rounded to the nearest hundred: 1779+700=2479

5. Subtract the mass number of Polonium: 2479-209=2270

6. Add the number of neutrons in Polonium: 2270+125=2395 (mass# -atomic# = neutrons)

7. Add the number of neutrons in Radium 2395+138=2533

8. Subtract the number of elements in the periodic table that exist naturally (as opposed to synthetically): 2533-94=2439

9. Subtract the year Madame Curie died. 2439-1934=505

10. Reverse the order of the numbers. 505

WORD SEARCH # 1

ELEMENTS

```
W  Y  M  E (P  L  A  T  I  N  U  M) A  M  F  E  R  Z  S  W  G  M  J  K  U
W  U  S  K  N  L  D  A  Z  J  R  E  R  Q  R  D  M  V  T  I  U  B  D  B  U
J  E  C  K  T  P  H  U  D  E  O  R  E  O  I  Z  N  Z  W  N  N  W  F  T  J
U  F  M  P  F  H  T  X  W  A  Y  C  D  U  F  H  K  Z  I  J  Y  K  M  B  Y
C  Q  U  U  V  C  P  A  B  B  C  U  L  Y  J  X  H  M  Q  R  E  C  U  J  H
E  Z  M  W  I  E  Z  U  H  A  W  R  O  B  C  W  U  S  D  O  U  J  I  A  K
W  V  Y  N  A  D  J  M  R  U  G  Y  G  J  L  L  H  X  M  D  F  X  N  L  V
R  D  Z  L  E  C  O  B  G  U  B  Q  Y  L  A  G  U  M  U  X  U  O  O  C  J
Q  L  M  P  D  G  O  S  S  P  K  K  I  X  J  B  P  M  I  A  I  J  L  S  Y
 (N  O  N  E  X  N  O) A  M  E  H  B  K  P  R  F  B  F  D  C  D  A  O  M  F
J  V  R  W  Y  U  E  R  W  A  Q  P  Y  X  W  O  C  D  A  B  M  D  P  C  N
N  F  O  C  Z  E  T  N  D  Z  P  M  P  E  I  S  W  U  R  J  C  P  D  T  A
Y  A  W  W  D  O (N  E  G  Y  X  O) Z  I  J  K  C  F  M  A  S  J  G  D  I
X  S  S  W  P  S  V  A  L  R  H  H  V  L  Q  K  C  W  E  R  O  N  A  Y  P
G  M  U  O  U  Y  Z  Q  X  L  C  W  A  A  R  A  R  N  L  N  Y  Y  R  E  M
G  D  P  L  X  E  C  R  Y  N  Y  W  L  E  U  W  A  Y  I  H  O  B  H  K  Z
V  F  F  H  R  E  J  O  S  N  Z  Y  V  D  V  V  J  G  P  Z  S  O  F  T  C
A  U  H  P  W  B  I  J  Z  J  K  L  Z  S  X  H  J  Z  B  T  X  N  C  N  N
R  M  B  N  H  M  M  Z  R  D  I  I  K  Y  Z  Z  H  Z  U  C  O  M  O  D  T
H  A  N  U  T  A  M  G  S  N  G  F  V  S  G  U  H  P  C  M  N  P  K  L
Y  W  O  P  V  C  S  G  M  J  M  K  R  Z  H  L  P  M  E  F  O  Y  P  W  F
L  E  V  U  C  I  Y  E  R  D (T  I  N) Y  F  O  V  D  E  L  P  H  E  F  W
N  D  E  N  G  C  C  N  G  R  E  F  R  Y (N  I  C  K  E  L) I  Q  R  F  W
A  U  V  Y  F  H  L  V  N  O  E  H  O  M  S  G  K  H  N  H  Y  U  W  G  Q
J  G  I  E  Z  D  T  R  C  A  N  N  H  R  L  T  S  F  R  B  F  M  U  D
```

ALUMINUM	MERCURY	SILVER
CARBON	NEON	SODIUM
COPPER	NICKEL	SULFUR
GOLD	OXYGEN	TIN
HELIUM	PLATINUM	XENON
HYDROGEN	POLONIUM	ZINC
KRYPTON	RADIUM	

WORD SCRAMBLES

PHYSICS

1. TOERCCALRAE . . . . Accelerator

2. NCVCIEOTON . . . . .Convection

3. MTOA . . . . .Atom

4. DCORLILE . . . . Collide

5. UNNRTEO . . . . Neutron

6. ROLTCEEN . . . . Electron

7. SEPOOTI . . . . .Isotope

8. SMSA . . . . .Mass

9. TMPSUCRE . . . . Spectrum

10. AURQK . . . . Quark

11. WHEGLNETVA . . . . Wavelength

12. JUOEL . . . . .Joule

13. EOITYVCL . . . . .Velocity

14. TZHER . . . . .Hertz

15. YRGVATI . . . . Gravity

16. PWEOR . . . . .Power

17. TOHPON . . . . Photon

18. NYEGER . . . . Energy

19. TCSNDAIE . . . . .Distance

20. CNINUTODCO . . . . Conduction

CIPHERS

GREAT SCIENTIFIC MINDS

1. WEH'B PT KLCKRW EL XKCW DECZ. HEBXRHY DECBXDXRGT JEATU TKURGS. WEH'B GTB EBXTCU WRUJEOCKYT SEO EC BTGG SEO BXKB SEO JKH'B WE RB. –YTCBCOWT TGREH

Hint: W=D

ANSWER: *Don't be afraid of hard work. Nothing worthwhile comes easily. Don't let others discourage you or tell you that you can't do it.—Gertrude Elion*

2. QNU QADU KEIM TJ EMQUXXEIUMPU EK MTQ LMTFXUWIU HDQ ESBIEMBQETM.–BXHUAQ UEMKQUEM

Hint: H=B

ANSWER: *The true sign of intelligence is not knowledge but imagination. —Albert Einstein*

3. VL MOWRI YBQJLGWOA CRQ WGWO SRYW CBINLPI R ULHY MPWQQ.–BQRRJ VWCILV

Hint: O=R

ANSWER: *No great discovery was ever made without a bold guess.—Isaac Newton*

4. THPK XLBSKHUOH YC GB XLBS GJH HMGHLG BN BLH'C YOLBTPLEH.–EBLNZEYZC

Hint: N=F

ANSWER: *Real knowledge is to know the extent of one's ignorance.—Confucius*

5. PBMFDTDH DBKBF BJIMSXVX VIB OTDU.–PBADMFUA UM KTDYT

Hint: O=M

ANSWER: *Learning never exhausts the mind.—Leonardo da Vinci*

(page 203) 8. TD PVWK ULQD ADCWDQDCLFXD LFO LSZQD LHH XZFERODFXD RF ZVCWDHQDW.–PLCRD XVCRD

Hint: H=L

ANSWER: *We must have perseverance and above all confidence in ourselves. —Marie Curie*

ACKNOWLEDGMENTS

The idea for this story was born several years ago while commuting home from work. Stuck on the so-called expressway, I started wondering, wishing, actually, to have the ability to teleport home and out of traffic. That idea percolated in my brain until it found its way to Lexi and her race around the world. But writing the story was only half the battle. A lot of people helped bring Lexi to life, and I am extremely grateful for their assistance:

My agent, Natascha Morris, at BookEnds Literary Agency, for her amazing editorial notes that injected more heart into Lexi's journey, and for finding this book a home at Running Press Kids.

My editor, Allison Cohen, who took a chance on a genre mash-up, and then fell in love with Lexi and her friends as much as I did. Her enthusiasm was infectious from the start, and this book would not exist without her.

To the entire team at Running Press Kids, especially Cisca Schreefel, Christopher Eads, Frances Soo Ping Chow, and Valerie Howlett, and illustrator Charles Lehman for such a dynamic and wonderful book cover.

I did quite a bit of research on the various locales and scientists mentioned in this book, but deserving of a special shout out is Bryan Kent Wallace, Assistant Professor of Physics at Fisk University, who was a tremendous help to my research into Elmer Imes.

Writing is a solitary profession, but I have been lucky enough to be part of an incredibly supportive writing community. For that, I owe a resounding thanks to Brenda Drake, creator of Pitch Wars, for welcoming me as a middle grade mentor in 2015. I've met so many wonderful writer friends through Pitch Wars since then, including Wade Albert White, Juliana Brandt, Naz Kutub, Taylor B. Gardner, Julie Artz, and Melyssa Mercado. They all read drafts of this book at one time or another and provided fantastic insight as to how to make the story stronger.

The best writing support group anyone can ask for—the ladies of March 39, Hymn Day: Lynnette Novak, Kelly Hopkins, Mónica Bustamante Wagner, and Fiona McLaren. Thank you for your encouragement and support throughout my writing journey. I am so glad we found each other!

Finally, thanks to my family, especially my parents, who passed on their joy of reading to their children. Weekly library visits were routine, as were summer reading programs and story time. To this day, the one thing we all have in common is always having a good book nearby. Hopefully, this one makes the cut.